D. B. SIEDERS

HELL

JINX MCGEE | BOOK THREE

BOUND

HELL BOUND

D. B. SIEDERS

CITY OWL
PRESS

HELL BOUND
Jinx McGee, Book 3

CITY OWL PRESS
www.cityowlpress.com

Cover Design by MiblArt. All stock photos licensed appropriately.
Chapter Headings by SiederTree Studios.

Edited by Tee Tate.

For information on subsidiary rights, please contact the publisher at info@cityowlpress.com.

Print Edition ISBN: 978-1-64898-283-5

Digital Edition ISBN: 978-1-64898-284-2

Printed in the United States of America

ALSO BY D. B. SIEDERS

Soul Broker Series:
Waking the Dead
Raising the Dead
The Quick and the Dead

Jinx McGee Series:
Catching Hell
Hell Bent
Hell Bound

Southern Elemental Guardians:
Making Waves
Lorelei's Lyric
Cross Currents
Fire Storm
River Spell
Forest Charmed

PRAISE FOR THE WORKS OF D. B. SIEDERS

"I was immediately drawn into *Catching Hell*, and the book never really let me go. Jinx is a snarky but lovable main character who really doesn't have much faith in her own abilities. Dominic is a great love interest, and I'm looking forward to finding out more about the both of them. Highly recommend." – *PenKay, Vine Voice Reviewer*

"A unique cast of characters drives this beautifully crafted tale that demands you keep a box of tissue on hand. *Waking the Dead* is a soul-wrenching look into the decisions one must make about life and death, not only for one's self, but for a loved one. Ms. Sieders knows how to put words on paper that touch the heart, and invigorate the mind." — *4.5 Stars from InD'Tale Magazine*

"Revolution brews in the spirit world of *The Quick and the Dead*. Vivian and Lazarus encounter a vibrant cast of allies—among them mambo woman Bijoux Briggs and Vivian's sister Mae, who was disabled in life but is powerful in the afterlife—and develop a love connection despite their complicated past." — *Publisher's Weekly*

"D.B. Sieders is a unique storyteller. *Crosscurrents* is a mix of science fiction and fantasy that is woven together perfectly. Ms. Sieders's characters are distinctive and the story is imaginative and fun." — *4.5 Stars from InD'Tale Magazine*

"For paranormal romance readers who are looking for something a little different, *Lorelei's Lyric* could be your first step into a whole new world." — *Romantic Reads and Such*

"D.B. Sieders has a charming way with language, bordering on zany, sarcastic, and gritty. *Waking the Dead* is realistic, unique, honest, humorous, bittersweet, a little flirty, and a dark journey of hope. It is an addictive must-read!" — *5 Stars from Liz Konkel, <u>Readers' Favorite</u>*

"D.B. Sieders' *Raising the Dead* is the second book in the Soul Broker series and an engrossing addition to the paranormal/supernatural genre... Surprises await and darkness lurks as Vivian's journey unfolds in a plot wrought with danger, heartache, betrayal, and mystery." — *5 Stars from K.J. Simmill, <u>Readers' Favorite</u>*

"I was immediately drawn into *Catching Hell*, and the book never really let me go. Jinx is a snarky but lovable main character who really doesn't have much faith in her own abilities. Dominic is a great love interest, and I'm looking forward to finding out more about the both of them. Highly recommend." – *PenKay, Vine Voice Reviewer*

For my dear friend and fellow author Jody Wallace,
who keeps me writing

CHAPTER ONE

As I walk through the Valley of the Shadow of Death, I remind myself that you can't always trust Google Maps— On a T-shirt worn by Jinx McGee, Demon Hunter

Something weird was in the air. Literally.

Unlike the last time, there were no exploding buildings or chaos, but the night was still young. There were strange glowing objects flashing to and fro above the downtown skyline before blinking out of existence.

Or to another plane of existence.

I scanned the sky looking for signs of imminent attack. D, my demon boyfriend, ran toward HQ with me in tow.

Then I stopped to get a better look.

The objects weren't flying demons, at least not any species with which I was familiar. The strange beings flitted between tall buildings, over the river and bridges, moving in sync with the music pouring from bars and honky tonks. They glowed with an unearthly light, the creatures. Beneath the glow, there seemed to be an abundance of feathers.

And eyes. So many eyes.

Celestials. Celestials were on the loose. Biblically accurate angels were powerful, hideous, and terrifying.

And they were flying around downtown Nashville in plain sight of modern humans who'd been blissfully unaware of the presence of these interdimensional beings, at least for the past few millennia.

D spotted them, too, and hesitated, tense and ready for battle. He was a handsome devil. Over six feet tall with dark hair, long dark lashes, deep brown eyes that sparked with red demon light when he was angry or aroused, he had a body hardened by training and battle in the depths of hell. Under other circumstances, I'd be admiring that body and making all kinds of delightfully evil plans of what I would do with it later.

It was what I should have been doing and was doing before we were so rudely interrupted by a flock of celestials flying out in the open for everyone to see.

My demon and I had been on a date in downtown Nashville—our first bona fide official date—and about to enjoy some live music, but duty called. When you're a demon hunter, you're always on call, especially when you're in charge of capturing seven deadly master demons and their celestial counterparts who had escaped their realms and come to earth to cause mischief, mayhem, and war.

Make that six.

We'd already dispatched the Master Demon of Sloth back to the hell realm and had her sister, who happened to be the Archangel of Diligence, in custody. We also had the archangel's sidekick imprisoned at HQ. Both had tried to kill me, but Pinstripe the sidekick came closer to bringing about my end with her massive tentacles. Contrary to popular culture, myth, and legend, master demons came in all shapes, sizes, and genders.

All of them were treacherous, vicious, and ruthless. The myths got that part right. And archangels could give their demon counterparts a run for their money in maliciousness.

Now, we had the Master Demon of Gluttony to contend with, not to mention the rogue angel who'd pretended to be our ally so she could steal the Sigillum Dei, an artefact that could open portals to the hell realm and the celestial realm.

Couldn't trust any of these creatures.

Having just received texts from my boss and teammates about the stolen artefact, playtime was over. We needed the Sigillum Dei to send our enemies on a one-way trip away from earth and back to the dimension where they belonged. It was the only way to permanently banish them and stop the coming war that high-ranking demons and angels planned to wage.

We had to get it back pronto.

More flashing from the idiot celestials above us, and the humans were starting to notice. That couldn't be good. They were already rattled. War was brewing between the celestial and hell realms with earth as the battlefield. The combatants were currently confined to Music City, but the barrier wouldn't last long.

And apparently, they'd abandoned the rules of secrecy that kept mundanes blissfully unaware of scary creatures from other dimensions.

The out-in-the-open flying circus of celestials couldn't be a coincidence. The stench of ozone permeated the air, overwhelming the city smells of food, beer, stale urine, and sweaty humans. My ears popped. The people in downtown were covering their ears, noses, and looking up in awe and the beginnings of terror.

When I found Cassiel, the celestial traitor who'd stolen the artefact, I was going to blast her ass into the far reaches of the known universe for pulling this little stunt and for ruining my date night.

I gave my date a look and we took off running.

Demoriel, who I called D for short, was on our demon hunting team, too, and had magic and powers that had helped our mostly human colleagues on demon hunting missions. So far, we'd managed not to run into any pedestrians and weren't garnering too much attention. There were too many other interesting things to see and hear in downtown Nashville, like pedal taverns full of tourists and unidentified flying objects.

HQ would have to wait. We couldn't ignore this.

"Okay," I said, trying to control my breath and focus on endurance running. The demon grafts that had saved my life and enhanced my abilities helped, but they still had to work within the limits of a mostly human body. But I'd trained hard as well. What I lacked in height I made up for with ferocity, tenacity, and an iron will.

My celestial half probably helped, too.

Yup. Part celestial, part demon, part human. That was me. The warrior of three realms or some crap.

"We need to find Cassie first and get the Sigillum Dei before we go after Beelzebubba the Real Estate Tycoon. And I'm thinking Cassie has something to do with this nonsense," I said, gesturing to the night sky above. "How do we track a celestial?"

D shook his head as he kept pace with me. "You'd have better luck than I would. Are you angry enough to tap into your celestial side?"

That shouldn't be a problem in theory. I hadn't fully trusted the angel who'd become my unlikely ally and source of information in my quest to stop the coming war that would destroy earth and all I held dear. But I'd liked her. Even grudgingly respected her. Then she'd stolen the Sigillum Dei. Since I had a real problem with betrayal, I could work up a proper temper flare that would unleash my celestial power, a gift from my deadbeat dad who'd withheld his true identity as a celestial.

Or possibly some kind of ancient deity.

Not that being half celestial, or some sort of demigoddess, was doing me much good right now.

I had power more potent than my borrowed demon powers. But I hadn't figured out how to bend that power to my will. It only seemed to work when I was pissed off or on the verge of death. Try as I might, I was too shocked to muster enough righteous anger at Cassie. And hurt, though I'd never admit it.

But I had another source to tap into, a deep well of rage.

I thought about the people who'd been damaged by the last demon we'd defeated—a demon who'd had help from two powerful celestials. They'd stolen the minds, will, and soul energy of thousands of innocent humans, tortured lesser demons, and had nearly destroyed my mind. The

Master Demon of Gluttony would be just as cruel in his pursuit of power, as would any celestial working for or against him.

That made me good and mad. My stomach fluttered with the bubbling sensation I'd come to associate with my celestial mojo. I focused my entire being on Cassie, a.k.a. Cassiel the traitor who'd stolen an artefact that was our only means of permanently banishing the powerful demons and celestials currently on earth. It could also let legions of demons and celestials loose on earth to wreak havoc. My team could never defeat that many.

I grabbed D's hand. A vision of Cassie formed in my mind. She wasn't at HQ, or any place in the city I recognized. She couldn't leave the city. None of the celestials or demons could leave so long as the ward our boss had crafted—or bargained for—held. But the city was big. She could be anywhere.

I focused harder. It was dark. No landmarks, no trees, no familiar skyline. It was a strange, misty landscape.

It was a place I'd been before. Bingo!

"She's in the space between," I said, coming to an abrupt halt. Cassie had transported me there once for a private conversation and to show me a vision. I knew how to get out of that pocket of reality. She'd given me the word—*reditus*—that had brought me back to earth. Some myths and legends were true. Demons and celestials loved Latin. No idea why a dead language held such appeal, but it was their preferred communication tool.

"I'm going to try something," I said. "I think I can take you with me."

D looked at me with an intensity that sent my stomach fluttering for an entirely different reason.

"I trust you," he said.

Invoking whatever higher power might favor me, I gripped D's hand tighter and channeled my power. Then, I spoke another Latin word.

"*Ire*."

Nothing.

Too easy, I supposed. Or maybe my pronunciation was off? I spoke the word again, growing angrier with each passing second.

"Deodamnatus! Filius canis!"

I opened my eyes to find D grinning at me. "That was creative, but swearing won't help, and I don't think *ire* is the magic word. Intent matters when it comes to magic, not language or specific words. Try again."

I took a deep breath, closed my eyes, and focused on Cassie and the space between. The fog and darkness filled my mind's eye. Then, throwing caution and good judgement to the wind, I opened my eyes and said, "Take me to the fucking space between. Now."

Downtown Nashville faded as we entered an entirely different reality.

CHAPTER TWO

D and I stood in the strange place and peered into its thick, billowing fog.

The space between was, according to Cassiel, a zone between the realms of earth, celestials, and demons. A sort of no-man's land that stretched for who knew how long and led nowhere. Under the multiverse theory, each universe was a bubble and the space between was just that—an unoccupied bit of reality's landscape between universes, or realms, or whatever existences were. The physics and mathematics of it were beyond me, but the concept made sense. Nashville had several portals that could be used to travel between earth and the hell and celestial realms, so it stood to reason that it resided at the junction of two or more bubbles, easing travel between them.

Or maybe it was just magic. Trying to reconcile science and magic made my head hurt. I'd leave that to Trinity and the tech demons on our team. They were the smart ones. I was a fighter. Right now, I was on a mission to track down a rogue celestial and get the Sigillum Dei back.

The last time I'd been here, Cassiel had shown me a vision of my past. I'd seen my father "gift" me with what I thought was a demon. I'd been possessed by her since the age of five.

Turned out she was a rogue archangel. Banishing her had nearly killed me. It had also unleashed the master demons and archangels on earth before the portal closed.

I reached out with my senses, searching the mist for signs of my target. My powers worked well in this place.

Those powers bubbled through me as if pleased to have brought us here. They seemed...excited. For battle? Familiar territory? Didn't matter. No doubt they'd come in handy when I let them out to play.

Other celestials who looked suspiciously like the entities flitting about in the Nashville sky appeared in the space between before being swallowed by fog. They illuminated the mist like enchanted flashlights, glowing blue with their celestial auras. I had one of those auras, but it usually only showed up when I was angry or in battle.

"Why are they here, and where are they going?" D asked, drawing his demon blade and working a little magic to give us some light. If he was worried about attracting the attention of the celestials around us, he didn't let it show.

His aura was demonic red, like a glowing garnet, brilliant and mesmerizing.

I channeled my powers to produce a cool light spear and shield. Having manifested a few celestial weapons before, it was easier this time. Must be getting the hang of it. Or maybe the space between was just a better space for magic use.

"Hey, is it easier for you to use magic in the demon realm?"

"It is," he said. "Earth doesn't have a lot of inherent magical energy, and that energy is concentrated in a minority of creatures and places. That's why your people developed technology. My kind never needed it."

"Neither do celestials," I said, remembering how difficult it was for an archangel we'd recently battled to blend magic and tech. "I'm guessing this place is fueled by magic. My cell phone isn't working, either."

D paused to check his mobile. "You're right. I expected no signal, but it was over ninety percent charged when I got the message from HQ. Now it's dead."

No chance of calling for backup.

My demon flicked his blade, dimming the light right before a massive celestial creature materialized in front of us. Like the other celestials I'd encountered in their true forms, this one looked alien to my human eyes. In addition to being massive and long like an oversized snake, it was covered in what looked like a shimmering coat of long iridescent hair. Another appeared, this one smaller. The smaller creature made a bleating sound like a sheep with a megaphone and floated over to the larger hairy snake-looking thing, which crooned softly to it.

"That is the most horrifyingly adorable thing I've ever seen," I whispered, my stomach fluttering. It was like the first time I saw a racoon in the backyard of my childhood home. Fluffy, rangy, chubby, with human-like hands and a boopable snoot. I'd squealed in six-year-old delight and got treated to an open-mouthed trash-panda grin full of teeth as it hissed. I'd been a goner.

This creature was easily one hundred times the size of a racoon, and a zillion times fluffier. "Great googley moogley," I said, "I totally want to pet it."

"That's what you said about Sully, but you're not wrong about the horrifying part. Don't try to pet it," he said, but I could hear amusement and wonder in his voice.

Sully was my demon realm battle cat. I had a thing for animals, especially weird ones that came from other dimensions.

As we watched, four more adult-sized versions of the creatures appeared, one of them with a set of large, curving horns attached to what was probably a head—hard to tell with all that hair, at least until it shook its body and a snout appeared. Wowzers. They were sheep. Celestial sheep. And the big one with horns had to be the ram. They all floated and undulated, bleating and snorting as if nervous. Classic prey behavior.

What were they afraid of?

"What's the plan?" D asked. "Do you sense your guardian angel anywhere?"

My snort gave way to a growl. "She's *not* my guardian angel. She's a thieving traitor. Anyway, she's somewhere in this mist but I can't get a handle on which direction." I was better at tracking demons thanks to the life-saving graft I'd received from Alexi, who shared his body with a ferocious wolf demon. Being a creature of the hell realm, my inner wolf wasn't instinctively wired to smell celestials.

Having only recently learned that I was part celestial, I wasn't very good at tracking them, either. But Cassie's power levels were high, about one or two notches beneath the mighty archangels. The artefact could be amplifying it. I sensed the power but couldn't trace it.

"Maybe it's this place," D said. "It's pretty disorienting."

The smaller serpentine sheep had wandered away from its mama and floated closer to us. I caught a glimpse of large purple eyes as the snout emerged to scent the air, presumably to figure out if we were friend or foe. The teeth in its open mouth were flat like animals that ate veggies instead of other animals.

"What are you doing here?" I asked the beast in front of me. "And what were you doing on earth? Not a safe place for your kind." I reached out and let it sniff my hand while D groaned and muttered about wild creatures and celestial rabies or something. I quit paying attention as a cold, wet nose bumped against my fingers, and it turned its head so I could stroke soft fleece. Holy guacamole. The celestial realm had animals, just like the hell realm. Shouldn't be so surprising, but having seen a cadejo, a.k.a. flying demon dog owned by a bucknutty summoner, and being the proud companion of a demon realm flying cat that could morph from kitten sized to bigger-than-a-tiger battle cat sized, I was hooked.

Maybe I could become an interdimensional wildlife biologist—after we defeated the other six master demons and their archangel counterparts, of course.

"The juvenile snake lamb is a curious creature," I said putting on my best approximation of a sophisticated British accent. "It leaves the safety of the herd to investigate the strange, hairless creatures sharing its territory. Clearly, it has no natural fear of the being whose hand it just licked, suggesting it is familiar with beings like this and possibly domesticated."

"Jane, what are you doing?" D asked, alarmed.

I broke character, switching from my best British naturalist narrator voice back to my own. "Planning my documentary series on the interdimensional animal kingdoms. Cooper can be my field agent."

Cooper was the bucknutty summoner and owner of the demon dog.

Before D could scold me, the herd began to float away, following something or someone we were unable to perceive. Mama bleated for her baby, whose flank I was still scratching. The young snake sheep bleated back but didn't move away. Instead, it leaned its long body into my fingers and moved back and forth until I hit the best spot.

As much as I wanted to keep it, even I understood the first law of nature—never come between a mother and her baby.

"Go on," I said, giving the critter a gentle push. "Go with Mama. We'll follow."

Purple eyes narrowed and the overgrown baby shoved my body with its flank. The thing was strong. Size and muscle made it impossible for me to get the damned creature to budge.

"Are you a celestial sheep or a jackass?" I asked, going nose to nose with the beast. It snorted, covering my face with a light mist of moisture.

"Ew! Celestial sheep snot."

The creature blinked and bleated.

"Told you not to pet it," D said. So not helpful.

Without thinking, I backed up, took a running start, and jumped on the celestial sheep's back. I grabbed fistfuls of hair, bracing myself for an interdimensional rodeo ride, but the creature simply bleated and started moving in the direction its flock had gone.

D jogged beside us, yelling at me. "I'm amazed you've lived this long. You do realize this thing outweighs you by thousands of pounds, is floating, is magical, and may be venomous?"

I giggled. "Don't be such a buzzkill. I've got a great view, and I don't have to run through the void for who knows how long to follow the herd. You do realize you could be up here experiencing a once-in-a-lifetime ride on a celestial beast, right? Come on! Consider it part of our date. It's super fun."

My companion muttered something uncomplimentary in the demon language before leaping onto the sheep's back. He scooted closer to me, my backside cradled between his thighs. I'd been half-joking about the date thing, but never one to look a gift horse in the mouth, or gift livestock, I snuggled against him. The sheep picked up speed, darting in and out of the mist and bleating, following the sound of its mother's answering call.

"Admit it," I said. "You're having fun."

He grumbled, but he didn't deny it. I'd never had the chance to ride horses, but I imagined this is what it felt like to ride free over open land, the wind in my hair and a sense of euphoria coursing through my body and soul.

Our sheep darted around other bizarre and presumably celestial creatures in the mist. There were so many. At least they were traveling in a direction that should lead us straight to Cassie the traitor angel. D and I would get the Sigillum Dei back and, if it seemed prudent, we'd investigate this congregation of celestials.

Baby caught up with the rest of the flock. Mama gave it a cursory sniff but ignored us. We'd stopped, and the throngs of celestials seemed to be waiting for something or someone.

"Demons! My flock is under attack by demons!"

We turned in unison toward the sound of the angry voice as a bearded old man wearing robes straight out of a Medieval Biblical painting pointed a giant shepherd's hook at us while shrieking.

I swatted the hook away with my celestial spear. "First of all, it's rude to name call. I'm technically half-human and half-celestial. These demon grafts saved my life after an archangel tried to kill me." I was probably something more than celestial on my father's side, but there was no need to derail the conversation with irrelevant details.

The shepherd's jaw dropped, as though he wanted to speak, but D gave him a hard stare that shut him up.

"Second, we aren't attacking your flock. We're looking for a rogue celestial who stole an artefact. What are all of you doing in the space between?" I asked.

The shepherd balked. "Why should I tell you anything, interloper? Remove yourself from my charoum this instant."

Great. I was going to have to negotiate with an indignant, outraged angel. I was terrible at negotiating, except with my demon steel knife and nifty celestial weapons. They made negotiating so much more efficient.

I was tempted to show the angel just how well I negotiated with a blade, but beneath the self-righteous anger lurked genuine fear. All the celestial creatures in the vicinity were uneasy. I sighed. Not being a bully —more's the pity for that in my line of work—I spoke in a slow, calm voice. My negotiating voice. I'd picked it up from retail workers and tele-marketers.

"It doesn't seem to have a problem with me being on its back. Tell you what—you tell me why you and the rest of these celestials are here, and we'll leave you and your creatures in peace."

Before the shepherd could answer, a chorus of roars echoed through the space, terrifying and familiar.

I'd heard them before. We were in deep shit.

The celestials screamed in panic. Damn it, they'd trample each other and do the job of the demon warriors who'd somehow infiltrated the space between and were after them. Or maybe they were after us. Didn't matter. We would fight them.

"Maaks!" D yelled. "Dragon demons. Run! We will cover you."

The celestial throng responded to D's booming voice, which I suspected he amplified using magic, and ran. D and I leapt off the beast's back and prepared for a fight. I channeled my celestial powers, conjuring a protective shield around us. Back-to-back, we waited, knives in hand and at the ready.

Instead of dragon demons, we were swarmed by wraiths.

CHAPTER THREE

I struck out with my knife, blinded by the cursed immaterial demons surrounding me. Large and dark, their mouths were gaping maws straight out of a nightmare, and they were damned fast, surrounding us like dark clouds. Individually, wraiths were not especially powerful, but at least twenty held D and I in place with a combination of shrieks and darkness. They fought in numbers and the strategy worked with deadly efficiency. Every time my blade sliced through one, another would take its place.

And so far, I'd only managed glancing blows, which compromised my protective shield.

Enough. The wraiths were a distraction. They were meant to keep us busy while the maaks went after the celestials. Maaks were solid demons, freaking strong, fast, and designed to tear their opponents to pieces with claws and fangs. They could fly, too, using great leathery wings that sprouted from their backs.

All the better to chase us with.

The shepherd and his sheep didn't look like fighters, and I wasn't sure if any of the celestials gathering in the space between were powerful enough to defend against the dragon demons' razor-sharp talons and magical attacks. The demons were predators and the celestial creatures behaved like prey. They'd never survive without our help.

I channeled my celestial powers and sent a wave of magic that blasted the wraiths into the mists of the space with wails of agony.

Damn. That actually worked! Score one for me, demon hunter extraordinaire.

Let's see what else I can do.

For the first time in my career, I voluntarily sheathed my demon steel knife in the heat of battle and conjured a celestial sword. It glowed a brilliant blue, like a light saber but with a core of sharp metal. With a roar of outrage, I charged into battle, slashing the first maak in my path, taking off an arm before moving on to the next combatant.

From the unearthly howl behind me, I knew D had finished the job with his demon steel blade.

Either the celestial sword was more powerful in my hands than demon steel, or D's magic was stronger. Maybe both. The last time we'd encountered this type of demon, it had taken both of us fighting together just to wound a single maak enough to make it teleport away.

Aside from master demons, maaks were the strongest demons I'd ever fought. And they were the tip of the iceberg. The hell realm was full of strange, beautiful, horrifying, and often deadly creatures. These demons shouldn't be on earth.

It was my job to stop them.

I cut through two more maaks while D dispatched three of his own in the chaos. Celestials screamed in terror and pain as the maaks savaged them.

Celestials, like demons, bled as red as any human.

Carnage. So much blood. This was just a taste of the war to come between these species if I failed to stop it. Humanity in the crossfire, it would make the blood and gore spilling in this space seem like a single drop.

I didn't know what these celestials were doing here, but they weren't hurting anyone by their presence. They were caught in the crossfire, too, like the tempter demons who sought refuge on earth and an escape from the master demons who would use and abuse them before sending them to be slaughtered.

So-called archangels, counterparts to master demons, weren't above using, abusing, and sacrificing less powerful celestials for their war efforts. These celestials were likely refugees, too.

I screamed a battle cry as I summoned and threw a series of celestial spears. Three dragon demons fell, their wings shuddering. One of the celestial sheep, the male, streaked toward the biggest maak and rammed its great horns into the fallen demon, crushing its chest with a sickening series of cracks. The shepherd impaled another with his hook.

"Fight!" D yelled at the other celestials. "Fight them!"

He didn't have to tell them twice.

Celestials in all shapes, sizes, and forms—from the ethereal and winged, the humanoid, the creepy with tentacles and loads of eyeballs, and even a few that looked like a mashup of leftover parts from humans and animals—entered the fray. Tentacles smacked dragon demons out of the air and strangled them. Those made up of feathers and eyeballs harried dragon demons, allowing the chimeric monstrosities among them to tear apart the demons. Other large celestials formed a defensive perimeter around the smaller celestials with no defenses or fighting capacity.

The maaks kept coming.

We settled into a rhythm. D and I dispatched or disabled each maak we encountered, and the celestials capable of fighting came in for the kill. At least the celestials that survived. The dragon demons had killed more than two dozen by my reckoning. How many were there? How many more would come?

We were seasoned fighters, but even a powerful demon like D and a half-celestial warrior like me experienced battle fatigue.

"How many can you teleport?" I yelled.

"Don't know," he said before slashing at the flank of a flying maak. "Maybe ten?"

There were more than ten celestials in this space.

I didn't want to decide which ones to save.

A blinding light shone through the mist of the space between, inter-rupting our battle. I fumbled, swinging my sword as I spun in a circle. I didn't have a lot of reach, but I was fast. Nothing could attack me except from above. And I wouldn't be able to see it coming.

Just as the thought flashed through my mind, I felt a helmet surround my head and armor materialize around my body.

I could conjure celestial armor—wish I'd known that before.

I thought about D's head and body covered with armor and hoped my celestial mojo would protect him, too.

At last, my vision came back online.

What I saw made my blood boil with rage.

It floated one hundred yards in front of me, a portal conjured by the Sigillum Dei.

A pentagram with an outer circle, three heptagons, and an inner circle decorated with glowing sigils. I'd last seen it at IIQ the night that seven master demons and seven archangels escaped their realms and invaded earth. The night I'd sent Lord Belial, the mastermind behind the brewing war, and Haniel, a rogue archangel, Belial's lover, and the entity that had possessed me since childhood, back to the hell realm where they belonged.

That's what the Sigillum Dei did. It banished the entities it targeted to their home realms permanently. Belial and Haniel couldn't come back to earth. But they could send their legions and loyal followers to wage war in their place.

I hoped they suffered a thousand daily terrors for what they had done to me, to D, and to countless humans, demons, and celestials.

Cassiel was here. She had to be. Our former ally had used the stolen artefact to open a portal, and now scores of terrified celestials were tram-pling one another to get to it.

Damn it! They'd kill each other in the process of escaping.

Then I saw *her*.

Cassiel, my former ally turned traitor, floated above the portal, her face contorted in agony. The portal widened. She'd worn her human grandmotherly glamour. It was how she looked when we first met and seemed to be her go-to form. Why that instead of a more intimidating warrior glamour was beyond me.

Guess she wasn't expecting the dragon demons. Or me.

The first wave of fleeing celestials flashed through the portal, the small riding on the backs of the large or being carried. Many carried their dead. The chimeric celestials who'd closed ranks around the shepherd and his snake-like sheep held their ground for a few breaths, but fear eventually won.

They fled to the portal, leaving the shepherd and his flock defenseless.

We ran to cover the shepherd and sheep, racing to catch three pursuing maaks and then slashing them to ribbons. The last celestial went through the portal, leaving the space between empty except for me, D, the shepherd and his flock, and the bodies of slain demons and celestials. And blood.

So much blood.

More maaks screamed from the depths of the mist. They were coming.

"Hey, Cassie!" I yelled. "You've got some explaining to do."

Cassiel turned her attention to me. The portal shrank, and celestial sheep stopped their mad dash toward it as if uncertain. The angel's body strained as she worked to maintain the portal, and she struggled to speak.

"Jane...I can't...hold the...portal."

"Fuck the portal," I screamed, taking out my anger on the fallen maak at my feet, stabbing him with my sword. "Get down here and give back the artefact right now. And how about taking out a few of these damned dragon demons while you're at it?"

The portal continued to shrink. Damn it. D and I herded the reluctant shepherd and flock toward the portal. They were fast, but not fast enough. I wasn't sure the ram would fit, but most of the ewes and lambs could get through if we hurried. First, save the innocents.

Then, kick Cassie's ass.

"Jane...save them..."

I had every intention of saving them, but it was the wrong thing to say.

"What do you mean, save them? You're the one who dragged them here and you were apparently dumb enough to be followed. You save them. Open that portal." Rage coursed through me, the tattoos from my demon grafts glowing beneath the celestial armor I conjured. The alchemy of celestial and demonic power coalesced, and I pushed it toward the portal, willing it to open.

It hurt.

My skin was on fire, stretched too thin over muscle and sinew as the power coursed through my body. My human body wasn't meant to hold this magic. Summoner magic wasn't a part of my heritage. I didn't have the right kind of power.

I pushed again. Nothing. Then, suddenly, the portal began to spiral back open.

It wasn't me. I wasn't sure it was Cassiel. Didn't matter. All that mattered was saving the celestials.

"D! Push them through," I yelled.

He sheathed his knife and in a burst of red demonic light he transformed with a roar that shook my bones. Great black wings emerged from his back. His body grew, doubling in size, and great horns tore from his skull. His skin was a deep red and his handsome features twisted, still handsome but somehow more.

Other. Demon.

I froze, caught up in awe at D's transformation. The portal wavered but held as something pushed more power and will into holding it open.

The sheep had frozen as well, until D howled—in rage, in pain, or perhaps in an agonizing blend of both.

Then the flock bleated in panic and fled from the terrifying sight and sound.

Holy guacamole. D was the biggest, baddest demon here and he used his power to make the celestials haul ass.

It made me wonder what else he could do.

"I can't hold it!" Cassie said, her face and body going limp.

Shit. Without her, I wasn't sure it could hold, either.

The portal snapped shut. The next wave of maaks were almost on us, and I was spent. D screamed in frustration and took flight, heading straight for Cassie.

"Save them," Cassie said. Then the cowardly angel disappeared along with the Sigillum Dei.

D's voice, deep and warped, echoed through the space between. "Hold on. I'm getting us out of here."

I barely dodged the swipe of dragon demon claws before it vanished along with the space between.

CHAPTER FOUR

"This is an office, not a celestial farm."

Boice wore a T-shirt that read, "Wait, What If Demons Don't Want to Fuck with Us?" He stood in front of his computer workstation, arms outstretched to ward off an enormous floating celestial ram that was eyeing him with mild interest.

One half of the twin demons of technology, Boice loved his tricked-out computers more than life itself and didn't take kindly to anything that threatened the delicate equipment's structural and functional integrity.

That integrity was currently being threatened by a bunch of celestial sheep roaming through HQ's main conference room. It was bigger than the average boardroom, but not nearly big enough for the flock and a band of demon hunters.

If the sheep pooped on the expensive hardwood floor, I'd be the one in deep doo doo.

At least the ram wasn't charging after Boice. The whole flock was calm, which surprised the hell out of me. But perhaps their instincts let them know they were safe.

"I know, I know," I said, rubbing one of the lambs, petting her soft fleece to keep her calm. After transporting what was left of the flock—

which incidentally consisted of twenty-five sheep, considerably more than the ten D said he could manage—and its shepherd to HQ, D had assumed his humanoid form and passed out. Sam, another of our resident demon teammates, assured me he would be fine after about ten hours of sleep and some food.

My demon had depleted himself to save celestial creatures.

Not for me, not to impress me or get in my good graces, but because it was the right thing to do.

Good men were hard to find. I found a good demon, and I was never letting him go.

I'd tell him when he woke up. I'd probably have to reassure him that his big, bad demon form with wings and horns and ginormous size didn't freak me out. He was rather sensitive for a demon.

It was part of his charm.

I was beat and beaten. Fatigued tugged at me like a rottweiler with a juicy bone and the adrenaline that had kept me on my feet during the battle was long gone. I dearly wanted to sleep for ten hours, but that would have to wait.

For now, I had a small flock of enormous celestial sheep milling around the offices of HQ. Even if we let some of them wander the hallways, the space wasn't big enough to accommodate the curious beasts. So far, they were content to calmly explore, but their bulk and curiosity were a destructive mix. They'd already smashed two conference tables and several desks.

"Where else could I take them?" I asked. If they stayed here much longer, they'd damage everything in the room and then there would be hell to pay. Literally. We needed to relocate them ASAP. Too bad I had no idea where or how we'd transport the giant celestials there if we had a place.

"Um, how about a farm? The woods? Cooper could add them to his zoo." Roice, the other half of the twin demons of technology whose T-shirt read, "Revenge is beneath me. Accidents, however, will happen," snarled at an ewe. The beast ignored him and continued to chew on the wires she'd pulled out of his combination computer and entertainment system.

It was so strange. The sheep had been terrified by the pursuing demons in the space between, but they didn't appear concerned about the twin demons yelling at them—and me—in the middle of unfamiliar territory. While the tech demons wore a glamour with greasy hair and the lanky bodies of teenaged gamer geeks, they were powerful demons who'd mastered both the magic of their hell realm homeland and the technology of earth.

And they were warriors in their own right, probably as intimidating as D was in their true forms.

Either the celestial critters couldn't sense the danger through demon glamour, or they were smart enough to sense that the grumpy pair of brothers were all bark and no bite. The secret softies were no threat to innocent animals.

I would call Cooper as soon as I had a spare moment. My favorite summoner maintained a base of operations in one of the city's largest parks and kept a menagerie of animals from earth and the demon realm. Who owned who was up for debate, but if anyone could wrangle these celestial creatures and keep them under control, it was Cooper.

Archimedes, his demon dog, could guard them, and Ricky the fox could help. Cooper was living the life of an enchanted fairy tale princess with his menagerie of talking animals. I was all kinds of jealous.

I could call Sully, my trusty demon cat, but she might decide to assume her big cat form and eat the sheep. While loyal to me, she could be unpredictable. She was still new to earth and learning what was fair game in her hunts and what was off limits.

"Cooper's next on my list, but we can't just haul them through the streets of Nashville. We're still trying to maintain secrecy," I said. Where had the shepherd gone? Maybe he could wrangle his flock until we figured out what to do with them. "Mara saved our asses downtown, but the good citizens of Nashville aren't going to buy the movie making angle a second time."

Our team succubus had fallen in love with action-adventure movies when she came to earth around the early 1950s and binged them on her downtime. It was her idea to gather a bunch of demons, glamour them to look like superheroes, extras, and a film crew, and announce to the panicked crowd downtown that Nashville had been chosen as the location for *Red Raven and the Devils*, the first film in a new franchise that would be the big summer blockbuster to beat.

She'd played off the flying celestials as proprietary new CGI technology that would feature in the film and would be popping up from time to time throughout the city. The succubus had even taken footage posted on social media and turned it into an unofficial "leaked" trailer.

Mara was a freakin' genius.

On the other hand, Lacey, Mara's girlfriend, and my partner, was a freakin' snark. She'd treated me to a rendition of Old McJinxie Had a Farm, ei-i-ei-i-o, and on this farm, she had a demon murder cat, two werewolf demons, and a herd of big ass celestial sheep, ei-i-ei-i-blah-blah-blah.

She was one to talk. Simon, her personal greed demon, took the shape of a spectral raven. And if anyone in this scenario had farmer vibes, it was little Miss Lacey Green the freckled redhead in overalls.

At least she was helping Mara convince the greater Nashvegas area that the flying circus of celestials were just movie magic.

Unfortunately, some skeptics were already on the Internet tossing out conspiracy theories, speculating on an invasion from Russia or China, and, naturally, predicting the end of days—Armageddon, the rapture, all the usual suspects that were ironically on the nose. For now, it was background noise. But if the celestials kept up with the flying eyeball-laden ariel jump scares, we'd have a full-scale panic.

"Already called Cooper," Alexi said as he walked in. Alexi Volkov was tall, blonde, muscle-bound, looked like he could kill you—and he could—but deep inside the guy was a marshmallow and was one of my favorite teammates. The Russian surveyed the scene with a big grin on his face.

Alexi winked at me. Then, he shifted into his wolf demon, a curse from his Russian mafia father that he used to track demons in the field.

"Dude, you're going to start a stampede!" Boice drew his demon knife backed away from our esteemed colleague and the sheep.

"Dude, *you're* going to start a stampede if you don't put that knife down," I yelled.

Alexi's wolf body contorted, muscles rippling and skin crawling. I fought the urge to vomit. It was grotesque and looked painful, nothing at all like his normal transformation. Roice froze, his mouth gaping open as he slowly reached for the demon knife at his hip. I would have been funny if not for the tension in the room and the very real danger we'd face with an out-of-control wolf demon. Boice kept his mouth closed while grabbing an office chair and brandishing it like a club.

After several agonizing minutes, Alexi raised his great head and stared at us, tail wagging.

Instead of assuming the shape of a terrifying demonic wolf man, he'd transformed himself into an enormous, adorable creature that looked like a husky German shepherd mix on steroids.

Neat trick. He must've been stretching his shapeshifting skills.

He barked, the sound echoing through the room and bringing the celestial sheep to attention. Circling with grace and speed, the giant dog corralled each beast, moving them away from computer equipment and furniture and wrangling them into the center of the room that we'd cleared.

With each pass, he tightened the circle until the flock stood flank to flank, and in some cases, head to ass, alert, but not frightened.

"Nice going, wolf man," Roice yelled. "You're getting ten ribeyes tonight."

We had the sheep under control, but their guardian was still nowhere to be found.

"Anyone see the shepherd?" I asked, scanning the room. I hoped his flock hadn't crushed him.

"Your mom took him to the kitchen," Boice said. He'd strolled to the center of the room and was scratching Alexi the wonder dog behind the ears. Too weird. Alexi seemed to enjoy the attention and praise, or maybe he was just excited about the promised steaks. At any rate, now that the situation with the flock was under control, I could go check on the shepherd and make sure he wasn't threatening my mother.

I took a moment to appreciate what Mom had done to the large kitchen on this floor of HQ. The industrial appliances and sterile stainless steel remained, but my mom had added her copper pots and pans, colorful accent pieces like the red coffee maker and air fryer, and decorative ceramics that blended beautiful form with function added a warmth to the space that almost matched the warmth of her presence. Plants, decorative plates, and candles gave the space splashes of color, as did the blue wooden stools that surrounded the kitchen island. Checkered placemats sat on the island in perfect alignment with the chairs. It was Gordon Ramsey meets cottagecore and it was magical.

I was so glad she finally had a dream kitchen worthy of the wonderful meals she prepared for the team.

Charlene McGee, a.k.a. Mom, looked younger than she was but reminded us daily that her body felt the mileage even if it didn't show on her face. Tonight, she wore an elegant and comfortable-looking set of blue lounge pants and tunic covered by a homey apron that read "Feed the Demons," a gift from yours truly. My sister had inherited her blond hair and height. The only physical traits I got from Mom were her Scottish facial features and full lips. The rest was all dear old dad, from my dark hair to my brown eyes and olive skin.

Not sure where the boobs came from, but I saluted whichever ancestress had bequeathed them to me.

Mom sat next to the shepherd, who clutched a cup of tea in his hands and took small sips as she spoke to him in gentle, soothing tones. A pang filled my chest and spread through my body. Longing. While we were close and working to mend our relationship, this was a side of my mother I'd rarely experienced. Simple, unguarded tenderness. Beautiful. A gift.

My father had robbed us of that when he'd let an insane archangel disguised as a demon possess me when I was five and then left our family shortly thereafter. Mom worked several jobs to make ends meet and keep us fed, clothed, and to provide occasional treats like toys and sweets. She'd had little left for cuddles and comfort.

Or maybe I thought I hadn't deserved comfort, so I'd pushed her away. That was something I was working on in therapy. It would take a while to resolve.

For the longest time, I thought I was a demon-possessed child. How could I be loveable? True, I'd had D for comfort and companionship when I was young, but deep down, I'd craved my mom's love and acceptance, knowing I'd never get it if she knew the truth about me. Evil demons didn't come to good children, so I figured I was an evil child. I did my best to hide my state of demonic possession, but it never failed to get me in trouble. The whole mess had become a self-fulfilling prophecy. Rage and sadness took me under at the realization that no matter how hard I tried to be good, I couldn't escape the evil inside of me. Then I'd spent the better part of ten years burying those feelings.

They hit me now, those awful feelings I hadn't fully processed. Knowing now that I'd always had mom's love but hadn't been able to accept it made the heartache worse. One of the side effects of therapy was finding and acknowledging uncomfortable truths and feeling all the feels.

Crap. I didn't have time for this right now. Mission first. Heartache later.

I took a deep breath, composed myself, and said to the shepherd, "Your flock is safe and guarded. You're safe, too. Why were you in the space between? Wait," I held up a hand and said, "let's start from the beginning. Why are you on earth?

Mom glared at me. It was like a slap in the face. My expression must have given my feelings away, since she softened her gaze and said, "Can this wait? I've only just calmed Nisroc and he needs food."

I swallowed hard, pushing down impatience and anger. Mom wasn't being mean. She was looking out for the shepherd. She wasn't angry with me, wasn't trying to hurt my feelings or scold me for always doing the wrong thing, for not doing enough or being enough.

My eyes stung. No. No, no, no, this was so not the time to spiral.

I turned my back and busied myself with the fancy coffee maker. When I was certain my voice wouldn't break, I said, "Food is a great idea. But we need answers so we can help Nisroc and others like him who may be out there."

I addressed the shepherd as I filled the grinder with delicious-smelling roasted beans. "My name's Jinx, by the way. I'm guessing you're a refugee celestial who's been hiding out on earth. With war brewing, I assume you took your flock to hide and came to the space between to get safe passage to another realm. Am I right?"

The shepherd spoke, his voice a beautiful tenor. "We came to earth long ago. I cannot say when—we don't reckon time the way your kind does—but it was when creatures like my charoum were tended by humans in vast fields, when steel and glass did not dominate the landscape."

Charoum must be the name of his celestial sheep. So, he and his flock had been hiding on earth for a few thousand years. Someday, when I had a spare moment, I'd have to work on discovering the secret of celestial longevity. Or the secret to demonic long life. Why did they get to live longer than humans?

I watched as the machine took the fresh beans I'd fed into the grinder and mixed the grounds with hot water to make earth's most magic elixir. Demons loved coffee. Celestials probably did, too. I thought about offering Nisroc the shepherd a cup, but my mom had set-in-stone notions about proper beverages for certain occasions. Stress called for tea and soup. I took a deep breath and inhaled the aroma of golden chicken broth with vegetables, herbs, and spices. Mom was baking bread, too.

I turned around while my coffee brewed and said, "So, why are you here? What made you leave your home?"

"My charoum produce the finest wool in our land and the sweetest milk. Their wool can withstand magic when woven with enchantments. I provided wool to archangels and sentinels who protected our realm. It was enough. Then, one day, more was needed. More than I could give. The archangels came and told me they needed four times the wool and double the milk. They were building an army, you see. I could not meet their demands."

He told the story like a robot, his voice slow and lacking inflection. It was jarring, but maybe it was the only way he could tell the story without shutting down or having another panic attack. Having been on the receiving end of more than a few panic attacks, I decided to cut the guy some slack. I nodded, coaxing him to continue while I busied myself adding hazelnut syrup, cream, and a generous shake of powdered chocolate to my coffee creation.

The first sip was heaven.

At last, the shepherd spoke. "If I could not give them what they demanded, they would take my flock and use their powers to extract it themselves. My charoum would not have survived. So I sought out those who ferried celestials out of our lands and to the safety of earth, promising my prize ewe as payment for passage. The celestial who ferried us was generous and kind, requiring no payment. She brought us to an isolated patch of land on earth, taught us how to hide ourselves with glamour, and visited us from time to time. Cassiel—"

I choked and sputtered, barely stopping a coffee spill down my clean white shirt. "Cassiel! That thieving traitor of a so-called angel who stole the Sigillum Dei and disappeared brought you and your flock here?"

Nisroc's gaze sent a shiver of ice down my spine as he regarded me, unblinking, and with rigid features that didn't hide the slight tremor in his shoulders. He rose with slow control and grabbed his shepherd's hook, holding it more like a weapon, and I had to remind myself that the appearance of a hunched old human man was a glamour. For all I knew, he had tentacles, or knife arms, or scales.

Being celestial, I'd bet money he had at least a hundred eyeballs in his true form.

"You will not speak of my benefactor in such a way. She is no thief, nor traitor. She has saved countless celestial lives."

I drew my knife and started flipping it from hand to hand, throwing in a few spins and showy moves to remind him that I had a weapon, too. He'd seen me use it. He'd seen me use a lot of weapons and magic.

Mom glared at me, but it couldn't be helped. I was fresh out of energy for a calm interrogation. "Benefactor, huh? She wasn't such a great benefactor when she left you behind to face a hoard of dragon demons. And Cassiel stole the artefact she used to make that portal from my team. We can't banish warring master demons and archangels from earth until we get it back. I don't want to hurt you, especially since I saved you from the hoard of dragon demons," I said, pointing the tip of the knife in his direction. "But I won't be bullied."

Nisroc scowled, but he put down his hook and planted his skinny ass back in the chair. I didn't look at my mom. I'd deal with her disapproval later. Right now, I needed answers.

"Okay, tell me the rest," I said, sheathing my blade.

The shepherd didn't drop the nasty expression, but that was okay. As long as he kept talking, I could put up with dirty looks. "Cassiel came to fetch us when the troubles began. Archangels and master demons are back in this realm. Earth is no longer a safe place for us... She needs the Sigillum Dei to transport us to a new place of refuge. Didn't she ask you for it?"

Well fuck a duck.

The question sucker punched me in the gut.

I shook it off and answered the shepherd's uncomfortable question. "As a matter of fact, she did ask. She tried to strike a bargain, but I refused to hand it over. We couldn't afford to let it go while master demons and archangels are still loose on earth." Before the grumpy shepherd could get up and grab his stupid hook again, I held up a hand. "Cassiel didn't tell me why she needed it. If she'd explained things, I would have helped her."

Maybe. I would have helped her get the celestial refugees to safety, but I wouldn't have given her the artefact.

"Would you?" He eyed me with suspicion. "You are a celestial, and yet you aligned yourself with demons. You aid and abet them."

I folded my arms over my chest and bit my tongue. I was only half celestial but pointing that out again would set us off on a tangent. I didn't care to explain my complicated heritage to him.

"Um, I'm a demon hunter, meaning I hunt rogue demons and protect the law-abiding demonic refugee population in this city. Your people aren't the only beings in need of a safe place. And for your information, the man who helped me save your ungrateful ass is a demon, as are the people out there taking care of your flock. I'm team protect the innocent —demon, human, celestial, doesn't matter. Understand?"

He opened and closed his mouth a few times before nodding.

"Where is Cassiel?" I asked.

Nisroc's face turned to stone. "You will cast me out if I do not tell you?"

Oh, for the love of licorice...

"No, I won't cast you out. But if you're cooperative, I'll make your stay comfortable and help you get off earth and to...where were you going, anyway?" I'd assumed the celestial realm was no safer than the hell realm.

Shrugging, the shepherd sipped his tea. My mother placed a steaming bowl of soup in front of him, and a plate with fresh bread and a neatly folded napkin. At last, he said, "Someplace safe."

So. Not. Helpful.

"Jane Aurelia McGee," my mom said. Why the hell was she using my full name like she had when I was a kid? I leveled my gaze on her, and she pointed to the seat next to Nisroc. "Sit. Eat. You need to take care of yourself so you can track down Cassie, get this gentleman and his flock to their destination, and defeat that master demon disguised as a real estate tycoon."

I stood there, dumbfounded. She wasn't mad at me. She wanted to feed me.

Sighing, mom came over and reached out tentative hand to stroke my cheek. I fought the urge to jerk away or lean in. This was too weird. I didn't trust it.

"I can't change what your father did to you, or make up for the years we lost because we didn't, I didn't..."

I took her hand in mine. "I know, Mom. Food sounds great."

Abandoning my interrogation—for now—I settled in to enjoy some good, homecooked comfort food. I'd eaten two bowls of delicious soup and was getting ready to check on D when Megan burst through the kitchen door, eyes swollen and face puffy from crying. My normally poised and polished older sister was a mess of streaked mascara, disheveled hair, and a fine tremor ran through her body.

"Who do I need to kill?" I asked, a growl in my voice. My inner wolf demon itched to get out and avenge our kin.

"Brad," she said, her voice cracking on a sob. "Brad left me."

CHAPTER FIVE

Brad. *Fucking* Brad.

I was totally going to kill him.

Megan's husband, who clearly never deserved her, had apparently decided that Megan's "focus on career" as a demon hunter was more than he could handle. True, he was a mundane human who had been thrust into the hidden and frightening world of demons and celestials and their brewing war. And yes, when they'd married, he had no idea she was half celestial. But neither had she.

Brad was a weak man, but I'd never pegged him as cruel or disloyal. I was a lousy judge of character, it seemed.

"He swore to take you for better or worse, till death do you part," I said, rubbing Megan's shoulders while she sobbed at the kitchen table. "I was there and heard him say it. Say the word and I'll make sure he keeps that promise."

"Jane, I did not raise you to be a murderer," Mom said, but she didn't sound like she meant it. Dad left her when we were very young, abandoning her to raise two children on her own with very little money. Seeing her daughter suffer a similar fate would make even the most moral, upstanding woman a little murderous.

At least Megan would get a boatload of cash in the divorce settlement. Or through Brad's life insurance policy. Either worked for me.

"I don't understand. We were good together. I kept him safe from all this," Megan said, gesturing to the space around her. She had kept him as safe as she could from our world. And herself.

I clenched my jaw tight and, for once, thought before I spoke and said something snarky and unhelpful. After a deep breath, I said, "You're the one out here risking life and limb to save the world. And before that, you were saving the world at a nonprofit. What's he been doing, other than working all hours and leaving you at home to be his cook, maid, and trophy wife?"

Megan looked up at me, a scowl on her face, and opened her mouth, ready to defend her man. Then she closed it as fat tears rolled down her cheeks. No defense.

Oh, Megan, I would give anything to spare you this heartache.

Guilt bloomed within me, as dreadful as it was familiar. I had dragged her into this world, along with Mom. When my former boss Sameal, the sometimes demon and other times Angel of Death, threatened my family if I failed to send Lord Belial's minion back to the hell realm, I'd had my team on surveillance to protect them. Alexi had been ready to move them to a safe house. I didn't fail, but Megan blew Alexi's cover and figured out that I was a demon hunter rather than the private investigator I pretended to be.

Megan had taken the news well. She'd been...proud of me. Me, the former weird kid sister and bad seed, who'd brought the family nothing but misery. Even better, when she figured out she was half celestial on our deadbeat dad's side, she joined up with our team of demon hunters. Brave, benevolent, generous—that was my sister to a fault.

And now she was losing the man she loved because of it. Because of me.

I swallowed hard and put the guilt aside. I was good at that. Right now, Megan needed moral support, not a sniveling brat of a baby sister.

"Drink this."

Mom, who'd been puttering around the kitchen while Megan spilled the tea about Brad the bastard, put a clear glass tumbler full of amber liquid and a giant ice cube in front of Meg.

"Thanks," Megan said, taking a sip and closing her eyes to savor the smoky whiskey and the slow burn as it went down her throat. Whiskey was Meg's poison. Part of me wanted to join her, but it would be too easy to make drowning my sorrows a habit. No more alcohol for me. I had too many responsibilities and too much to lose.

I stood up and stretched. With one crisis after another, I'd been ignoring the aches and pains of recent battle. Fresh out of adrenaline to mask it, I was in a world of hurt. Nothing compared to Megan, though.

"Can I get you something to eat?" I asked. The shepherd and I had polished off Mom's soup, but HQ was always stocked with good stuff. I made a mean grinder sandwich.

"No, thanks," Megan said, offering a wan smile that didn't reach her eyes. "I don't have much of an appetite. What I really need is something to do."

Typical. Megan dealt with her problems by staying crazy busy. Dr. Khatri, therapist and temporary addition to our demon hunting team, would call it "avoidance," but there were worse ways to cope. I could loan her my demon kitty if I could find her. Sully's purrs had soothed my ravaged soul a time or twenty.

"Mistress? I am sorry for your troubles. Would you like to come and meet my charoum? They are a great comfort to me, and I would share the solace they offer." The shepherd had been quietly following our family drama from a quiet corner of the kitchen. He bowed to Megan, the little creep. I save him from a band of maaks and get yelled at, but Megan cries and suddenly he's a gentleman?

Ugh. But it might take Megan's mind off her troubles.

"They're pretty cute," I said. "Cooper's going to take them off our hands, but if you hurry, you can watch the twins have a conniption fit over damage to their computers."

That earned a genuine smile.

Instead of chaos, we were greeted by the sight of the entire team interacting with the flock of celestial sheep. Alexi in his good dog form had settled on the floor to cuddle the lamb while the twins scratched the ram behind the ears. The ram's head was raised, and his eyes were closed in ecstasy at the attention. Mara in her preferred humanoid blonde bombshell form had returned with Lacey, her girlfriend and my demon hunting partner. The two of them were lavishing an ewe by brushing its silky, otherworldly wool. Lacey's red curls bounced as she giggled, earning a look of adoration from Mara.

At least one pair of lovebirds in our group was happy.

Make that two. Sort of.

Trinity, our fearless leader and the smartest person in every room, surveyed the scene with Marquess Samagina of the hell realm, her personal demon and beau. Her dark hair was pulled back into an elegant bun, and she wore an exquisitely tailored suit of royal blue that paired beautifully with her brown skin and matched the frames of her glasses perfectly. I should really get some fashion tips from her.

She dressed like a grown up. I generally wore combat gear or snarky T-shirts and jeans.

Sam, by contrast, wore sumptuous robes befitting his station as a hell realm Marquess. Handsome, with black hair, a neatly trimmed beard, and olive skin a touch darker than mine and Megan's, he had the bearing of a scholarly warrior mage. It fit. He clasped Trinity's hand in his. It was adorable, aside from the stiffness in Trinity's shoulders and her clenched jaw. If you looked up tension in the dictionary, it would look like our team leader.

I would have been sorry for her if Trinity wasn't being a jerk about D.

When we returned to HQ bloody and exhausted with the celestials we'd rescued in tow, Trinity had eyed D with what appeared to be shock and anger before Sam hauled him away to rest. That made no sense considering he'd saved the day and proven himself to be an even bigger asset to our team.

I mean, shock I understood. Seeing D turn into a giant of a demon with wings, horns, and menace a plenty had shocked me, too. But only for a second. After that I'd just been grateful he was in good fighting form.

What the hell was up Trinity's ass? I'd fight her to defend D's honor and position. Besides, it wasn't like she had room to talk. She was dating a Marquess of the Hell Realm. There was no reason for her of all people to have a problem with my demon sweetheart.

Angry boss or not, I still wished D was here. Kind of hard to be surrounded by couples while on your own. Then again, Megan and Mom had it worse. My love was resting and would return to me after he recovered.

Alexi sat up, ears pricked and gaze intent as he watched Megan walk slowly toward one of the smaller ewes. Her eyes were red and her face puffy and tear streaked. Alexi's eyes flashed red. The Russian had a thing for my sister but had never acted on it out of respect for her and her marriage. I'd seen the shy smiles and looks of raw longing he sent her way when he thought no one was looking. Ever since he'd served as guard for her and our mother, Alexi had been staunchly protective of Megan.

She needed time. Maybe, someday...

In the meantime, he could help me get a little revenge on Megan's soon-to-be ex.

Something niggled the back of my brain. Brad was a money man. He was good at his job and practical by nature. Was he terrified of the hidden world he'd been thrust into? Sure. But why leave now? Our team had defeated one master demon and two celestials, proving we could hold our own. Plus, Brad had made a killing on his investments in the start-ups that filled the vacuum left by the video game development company that served as a front for celestial weapons manufacturing.

If he stuck around, the twins could make him a billionaire five times over with their insider knowledge. They'd offered. Boice and Roice liked making money, too, and in their twisted code of ethics, helping Brad would be compensation for his entanglement with our operation. The guy was only human. No magic powers, no ties to the demon or celestial realms other than through his wife.

Soon-to-be ex-wife.

It was a hell of a risk, but the payoff would be worth it. He and Megan would be set for life. Hell, their great, great, great grandchildren would be set for life.

So why walk away?

He must have gotten a better offer. But where?

I had a thought. I terrible, infuriating, awful thought. Brad had been dabbling in real estate recently—very recently. As in around about the time that a powerful demon disguised as a real estate tycoon started wheeling and dealing in Nashville. Beale Bub of Bub Realty, our next master demon target and, with a name like his, the embodiment of gluttony and excess, had to know what happened to the Master Demon of Sloth. He'd want to know who sent her ass back to the hell realm permanently, and he'd want to gather intel on his enemies to make sure it didn't happen to him.

Damn it, I hoped I was wrong, but if I wasn't, we were in a deeper pile of shit than any of us had imagined. I took out my phone and fired off a text to Boice and Roice.

Need surveillance on my douchebag brother-in-law. He may be embedded with our next demon target.

CHAPTER SIX

By the time we got Nisroc and his sheep settled on the lower levels of HQ, I was too wound up to sleep. We'd offered the shepherd his own room with a comfortable bed, but he refused to leave his flock. At least Mom got him to eat.

Still hungry from fighting and expending my powers, I wandered back into the kitchen to scrounge up some leftovers. Mom sat at the table with Megan, sharing steaming cups of coffee and their troubles. It was a familiar scene. They'd always been close. I'd spent many a night creeping just outside the kitchen of my childhood home, listening to my mother and sister talk about everything and nothing at all. Mom's jobs, Megan's classes, boyfriends—Megan's and Mom's—and every now and again, me.

On one memorable night, I heard them talking about some trouble I'd had at school when I was seven years old. I didn't want to think about it, but hearing the low, murmured conversation just outside my reach brought it all back.

"Did Jane's teacher call you?" Megan asked.

"She did," Mom said, her voice flat. "Said she was disruptive in class.

Talking. To herself. Or maybe an imaginary friend. It's not that unusual for a kid her age."

I shrank and tried to hide the hitch in my breath. Trouble. I was in it. Again. I was trouble. But I'd just been trying to get the demon inside of me to stop distracting me so I could read the passage we'd been assigned. Hannah didn't like the story. She was bored and wanted to go explore the woods on the other side of the playground fence.

I wanted to go, too, mostly because D was hiding there.

I didn't know where my secret demon friend spent all his time, but often enough he came with me to school. Sometimes I'd sneak him in. He never got caught, and he learned a lot. He was way faster and way smarter than I was, and he even helped me with my homework. Thanks to him, I could read better and faster than all my classmates. They used to think I was stupid and weird. Now, I was just weird. Thanks to D, I was smart.

And with him around, I wasn't alone.

No one liked me at school because I was trouble. They sent me to talk to the school counselor a lot. I knew better than to talk about Hannah. Only crazy people heard voices, and anyone who said they were demon possessed would be called crazy. Those people got taken away from their families and locked up in bad places.

I didn't want to go to a bad place.

But I belonged in a bad place. Only bad people got demons. D said that wasn't true, but deep down in my heart, I knew it was. My daddy left because I was bad. Mommy had to work extra hard because I was bad. I tried to be good, but I was bad, and I was trouble.

"One of her teachers told me we needed to take Jane to a special doctor. Maybe she has autism or something. They can help her," Megan said.

Megan was wrong. No one could help me.

"We can't afford it," Mom said. "Besides, I've been reading up on autism, ADD, ADHD, dyslexia, all that. That's not Jane. She's just...different. It's been hard for all of us, but I think it hit Jane especially hard. I told her teacher about our...situation."

Mom never mentioned dad or how he left. Not to me or my sister. I think it made her sad. Sometimes at night when I was hanging out with D, I heard Mom cry.

"Don't worry," Mom said. "You should focus on school. Let me worry about Jane."

I crept back to my room and crawled into bed, pulling the covers over my head. D poked me. He was hungry. I'd have to go back when everyone was asleep to get him some food. He hid in our house, and I kept him in my room, gave him food, and he kept me company. The little demon had come to me just after I found out I was possessed. Like attracted like. He was trouble, too. That's why someone abandoned him on earth and left him all alone.

Only, I didn't think he was trouble. He was just a kid, like me.

"No food yet," I said, burrowing deeper under the covers. "Try to sleep. I'll go get you something later."

"Why are you crying?" D asked.

D always knew when I was crying. He knew things. Demons knew things. They had magic and they watched people. There were lots of them around. I saw them because Hannah did. I had to pretend I didn't. D told me bad things would happen to me if the demons knew I could them. Most of them just did normal things, but others hunted.

They hunted people.

D sometimes hunted the demons that hunted people. Mostly, he just looked out for me and my family.

"I got in trouble today at school."

D snorted. "What else is new?"

I laughed. D was good at making me laugh. I wiped my eyes and poked my head out of the covers. My secret friend looked like an ordinary boy. Except for his eyes. They glowed red sometimes. Mine did, too, when Hannah got mad.

"Hannah wanted to go run in the woods," I said. "I got in trouble for talking to her."

D sat on the bed beside me and gave me a lopsided grin. "Well, we can go now."

I grabbed my pillow and slugged him with it. I was already in trouble, and he wanted me to sneak out of the house and go someplace I wasn't supposed to go?

It would be fun to go to the woods and run, though.

D knew he was getting to me. "If you go now, it'll make Hannah happy. Then she won't talk to you in class, and you won't get in trouble."

He held out his hand. His dimpled grin and sense of adventure were irresistible. But how was he planning to get us out? We had to go past the kitchen to get to the front door. Our floors creaked. And my mom had supernatural hearing. If we got caught...

"Trust me."

I took D's hand, and he led me to my bedroom door, opening it without a sound and tugging me through, then closing it behind us. We crept down the dark hallway. I braced for the squeak that would give us away, but it didn't come.

We weren't making any noise.

D stopped in front of the kitchen doorway. I bumped into him and yelped. Well, I meant to yelp, but when I opened my mouth, no sound came out. I tried to ask D what he was doing. He just stood in the doorway as if daring my mom to turn around and spot the stranger who'd been living in her home for two years without her knowing. I tried to whisper his name. Then I tried to yell.

I poked him in the side. Instead of jumping or moving us along, he pulled me close to him so I stood in the kitchen doorway where Mom or Megan could see. Mom turned away from the kitchen sink, busy drying a dish. The dishes were one of the few nice things we owned. We'd had nice things before daddy left. They disappeared a little at a time. Megan told me Mom sold them.

Mom looked up. I froze. She stared at me. I waited for her to drop the dish or yell at me or D. My heart raced, but D's arm around me was reassuring.

Mom turned toward the kitchen cabinet and put the dish away. Megan chattered about a school project, and they acted like D and I weren't even there. How did she not see us?

D pulled me away from the kitchen doorway. We walked soundlessly through the living room and out the front door. After we made it down the sidewalk and past three houses, I tried speaking again.

"How did they not see us?" I asked. "What did you do?" He'd snuck us out of the house. We didn't get caught. Even though Mom looked right at us, we didn't get caught.

D grinned. "Magic. We can come and go whenever we want to. They won't notice you're gone."

"Whoa," I said. "You can do magic? Like, magic, magic." Not like that stupid magician we'd seen at school. He was a phony. Hannah told me so and showed me how he tricked us.

"Yeah," he said, lowering his gaze and kicking a rock. "Some. You can, too, with Hannah."

I seriously doubted that. D must've guessed what I was thinking because he scowled when he looked at me. He was mad. I didn't want him mad at me. D was my only friend. Tears welled in my eyes, and I looked away. No way would I cry like a little baby in front of D.

"Look," he said, his voice soft. "I only just learned how to do the sneak out trick. If Hannah wants to try, I can teach you both."

I nodded, blinking back tears. He wasn't mad. I looked back up and met the gaze of the smirking demon boy.

"So, you wanna go to the woods? There's something you need to see."

"Okay," I said, a big grin splitting my face. "I've got a little money. We can go get some hamburgers."

And just like that, D turned one of the worst nights in my young life into the best. We grabbed some cheap fast food and took it with us into a patch of forest at the edge of the neighborhood. Okay, it wasn't really a forest, but in my child mind, it was a magical fairy tale land full of wonders and monsters, where I could run and be free. I spent as much time as I could there, especially after I found out I was possessed.

That night, I found out I was right about the wonders and monsters.

For the first time, I saw demon realm creatures lurking in the woods and mingling with native animals. And, deep in the forest and hidden behind magic I would later learn was demon glamour, I met other demons like D. D made the glamour go away. And I didn't have to pretend like I *didn't know they were demons. D told them they could trust me. They were hiding on earth from the bad demons in the hell realm. They came here using portals and they had to stay hidden or else something would come and get them.*

Someone worse than the demons they'd fled.

I didn't know it then, but later, I'd be working for that someone.

That night, I learned that most demons were just trying to get by, that worse things hunted them, and that D had a lot more power and influence in the demon community than I imagined.

"Jane?"

My mom's voice jolted me out of the memory and back to reality. She looked tired. So did Megan. I shouldn't bother them.

"You okay?" Megan asked.

I shook my head and tried to act casual. "Fine. I'm fine. Just came to grab a snack before bed. How you holding up?"

Megan sighed and looked down at her clasped hands. She wasn't wearing her wedding ring, or the giant diamond Brad bought her for their last anniversary. I hoped she'd pawned them. "Still in shock, I guess. Talking to the doc tomorrow, but I'm still cleared for field work."

Mom frowned. "You need to take some time for yourself."

Megan shook her head. "No, I need to work. Besides, the team needs me."

She was right. Working was better than sitting alone with her thoughts. I got that. I also got Mom's point. I wished we had more demon hunters, more time, more resources. If I wasn't a demon hunter, Mom and Megan would never have gotten involved in this mess. I'd been wrong all those years ago. I hadn't done anything to deserve demonic possession. Hell, it wasn't even a demon. My father had infected me with an insane archangel and then bailed. He was the bad guy.

But I was still trouble, it seemed. Trouble to Mom, Megan, and everyone around me.

I went to the fridge and rummaged around. I pulled out a mostly empty pie pan with a single slice of quiche. That would do. I grabbed it and pulled a pint of ice cream out of the freezer to take back to my room. If I had to wallow in bittersweet memories, I may as well have comfort food.

"Hey, Jane," Megan said. I turned around and met my sister's red-eyed gaze. She was giving me such an odd look, like she could see through me. "Would you like to join us for a cup of coffee?"

My chest went tight, and I blinked back tears. I'd never been invited to the table before. Then again, I'd never asked.

"I don't want to intrude," I muttered, looking away.

Mom stood up and pulled out an extra chair from the table. "You're not," she said.

I walked slowly, moving on autopilot, and sat down. Mom grabbed my quiche and busied herself grabbing a plate. She put three spoons on the table and a cup of coffee in front of me. The warm scent of hazelnut wafted from the cup, soothing my senses and my soul. Megan opened the container and shoved a large spoonful of mint chocolate chip ice cream into her mouth, closing her eyes as she savored the delicious frozen concoction.

I smiled and took a bite of my own. Comfort food was always better shared.

Mom put the plate in front of me. I took a sip of coffee and dug into the egg, ham, and cheese delight.

"Thanks," I said between bites.

"You're welcome," Mom said. "I'm glad you joined us. We need to family up right now."

I nodded.

"And just so you know," Megan said. "You've never been trouble."

I almost choked. How did she know?

Mom clapped me on the back and said, "Can't have you lurking out in the hallway like you did when you were little. I should have known you needed something...I wish..."

I shook my head. "You didn't know. It wasn't your fault. You did the best you could. You did great. I don't want to live in the past."

Mom nodded. "Okay. Megan and I were about to break out some cards. Want to play?"

I smiled, the tightness in my chest melting. "I'd love to."

Tomorrow, there would be demons to fight and summoners to find, a cheating brother-in-law to punish and an artefact to retrieve. But for now, I'd savor the moment with the McGee women, this time as a part of them.

And I did. Except for one thought that niggled in the back of my brain.

Today, I'd learned once again that D had more power than I realized. How much did I really know about my demon?

CHAPTER SEVEN

The next day brought undercover work—my favorite kind of work. Or it used to be.

The last time I'd gone undercover, I'd been caught in a mind trap concocted by two rogue angels. They'd made me as soon as I walked in the door. Of course, I'd been under the impression I was infiltrating a den of demons.

We'd all been surprised.

Nothing else to do but get back up on that horse. This time, however, I was better prepared. And I had backup. Lacey, my partner, BFF, and sometimes pain-in-the-ass was unusually nervous.

"Are you sure we won't be recognized?" Lacey asked. Again.

I checked my glamour in the rearview mirror of D's Mustang and stroked my goatee. The glamour sessions with Mara were paying off. I looked every inch the nouveau riche redneck dude bro from my light brown hair that was shaved with an undercut and long on the top in a "fashionable" man bun, facial hair, overpriced suit, and gaudy as hell cowboy boots. The car was part of our disguise, on loan from D. He trusted me with his car. It made me all warm and fuzzy inside.

And the Mustang purred like a kitten and was a dream to drive.

Too bad he wasn't returning my texts or calls. Maybe he was still wiped out from our battle in the space between followed by his feat of amazing teleportation with a giant flock of celestial sheep. Or maybe he was avoiding me. Ugh, after all the sessions I'd had with Dr. Khatri I should be able to shut down the stupid voices in my head that filled me with doubt and anxiety.

Right. If I couldn't shut them off, I'd drown them out with work. D would call when he was ready. There was no need to worry about him or what he could do, no matter what Trinity said.

"We've got glamour," I said. My deep voice was kind of sexy. "We've got spells from the twins and Sam to hide our demon essences—"

"Your demon essences and celestial essence that could blow our cover." Lacey's lips, glamoured to look like she'd come straight from the cosmetic surgeon's office after an injection of fillers, pouted. Oh, goody. The welcome wagon would have a great time watching us have our first domestic dispute.

"Are you still mad you didn't get to be the man?" I smirked, leaning back in the leather seat and spreading my legs. "I won the coin toss fair and square."

Lacey snorted. "No. Everyone knows you're a dick. You might as well wear one."

The buxom blonde glamour my partner wore was the perfect pairing with my own glamour. Lacey shifted in her seat, adjusting the short leather skirt that covered her long legs and adjusting her boobs in the low-cut T-shirt. Mara had glamoured them to look natural. I was pretty sure Lacey was enjoying them, and both she and Mara would enjoy them together later, in private.

The gaudy jewelry really tied the look together.

Hmm, I wondered if D might enjoy fooling around with me in this form...

We were parked on the street of Nashville's newest luxury subdivision that featured custom McMansions on small, perfectly landscaped lots. Gated community, of course, and immaculate despite the ongoing construction. Underground utilities, world-class security, a golf-course, four tennis courts, three pools with private cabanas, a "modest" convention center for HOA meetings and community events, exclusive on-site dining and a fine wine and spirits bar were among the amenities available.

They even had a luxury dog park.

Swan Springs, a custom community designed by Beale Bub of Bub Realty, lived up to the Master Demon of Gluttony's vision of world-class homes and their motto, "The sky's the limit. Come live the dream and take what's yours!" Lacey and I were here to take a tour as prospective buyers and find out all we could about Beelzebub's operation and his end game. Sure, the excesses promised to those who could afford to live in this sprawling private paradise were right up Beelzebub's alley, but what did it have to do with the coming war?

What nefarious plans did the demon have for the hapless mortals who lived here?

Only one way to find out.

A tall brunette in a beautifully tailored business suit was heading toward our car. She held a clipboard and sported a megawatt smile. This must be the on-site agent.

"Come on, darlin'," I drawled, flashing my skeeviest smile at Lacey. "Let's go talk to the nice lady and see if she can get us in with the head demon in charge."

Lacey unbuckled her seatbelt and glowered at me. "Don't call me darlin'."

I blew her a kiss. "Whatever you say, sweet cheeks. Simon ready to go?"

Simon was Lacey's personal demon. An immaterial mammon, a.k.a. greed demon, he was a master of stealth, digital research, and always had his mistress's back. They made one hell of a team. The pair had been professional shoplifters before being recruited to our demon hunting team.

It was that or go to jail.

Our former boss was the king of shitty bargains. Still, I was glad to have Lacey on our team, and with the change in management, she worked as a demon hunter and guardian of humanity because she wanted to, because it was the right thing to do.

Lacey traded her angry look for a smile. "Simon is already on it. He's in that agent's phone collecting all kinds of records on Bub Realty's sales force, financials, buyers and prospective buyers. He'll send it all back to the twins so they can work their tech mojo."

The pride in her voice made me smile. I didn't have a personal demon I could bring with me into the field. But I did have a demon battle cat. Sully was sitting in the backseat of D's Mustang glamoured to look like a ginormous Rottweiler—though not nearly as ginormous as her oversized winged battle cat on steroids form.

She referred to the Rottweiler glamour as a "stupid dog."

At least, I think that's what she said. The cat was smart. Smarter than some of my teammates, I suspected. But she was still working on learning the finer points of human speech. She'd hissed and said, "Stoo-pit dog! Pi-zza."

I got the last part. I owed her lots and lots of pizza for this. That cat could eat anything and everything, and she usually did. Frequently. In vast quantities. Pizza was her favorite.

I nodded and exited the vehicle, walking around to open Lacey's door like the nouveau rich gentleman I was pretending to be. Lacey got out and opened the backdoor for Sully, who'd pitched a fit about the collar and leash but was now playing her part. The brunette waved and said, "Mr. and Mrs. Dixon! Hello, and welcome to Swan Springs, your future home. I'm Lindsey Swathmore."

Lindsey held out a perfectly manicured hand. I took it in both of mine and shook it gently, turning on the charm. "Pleasure to meet you, Miss Lindsey. I'm Jesse Dixon, and this is my fiancée, Brittany Branson."

I let go of her hand and Lacey finally got with the program and started playing her part. "It's so nice to meet you," Lacey said, shaking Lindsey's hand, making sure to flash the giant rock on the engagement ring she wore on her left hand. Sully heeled like a good dog but eyed Lindsey with interest. A little too much. "Jesse told me this place was a dream, but he didn't do it justice. It's so...incredible."

Lindsey smiled and spread her arms to encompass the wonder that was Swan Springs. "Isn't it just? We're in Phase I, so it's a great time to buy. Prices will go up as we expand, but don't worry. We never, ever skimp on quality. The home you buy today will be just as spectacular as the one we sell to your neighbors a year from now."

"Well, I'd be proud to call this place home," I said, winking at Lindsey. "Reckon you can show us around?"

Lindsey smiled. "Of course. First, let's step into my office so we can verify the information you provided us on your pre-application."

We followed the sales agent to a small building that looked like a replica carriage house that sat outside the gate of what was likely a large mansion. The ten-foot-tall stone fence and landscaping hid the home from view, which was odd. The other homes were visible from the street, even the ones set far back on their lots, their ostentatiousness on full display.

Lindsey held open the door for us. Lacey went inside, but I stopped our hostess. "You wouldn't happen to have a water dish for Peaches?"

Lindsey's smile faltered as she looked from me to my demon cat in disguise. "Peaches?"

I sagged my shoulders, feigning embarrassment. "She's Brittany's dog. I would've named her Mayhem, or Danger, but I gotta keep the little woman happy."

Lindsey laughed. "Sure thing. She's a good dog, right? I won't have to worry about her running off and biting a neighbor? Or," she lowered her voice to a whisper, "doing a number two on one of the yards?"

Wow, this place was so fancy they didn't allow dog shit? Guess it didn't fit the aesthetic.

"She's very well trained," I said. "Peaches, up!"

Sully glared at me but obliged, standing on her hind legs with perfect balance and poise.

"Good girl," I said, patting her on the head. "Beg."

"No..."

The word came out in a low, growly tone that sounded like an asthmatic wolf.

Sully was stubborn. It was her first time doing undercover work. I'd trained her as best I could with Alexi's help. She'd done perfectly during our simulations. But, in typical cat fashion, she'd decided to be uncooperative at the worst possible moment.

"Did...did she just say no?" Lindsey asked, gaze wide with awe and fascination.

I laughed. "It sure sounds like it. She's a smart girl, but she's being a little ornery right now. Come on, Peaches. Show the nice lady a pretty beg and I'll give you a treat." I held out a small piece of beef jerky.

Sully kept her ass planted and opened her big fat mouth to scream, "Pi-zza!"

"No," I said through clenched teeth, hoping Lindsey didn't understand Sully-speak. "This treat now, the other treat later. If you're very good, I'll get you a pup cup from the ice cream shop on the way home."

Sully barked and wagged her stub of a tail like a good dog and, grudgingly, assumed the beg pose. Her look promised revenge, but she came through. I gave her the beef jerky. Lindsey brought her hand to Sully's nose after she scarfed down the treat. Sully sniffed, then head butted the woman. I groaned internally. We were going to have to work on canine behaviors before our next undercover gig. The demon cat was totally in danger of blowing our cover.

"She's unusual, but seems like a very well-behaved girl, don't you, Peaches?" Lindsey scratched behind her ears and baby-talked her until Sully rolled over and showed the agent her belly. Okay, maybe Sully wasn't so bad at the undercover work after all. Or maybe Lindsey gave good scratches.

Lindsey rose and straightened her skirt. "I'll go get a bowl and some water. Be back in a sec."

Once the agent disappeared inside the door, I knelt and rubbed Sully's belly. "Good job. When I go inside with Lacey, I want you to go check out what's hiding behind that gate. Don't let anyone see you, especially flying. Got it?"

"Pi-zza."

This cat had a one-track mind. Then again, I was food motivated, too. "Yes, when we're done here, you get all the pizza you can eat."

"Ice cream yum, Ink. Pi-zza ice cream yum."

The "Ink" referred to yours truly. It was as close as she could come to saying Jinx, and it made my heart melt whenever she said it. "Okay, fine, yes, ice cream, too. Be careful. And don't take too long. We don't want Lindsey to have a panic attack over potential dog poop."

Sully sneezed and sat up, a look of indignation on her adorable Rottie face. She wasn't fooling me. Given half a chance, she would poop all over the neighborhood, but at least she'd bury it in the front flowerbeds. I was tempted to let her. Good thing she could use the toilet. The thought of scooping a demon cat's toxic litterbox made my stomach turn.

Lindsey emerged with a fancy red enameled metal bowl decorated with pawprints and bones. "We give one to all our residents with pets when they move in. Engraved, of course. We can even get you one in peach."

I'll bet you could.

I thanked her and we headed inside the carriage house that looked more like a regency parlor straight out of a romance novel with powder blue covered with gilded mirrors and a framed landscape on canvas that hung neatly over the mantle of a fireplace. Lindsey's desk sat on top of a thick Persian rug. Lacey was already seated in an antique upholstered chair, perched on the edge of her seat and seemingly engrossed in her manicured nails.

Great acting, but she didn't fool me. She'd been discreetly scanning the space for signs of demon and celestial activity while I distracted Lindsey with our "dog." She looked up at me and smiled, placing her hands neatly on her crossed legs, the code sign for no supernatural beings detected. Figured. We'd lucked out with our previous case and followed demonic activity straight to our target.

Beelzebub was smarter, apparently, putting humans in charge of his public-facing activities.

Lindsey sat and opened her sleek laptop. "Now, we ran your background checks. You both have excellent credit scores," she said, smiling.

"Your portfolio of investments, assets, and, of course, your cash-on-hand qualify you for purchase. But that's only the first step in the process."

I arched a brow at her, leaning back in my chair and manspreading like I owned the place. "That a fact?"

Lindsey held up a conciliatory hand. "Mr. Dixon, you must understand that Swan Springs is a planned community. Exclusivity is part of the package and the appeal. Our clients could purchase property in a variety of upscale neighborhoods or purchase a large parcel of land for a custom build. What we offer is community. You and Ms. Branson fit our profile, but we need to be certain you fit the neighborhood and that you can represent the dream we provide, following our Covenants, Conditions, and Restrictions, and being the kind of neighbors our current residents desire."

I opened my mouth to say something snarky, but Lacey cut me off. "Oh, I assure you we're neighborly. I won the congeniality award in my sorority. And we'll follow the rules."

"I'm sure you will, Ms. Branson, but in order to purchase property in Swan Springs, we require an interview with our community board."

"Who's on the board?" I asked, feigning boredom.

Lindsey smiled. "The board is made up of our community founders as well as Mr. Bub, our founder." She beamed with pride. "As far as the interview, it's rather informal. You'll be invited to the home of one of our founders for a cocktail mixer and will have the chance to get to know your future neighbors while they get to know you. After that, you'll speak with the board and Mr. Bub. I cannot disclose the interview questions, but please don't worry. Just...be yourselves."

Uh-huh. No way was this legal. Or maybe the profiling was coded in legalese to make sure the residents of this community were rich, white, and snotty. Growing up poor, I hated everything this community represented. And if I walked in for a viewing as myself, I'd never make it past the gate with my olive complexion and blended Anglo-Persian features. Elitist, classist, and most likely racist and homophobic, most of my team wouldn't be welcome here as ourselves. Hell, most of the residents of Nashville wouldn't be welcome.

When I banished Beelzebub back to the hell realm, I'd take every last asset he owned on earth and donate it to folks in need. That would ruin his gluttonous appetite.

"So, when's the interview?" Lacey asked, laying the Southern belle charm on thick.

Lindsey busied herself typing and said, "How about Thursday evening at 7:00 pm?"

"We'll be there," I said, sitting up straight. "But there's something I'd like to know before we get too far into the process. I did a little research, and it seems like there may be a few issues with Swan Springs' environmental due diligence. Care to comment?"

Lindsey went still and while she maintained composure, her face paled, and her knuckles were white where she gripped the desk. Score one for Boice and Roice, the dream research team and diggers of all dirt and shady deals. Beelzebub had covered his tracks, probably spent a boatload of cash and/or made a few demonic bargains, but it hadn't been enough to get past the twin tech demons.

Lindsey cleared her throat and said, "I'm not sure what you've heard, Mr. Dixon, but I can assure you Swan Springs is clean, pristine, and free of any legal concerns."

"So it's not sitting on top of a graveyard?" I said, chuckling. "Like in that 80s movie?"

Lindsey laughed without a trace of nervousness, but the color hadn't returned to her face. "Not at all. This was farmland for centuries. What could be more all-American?"

All American indeed—it had probably been a tobacco plantation at one-time, run on slave labor after the "owner" stole it from the indigenous peoples who'd lived there for millennia. But more recently, the land had been investigated for illegal hazardous waste dumping. Bub Real Estate had purchased the land for Swan Springs at an unusually low price. It should have raised all kinds of red flags, but money and demon bargains hid all manner of sins. Simon was checking out the land and taking soil and water samples.

We'd analyze them and collect more when we came back for our interview.

Speaking of Simon.

The immaterial greed demon appeared behind Lacey, his spectral raven form terrifying to most, but a welcome sight for me and my partner. Lacey leaned back in her chair as if stretching and stroked the demon's feathers. Lindsey couldn't see him, of course, but she would notice if we acknowledged him. He preened, then he took a dive into Lindsey's phone. Supernatural bugging complete. Score.

I stood, taking Lacey's hand like a good fiancé, and was getting ready to politely make our goodbyes when a loud bark boomed outside like a hellhound on Adderall.

Shit! Sully.

CHAPTER EIGHT

I threw the door open and was greeted by a ginormous Rottie holding an ugly rodent in her mouth while drooling. To borrow a phrase from *The Princess Bride*, it was a rodent of unusual size. Several neighbors had gathered outside of the carriage house turned office to see what the ruckus was about.

Great. This fucking cat was going to get our interview invitation rescinded.

"Peaches!" I yelled, putting on my sternest man voice. Everyone turned to look at me. Wow. So this was male privilege. I walk into a situation in my natural five-foot nothing woman form and have to yell five times to get anyone to listen. Come out as a dude bro, and poof—everyone stands at attention.

"Drop it," I said, which caused the sea of neighbors to start yelling over top of one another.

"No—"

"It's still alive!"

"That thing's been digging in my garden—"

"Give that dog a medal!"

Naturally, Sully didn't drop the hideous creature held in her jaws. It was indeed moving, and it had sharp teeth. Maybe the neighbors were right.

"What is going on?" Lindsey yelled over the chatter of neighbors who appeared to be pleased with Sully. Whew. We could definitely turn this to our advantage.

A slim man in his sixties dressed for golf and sporting a tan spoke and a hush fell over the crowd. Huh. This guy must be one of the founders. His white hair was perfectly coiffed, and he had an air of authority about him, like he was used to getting his way. The very archetype of white male privilege.

The man approached me, giving me a thorough once over. Probably looking for tattoos or other signs of disrepute. He'd find none on my glamoured body. I molded my features into what I hoped would look like D's I'm-large-and-in-charge-and-I'm-not-afraid-of-you face and offered my hand.

"Afternoon," I said as he took my hand in a surprisingly firm grip. "My name's Jesse Dixon. I apologize for my dog. She's well-trained but protective and, well, she'll chase any critter she sees as a threat."

"Pleased to meet you, Mr. Dixon. I'm Lawrence Duneberry. No need to apologize. The...critter in question has been the bane of my existence for several weeks. No exterminator has been able to capture it, no trap will hold it, and it's been causing wide-spread property damage and frightening our community."

Lacey sauntered over to Sully and stroked her head, whispering soothing words to her. Or possibly asking if she was okay. The creature in her jaws looked like it might be rabid. Cooper said hell realm animals weren't susceptible to earth rabies, but I'd have him check her out anyway once we wrapped up this meet and greet session.

"Glad to be of service," I said. "I hope this means y'all might be inclined to welcome my fiancée and I to your beautiful community."

Duneberry smiled, flashing a mouthful of unnaturally white teeth. "We look forward to your interview. It isn't solely my decision, but I will put in a good word. Now then," he said, addressing the crowd. "As you were. Everything is under control. Lindsey, be a dear and grab one of the traps out of storage. Mr. Dixon and I will take care of the animal."

"Mind if I take it with us?" I asked. "I'll have our veterinarian check it out. Peaches is up to date on her shots, but I don't want her catching anything nasty from it."

"Very well," Duneberry said, but I caught a hint of reluctance. Interesting.

When Lindsey retrieved a trap that I doubted would hold the creature, Lacey and I wrestled the damned thing away from Sully and shoved its uncooperative furry ass into the trap. Dunberry kindly provided a tarp, suggesting it might "keep the creature calm." When I grabbed it by the scruff, my demon senses went nuts. I could feel my demon grafts, which looked like glowing sigil tattoos, vibrating beneath my glamoured skin.

Lacey must have sensed something, too, since she arched a brow at me. Sully hacked as if dislodging a giant hairball, which looked pretty weird in her glamoured dog form.

Yup. This was our first official clue. Time to pay a visit to our resident hell realm animal expert.

CHAPTER NINE

With some persuasion and plenty of beef jerky, we finally convinced Sully stop hacking and get into the car. She contented herself with growling at the tarp-covered trap sitting on the seat next to her. We drove off with Duneberry's business card, which I screenshot with my smartphone and sent off to the twins to do some investigating.

Once we were well out of the neighborhood and headed toward Percy Warner Park, we dropped our glamours. Lacey went from blonde and buxom to a curly redhead who was still rocking a nice rack. I breathed a sigh of relief as I resumed my feminine form. Beards were itchy as hell. I had no idea how men tolerated them.

And I had newfound sympathy for men and ball sweat.

Sully dropped her "stupid" dog form and immediately started screaming for pizza and ice cream.

Fortunately, we were able to grab pizza on the way and promised to get ice cream after we visited Cooper.

"Pi-zza, pi-zza, pi-zza, nom, nom, nom." Sully liked to sing-song talk and growl while eating. She sat inside the pizza box as she ate, having assumed her tiny cat form complete with a double set of ears, fluffy tail, and wings. Two tiny lumps had grown on her head since I got her. I hoped it wasn't another set of ears. She already had two pairs, but I'd take her as she was.

"How can she eat so much in her tiny cat form?" Lacey asked as she turned in her seat to watch Sully in morbid fascination.

I shrugged. "Magic? And I'm guessing it takes a lot of calories to shift back and forth between her big cat form. Wearing glamour makes me hungry. Maybe the same is true for my kitty."

Lacey and I had opted for calzones. I took a bite and moaned in delight as tangy tomato sauce, melted cheese, and pepperoni hit my taste buds.

Lacey paused to take a bite of her own Italian delight. "True, but she ate a whole pizza, and you *know* she's going to start screaming for more food when she finishes."

I parked as close as I could to the trailhead and waited while Lacey finished eating and Sully gave herself a cat bath. The tarp over the trap rustled. Then a hole appeared as small, sharp teeth bit through it.

Uh oh.

A tiny nose poked out and began sniffing furiously.

I unsheathed my demon steel knife while Sully paused her washing to crouch and growl at the trap. Then the most remarkable sound came from inside the trap.

"Pi-zza."

Lacey almost jumped out of her seat.

"It fucking talks, too! Does every freakin' animal from the hell realm talk? Why didn't we hear about that in training?"

It shouldn't be surprising, since Sully could talk. Sort of. The squeaky, rasping voice was creepy, but it confirmed our assumption that this creature was from the hell realm. I'd never heard an earth realm animal speak, except for parrots and other birds capable of mimicking human speech.

"Maybe," I said absently. "Or maybe we've only ever dealt with hell realm critters that can't talk. Or maybe they're evolving."

Wasn't that a horrifying thought.

"Apparently it's hungry," I said. Sully had scarfed down the pizza, and there wasn't much left of Lacey's calzone, but I always kept plenty of beef jerky handy as bribes for the demon cat.

I turned in my seat and held a stick of spicy meat over the hole in the tarp. "No pizza, friend, but you can have this. It's called jerky. You'll like it. If you're good, Cooper will feed you, too."

Preternaturally quick, a forked tongue shot out of the hole in the tarp and grabbed the jerky, forcing it through the hole. Muffled growls, grunts, and chewing sounds came from the trap, followed by a loud burp. Then a small paw emerged from the hole.

"Jerk-y?"

Lacey scowled as I fed it another meat stick. "You are so not adopting this one." Sully hissed, letting me know she agreed with Lacey.

"Of course not," I said. "It's evidence. And we'd better get it to Cooper before I run out of jerky."

Cooper Pendergrass, my favorite summoner and fellow animal nut, lived in Percy Warner Park near a hideous tree that served as his personal portal. At least, I think he lived there. No one really knew for sure since he was secretive and trusted no one. He was tall, good looking, and his mental health was questionable. He hadn't been well even before being bound and tortured by a powerful demon who illegally used his portal to invade earth. That probably had to do with the family business of summoning.

His late brother, Keith, had been an illegal summoner who let Belial's minions loose in Nashville and had plans to kidnap yours truly. Keith's and Cooper's father was the bastard who summoned D all those years ago and sent him to back to the hell realm, taking my best friend away from me and putting him in the clutches of Belial, D's deadbeat dad.

D and I were currently fighting over who got to kill Papa Pendergrass when we found him. From what little Cooper had told us about his family and upbringing, I figured we'd have to fight him to kill his dad, too.

We hiked to the boundary of his territory and stopped, waiting for permission to enter. Unlike last time, the foliage was lush and green, though last year's leaves still littered the forest floor. Magic pulsed through the clearing in warning. Cooper had reinforced his wards after Barbatos the traitor demon breeched them, and had no doubt added a ton of magical and mundane booby traps.

The guy was paranoid as all get out and I didn't blame him.

Lacey could have entered without Simon, since the perimeter ward was keyed to demon—which excluded me with my demon grafts, Sully the demon cat, and the thing we carried in the trap. But Lacey was as cautious as Cooper.

She'd been possessed and forced to open Cooper's portal by Barbatos. Cooper didn't blame her, but she carried the weight of guilt all the same. So we all waited.

They'd have to work it out on their own. I'd been interfering in my teammates' relationships and had been told more than once to back off and focus on my own issues. I'd have to work those out on my own. Right now, we had a job to do.

A streak of rich, reddish brown and white flashed out of the clearing on a collision course with me.

"Ricky!" I squealed with delight as the little fox leapt into my arms. I snuggled her close, scratching her ears and planting tiny kisses on her head.

An angry hiss from my side made me pause in the love fest.

Uh oh. Sully was jealous.

My demon cat transformed from a tiny ball of adorable fuzz into an enormous battle cat straight out of a nightmare. Large enough for two humans to ride comfortably, her massive wings spread in a display of feline rage. She growled and spat, displaying deadly fangs while digging lethal claws into the forest floor.

"Jinx," Lacey said, drawing her knife and assuming a fighting stance. "I hope you have more jerky."

I tossed Ricky at Lacey. Lacey dropped the knife and caught the fox, de-escalating the situation. My bestie would never recover if she hurt that cat. And Sully would never forgive herself for ripping into Lacey.

I turned to face my angry kitty, placing my hands on my hips and doing my best to look bored and thoroughly disgusted. My rapid pulse and aura of fear and anger were impossible to hide, but bravado went a long way.

"Sulphur Springs McGee, drop the cattitude right meow or no ice cream."

Sully stopped growling and cocked her head at me as if confused. Was she expecting a fight, or worse, for me to cower from my own damned cat? I didn't need to dominate her. We operated on mutual respect and cooperation. She knew that. I just had to tap into her rational brain instead of her feral I'm-going-to-tear-apart-that-little-fox attack cat brain.

Sully was eyeing Ricky like a tasty morsel.

Ricky, oblivious to the danger Sully presented, wiggled her red furred butt in Lacey's arms and growled at my cat. The little idiot vixen had a death wish.

"Lacey, how about you back slowly away with Ricky while I distract my sweetie peatie wittle kitty baby that I wuv so much," I said, dropping into the baby talk I used when spoiling my feline companion.

"Jerky," Lacey said in a harsh whisper. "Jerky."

"Jerk-y!"

Oh, for the love of lemons, the critter in the cage was yelling for jerky now. Damn it, could this situation get any worse?

Never tempt fate, even in your head.

My cat's attention diverted to the cage in which another tasty snack awaited. She opened her maw and roared. The critter in the cage began to scream with ear-splitting intensity and the cage began to shake.

The critter was expanding. Not good.

"Wild Kingdom's coming. What now, genius?" Lacey asked.

Sully crouched and leapt in the air on a collision course with the cage.

CHAPTER TEN

As soon as Sully crouched, I followed her example and prepared to leap in and intercept her. If I landed on her back, I could jerk on her scruff and subdue her for a nanosecond. If I hit her flank, I could knock her off course.

Either way, it wouldn't do much good.

In mid-leap, I channeled the demon graft donated by Alexi and assumed my phantom wolf demon form. I'd wrestled with Sully in that form before. If I could subdue her and turn it into a game, we might all just walk out of here in one piece.

That was a big if.

Suddenly, a wave of magic in the form of sparkling dust hit me and I fell to the ground. My human brain rebelled against the magic that was a little too close to the mind control I'd experienced at the hands of some not-so-nice angels. The wolf, on the other hand, was caught in euphoria with golden retriever energy and had us rolling on the ground with her phantom tongue lolling like a blithering idiot.

No, not this again. I had to save Sully from herself, protect the critter in the cage—our first and only piece of evidence in the case to stop the Master Demon of Gluttony—and save Lacey, Ricky, and possibly nearby hikers and residents of the greater Nashville area if Sully completely lost her shit.

Zer, my inner demon wolf, rolled us onto our belly shook her head, which allowed me to look at Sully.

The damned cat was rolling around on her winged back and batting at air like an overgrown kitten. Her purrs were deafening. But what really blew my mind was the critter in the cage.

Scratch that—critter formerly in the cage. It was huge and, now that it was no longer dripping with cat drool and muck from wherever it had been when Sully captured it, resembled a ginormous vole with tiny ears, a stumpy tail, and rodent-on-steroids teeth. Not just incisors, either. Its entire mouth was filled with sharp teeth.

I got a good view of those teeth because the damned thing was smiling. Sitting on its haunches and grooming its fur to remove the sparkly dust so it could eat it, it was grinning like a cartoon critter.

A man dressed in green camo, stood at the boundary with Archimedes, his winged demon dog cadejo, and smiled maniacally. Cooper. Cooper had done this.

As usual, his face was covered in a haphazard pattern of greens, greys, and black with a splash of brown here and there. The summoner looked cleaner than when I'd last seen him. No leaves or forest detritus stuck out of his hair. That could have been because he'd cut his hair and wore a camo hat. Tall, lean, with wiry muscles and striking blue eyes, Cooper was a hottie cursed with mental instability thanks to his occupation as a demon summoner and, I suspected, his upbringing.

The smirk was one-hundred percent sane smartass. It was impressive if a little infuriating.

With monumental effort, I wrested control from Zer and shoved her phantom furry ass back into my subconscious. I got to my feet, shook leaves and debris out of my hair and dusted my ass and the rest of my person off. Then I marched up to Cooper, who wisely remained inside his protective boundary, and yelled.

"What the hell did you do to us, Coop? Not cool, man. I had it under control."

"No, you did not, Jane McGee. Your motiaummerr was attempting to attack the rallmath."

Naturally, Cooper was more concerned with danger to the animals in his domain than the people.

"And I was poised to stop her. I don't know how you did that awful mind control shit, but don't you *ever* pull that on me again."

I collapsed on the ground as panic overtook my mind and body. Fucking PTSD. Damn it, I'd been doing better. The panic attacks hit me less frequently and didn't last as long. But being controlled by whatever magic Cooper released had set me back by taking away my free will like the horrible rogue celestials had during my last case. I was still working through the trauma.

How infuriating. And embarrassing.

Arms enfolded me and I focused on the warmth of Lacey's embrace, the scent of her shampoo, the way clumps of grass poking through leaf litter tickled my legs. A small furry head poked through my arms, which I was using to cover my head and hide from the terror, and a wet nose met mine. Sully had shrunk to her bitty kitty size and was purring and doing her best to soothe me.

So was Ricky the fox. And they weren't even fighting.

I caught Cooper's earthy scent and let his gentle hand running over my arms ground me and chase away the panic.

"I'm sorry, Jane," he said quietly. "I should have remembered."

"No," I sobbed. "I shouldn't have overreacted. I know you would never hurt me. I—"

"Shh," Lacey said. "We know you know, you short little psychopath. And we know all about panic attacks and PTSD, too."

I had really great co-workers. Fucked up, sociopathic, and a little homicidal at times—like me. But they had my back. And I let them. Go me with the personal growth.

"Okay, okay," I said at last, gently pushing away hands and arms and furry bodies. "I'm good now."

I raised my head and looked around at my team and fuzzy companions. Wait a minute...

"Um, where is the rallmath?"

Cooper laughed. "He's behind the tree eating your jerky. Guess you're going to have to restock."

While Cooper was busy examining the rallmath, I was chewing Lacey's demon a new one for failing to intervene. The little greed demon in his phantom raven form perched on a tree and ignored us. What was up his ass?

"Look, you little ingrate, I totally saved your life during our last mission. What gives?"

Lacey sighed. "He's pissy because he thinks he's being 'underutilized' in the field."

Like that was my fault. Lacey's personal demon was a pro at reconnaissance and Internet research. Assigning him to stakeouts and having him review information from all corners of the web made sense. But I could see his point. Back when we still shared a connection through his demon graft, which I'd returned to save his life, I'd been able to communicate with Simon. Now, Lacey was the only one he could talk to, but I'd gotten to know the demon better and understood that he wanted to take a more active role in our fieldwork. Like most demons who fled to the earth realm over millennia, Simon came to our dimension to escape persecution in the hell realm. He resented the powerful demons who now wanted to wage war with powerful celestials on earth.

If they succeeded, all the refugees from both realms would be dead or enslaved along with humans.

This was a situation for Dr. Khatri, former demon hunter turned psychologist. But I supposed I'd have to suck it up and take on the mantle of amateur mental health expert.

"Simon, you are one of the bravest, most capable demons I know. And you can fight. I've seen you do it. But look around," I said, waving my hands at Lacey, Cooper, and the throng of animals that had joined Ricky and Sully. "Battle is just a part of what we do. Before we can fight

—and I promise you there will be more fighting—we have to learn what we're up against. That's where you come in. Without you, we'd be fighting blind. Understand?"

Lacey snorted. She'd planted her ass on a fallen tree next to me while waiting for Cooper. Sully had climbed onto my lap for a cat nap. Assuming her big cat form always wore her out and made her hungry, I'd definitely need to feed her soon. Ricky perched next to them while Lacey absently stroked the little fox's head.

"Nice speech. I'm so sure he'll listen to you. I mean, it's not like I've told him the same thing a bazillion times."

She was such a snark. That's part of the reason we worked well together. "Well, clearly, he's not getting the message. I have better communication skills."

Lacey ignored me and looked up at her personal demon. "Stop sulking and come down here. You can battle the mosquitos trying to eat me alive."

Simon perked up and treated us to a fantastic aerial acrobatics display. I said, "Maybe we should put him on pest control detail. It's not like our normal demon hunting gigs dried up just because the big baddies came to town."

Lacey nodded. "True. Or we could recruit Cooper since he can talk to the hell realm animals."

Cooper did indeed appear to be chatting with the demon realm rodent. I had no idea how a human could make the high-pitched squeaks and yips that came out of his mouth, but that was one of the summoner's gifts. I struggled to find some pattern, but its speech was so alien. At least it was capable of learning English if properly motivated. Like with food.

At last, Cooper patted the rodent on its head and gave it something that looked like homemade beef jerky from one of his many pockets. I needed more pants like that.

Turning his attention to us, he said, "The rallmath told me that he and two dozen of his kind were smuggled from the hell realm recently. They were given to a powerful demon, presumably Beelzebub, and told to dig tunnels underneath each home in the subdivision where you found him. Perhaps for surveillance or to cause sink holes. That's something you'll need to investigate. And before you ask, no, I have no idea who opened a portal that brought them here—if a portal was involved—or how they crossed Trinity's city barrier."

"Maybe it isn't coded to animals?"

Lacey's thought was a good one, but I couldn't see Trinity, our brilliant team leader and master strategist, leave out such an important contingency.

"No," Cooper said. "What he described wasn't a city. It was a dark and foggy place with no distinguishing landscape features or buildings."

I jumped up and snapped my fingers as understanding washed through my addled brain. "That's it. That's why the demons infiltrated the space between. It wasn't to attack celestial refugees, though I'm sure they're after the Sigillum Dei. It was a way in for other demons and demonic creatures."

Lacey stood up and started pacing, too. "That would explain a lot. But how did the demons figure out how to get there? I thought it was a celestial construct."

I shrugged. "D had no trouble getting in, and the dragon demons who attacked us were fine, too. And they're all full demon. Maybe..."

Oh. Crap.

When Cassiel invited me into the space between, I'd had my demon grafts. She'd only meant for me to enter, but demonic magic was sly and operated by trickery and loopholes.

"What is it?" Lacey asked.

"When Cassie brought me to the space between, I had my demon grafts." I motioned to the swirling, multi-colored sigils swirling along my arms like animated tattoos. "What if I trained the space between to recognize demons?"

And if demons could get in...

Cooper's gaze went wide and met mine. He'd had the same thought. He turned and said something to the rallmath in what I presumed was its native tongue.

The rallmath started chittering at Cooper, and the summoner's face turned to a mask of stony rage as the creature spoke with speed and animation, its small arms waving with excitement.

"From what the beast described combined with my own intel, I believe my father has returned and set up shop just outside the city where he's smuggling demons into Nashville through the space between. He's building a new portal and this," he said, pointing to the rallmath, "is his test case. If we don't stop him, he'll unleash the legions of the hell realm on earth, and we'll be his first targets."

CHAPTER ELEVEN

We drove back to HQ in silence, except for the dulcet sounds of my demon cat devouring a gallon of ice cream. A promise was a promise. Even if the shit just hit the fan, I still had to feed the cat.

Cooper kept the rallmath, who I'd named Raus in honor of *The Princess Bride* and because it was easier to pronounce. He'd check the animal out, make sure he was healthy, and see if he could learn more about what Raus and seen, heard, and sensed since coming to earth.

If we got lucky, he could lead us back to Pendergrass Senior's portal-in-progress and possibly even act as a spy for us in Beelzebub's neighborhood.

"This is bad," Lacey said, breaking the silence to state the obvious. "We can't let Cooper's dad open a new portal."

"No, we can't," I said. "But it's going to be a bitch going after Pendergrass Senior and Beelzebub at the same time. We just don't have the personnel."

When we fought Belphegor, The Master Demon of Sloth, we'd been a united team with everyone working together. And we'd barely won. We needed help.

I had an idea, but no one was going to like it. I didn't even like it. But it might be our only chance.

And I wanted Pendergrass alive. So did D. That bastard had a lot to answer for and didn't deserve banishment or a quick death.

Jeez, I really was a little psychopath.

"I don't see steam coming out of your ears, but your demon graft tats are swirling. You either have a totally brilliant or a completely dumbass idea of epic proportions," Lacey said.

"Ass?"

My kitty's tiny voice screeched through the car as she said the word again. Great. "Auntie Lacey taught you a new word," I cooed, scowling at my partner. "It means your butt."

"Butt?" A look in the rearview mirror revealed my adorable demon kitten with her head cocked to the side, her double ears perked with interest. Then she proceeded to lick her rump.

Ew.

"It's a human expression," Lacey said, helpfully. "It means Jinx isn't smart, or that she makes stupid decisions."

"Stoo-pit? Stoo-pit dog! Ass butt dog dumb!"

It was too adorable. I couldn't even be mad at Lacey for insulting my intelligence and decision-making abilities. My cat was learning the intricacies of human language, and it was the coolest thing I'd ever seen.

Sully stopped and flattened her ears, growling at my partner. I held my breath. We'd been practicing and I hoped she'd self-correct. "Ink no stu-pid." She shook her head and said, "Lacey stu-pid dumb ass butt."

"That's right!" I said, my face splitting into a huge grin. "Lacey is a stupid dumb ass butt." My sweet, smart kitty was learning so fast! She'd mastered "stupid" and used her new words in a sentence to insult my partner.

Damn, I loved that cat.

Lacey looked indignant and said, "We'll see who the stupid dumb ass butt is when Jinx runs whatever crazy plan she's concocted by the rest of the team.

"Absolutely not."

Our fearless leader hadn't even bothered to look up from her paper-work. Nope. I didn't merit her full attention. She sat at her desk, the one she'd inherited from our former demon-slash-Angel-of-Death boss who went AWOL. Trinity had put her own stamp on the space, making it her own with upgraded computer equipment and multiple screens, an expanded library of demon and celestial lore, and a copy of the so-called prophecy from the pages of *Compiled Grimoires of the Wicked and Wise* illuminated in floating sigils that hung suspended above her desk like the sword of Damocles.

The celestial books and scrolls were new. Trinity had been gathering them, since our team was woefully unfamiliar with creatures from the so-called angel realm compared to the hell realm. The prophecy was a reminder of what we were up against—seven master demons, one for each deadly sin, and their corresponding celestial archangels who were less about virtue and more about demon genocide with humans as collat-eral damage.

Well, make that six. We'd defeated one master demon, Belphegor. Her celestial sister, Judaliel the Archangel of Diligence, and Judaliel's sidekick/administrative assistant I'd nicknamed Pinstripe, were currently locked up in our highest security holding cells in the bowels of HQ and waiting to be sent back to the celestial realm permanently with a mandate to never return and never to interfere with the earth realm again thanks to the Sigillum Dei.

Only we didn't have the artefact. And the two devious and multi-eyed celestials were no doubt plotting their escape while we scrambled for a plan. A plan was what I had.

But Trinity hadn't even let me finish describing my plan. Not cool. "You know, great leaders listen to their teams and draw from their strengths. I read that in several of those business books you made us read when you took over."

Trinity sighed and looked up at me over her elegant glasses. Her eyes were bloodshot from too many sleepless nights, too much pressure, and that pesky little debt she owed some powerful demon for securing the city. I didn't know what she'd traded to ward Music City and the surrounding counties, trapping the escaped master demons and archangels in to prevent wide-spread mayhem.

But it had to be big. Her soul, to be sure, but the kinds of demons who had the power to make deals with magic at a level to protect a city were as twisted as they were powerful. Those demons were cruel and would take the person Trinity loved most and destroy them slowly, with as much pain and suffering as possible, and then heal that person and do it all over again.

Sam was that person. And I wouldn't be surprised if the rest of the team were part of the bargain, too.

"I know how your mind works, Jinx. Your training was in human law enforcement, and you want to cut a deal with Judaliel and Pinstripe to fight Beelzebub or track down Damien Pendergrass. It won't work. They aren't human."

Damn, nothing got past that woman. And Damien? That was Pendergrass Senior's name? A little on the nose. He probably took on the name when he started dabbling in illegal summoning.

I played it cool. "I'm not stupid or naïve, Trin. I know I'm not dealing with humans, but demons and celestials aren't all that different from humans when it comes to self-preservation and self-interest."

"True," Trinity said, turning her attention back to paperwork, which appeared to be translating some ancient scroll or another. "But if you want to cut a deal, you have to have something to trade. You've got nothing."

"Not true. Judaliel is a lost cause. She's practically catatonic—except for the wailing. But Dr. Khatri has been interviewing the Pinstripe. Doc thinks Pinstripe is terrified of returning to the celestial realm after their monumental fuck up here. First, she didn't report Judaliel's little side project with Belphegor. Then Belphegor ran off with their celestial weapon and instead of retrieving it, and later she lost it to a band of demon hunters?"

Trinity stopped scribbling, a sure sign that I had her attention. Now, I had to keep it and get her on board with the program.

"I don't think she'll be keen on going up against Beelzebub, but she may be interested in stopping Damien Pendergrass from opening a portal to the hell realm, giving the demons an advantage in the war they're planning."

I started pacing, piecing together the details of a deal that might appeal to a vindictive archangel. Dr. Khatri had made it clear that her interpretation of Pinstripe's possible fears, motives, and likely reactions were mostly conjecture, but I trusted her. She had decades of experience in the field as a demon hunter and had crafted deals for asylum with many lesser demons like the one we had made with Mara before she joined the team. Sanctuary in exchange for keeping a low profile, succubus feedings only on approved humans, and serving as an informant for the Nashville demon community.

Pinstripe would want safety, and if I judged her right, she'd be looking to regain her honor and show her commitment to the mission by stopping a demon invasion.

The boss lady looked me up and down as I fought to stay cool, calm, and collected. "I'm surprised you aren't asking to go after Pendergrass yourself. You and Demoriel have a score to settle."

She grimaced when she said D's name. Seriously, what was with her and my demon? I'd ask, but I didn't want to derail the conversation and blow my chance to cut a deal with our celestial prisoners so we didn't have to fight on two fronts.

"Yeah," I said. "And we will. But we have to find him, capture him, and stop whatever demon smuggling operation he's cooking up first. Keeping more demons out of Nashville is part of the mission. I can put my personal vendetta aside for the greater good."

Trinity didn't look convinced. "What about D?"

Again with my demon... Still, she had a point, and it was a fair question. There were favors, and there were *favors*. Would D see this as a betrayal, or would he work for the greater good? He was a demon, but he'd spent his formative years on earth, so he had some human sensibili-

ties. The twins' voices echoed in my head, scolding me for demon preju-
dices and making assumptions, but even they would admit that no one
held a grudge like a demon.

Or a celestial. I was counting on that premise for my deal with
Pinstripe.

"D won't like it, but he's part of the team and he'll follow your orders.
It's your call." And it was. If I was in Trinity's position, I would have
weighed the risk that D and I would go off the rails and follow our own
agenda against the benefit of having a powerful celestial working for our
team.

That was my fault, not D's. I was a reformed rogue and I still had to
prove my reliability.

Waiting for Trinity to judge my intentions on the scale she kept in
her brilliant mind, I stood very still and made myself not fidget.

Trinity sighed. "How do we know she won't double cross us?"

I shrugged. "She can't leave the city. Pendergrass's portal in the
making is the only way in or out and he wouldn't grant her safe
passage. Hell, he'd probably hand her over to the demons to gain favor.
And word of what happened to Belphegor has spread like wildfire
through the demon community. That means the celestials have gotten
wind, too. She'll need our protection from other archangels and
celestials."

"Can we protect her?"

I reached toward my neck and grasped the small, battered ring that
hung on a chain next to my black mirror. The ring, a gift from my deadbeat dad, was more than an old trinket.

Just like dear old dad was something more than a rogue celestial.

During our last mission, the ring had granted me power beyond
anything I'd ever experienced from celestials or demons. It helped us
defeat Belphegor, but it scared me with its wild magic. I hadn't controlled
it. It had taken me over.

It terrified me.

But it might be the key to defending traitorous angels and defeating
more master demons.

Trinity arched a brow. She didn't look at my ring, but she was acutely aware of it and wanted to ask me what it was, what it could do.

But then she'd have to answer uncomfortable questions about what she'd traded to keep the city safe.

"Go," she said. "You get one shot."

Trinity didn't say "don't blow it." She didn't have to.

CHAPTER TWELVE

Dr. Khatri accompanied me to the lower levels of HQ. I figured having her run interference during negotiations couldn't hurt. We'd worked out a few non-verbal cues the doc could use to communicate her thoughts on the celestial's intentions. A head tilt meant Pinstripe was bullshitting us, crossed legs meant she was listening, note-taking meant she was scared and I should push harder with the threat of turning her over to her celestial masters or the demons.

We'd play it by ear. If nothing else, getting out of the cell she shared with Judaliel the snot-crying angel might be incentive enough. Talk about torture.

The noise hit us before the elevator doors opened.

Not the cries of Judaliel, though we could still hear that. The sounds and smells of celestial sheep threatened to overpower our all-too-human senses.

"What fresh hell is this?" The doc's voice was muffled by the collar she pulled over her mouth and nose to drown out the stench.

"Celestial livestock," I said. "The twins were supposed to send them with Cooper, somewhere in the great outdoors with plenty of room and far away from people."

Maybe my sadistic roomies decided to add to the caged celestials' torment by keeping the flock of charoum in their vicinity. Or maybe they were just lazy little shits. It was a toss-up.

Nisroc the angry shepherd sat in the corner just outside the elevator, sulking.

"They left you down here, too?" I asked, appalled. Mom would be furious.

He scowled at me, his mass of grey hair and beard a mess of tangles that matched the disarray of his robes. He still pulled off an air of dignity when he said, "I refused to leave my flock. We've been waiting for our transport."

Transport...

"Was D supposed to teleport you and your flock out of here?"

The shepherd cocked his head, brows furrowed in confusion. Right. He'd been through some serious trauma and probably hadn't been paying attention to introductions. I started over, "D, the demon who rescued you and your flock and brought you here?"

"I know of whom you speak," he said. "How could I forget that hideous visage and beastly frame?"

Oh, no he didn't. He did not insult my boyfriend in front of me.

"Hideous? Your kind are all eyeballs and attitude. What do *you* look like under that glamour?"

"Better than you, you hairless ape wench!"

"Enough!" Dr. Khatri got between me and the shepherd before I could act on my urge to pummel him. Turning her attention to Nisroc, she said, "You are our guest and would do well to remember that we took you in after saving you from obliteration by demons. A good guest respects their host."

"As for you," she said, turning her hard gaze on me. "Your hostility is misdirected. The shepherd and his flock are not the enemy. They are refugees and our guests. I'll inquire about their relocation after our interview with the celestial."

Nisroc perked up. "Celestial? There are others here?"

"Yup," I said. "We're holding two prisoners, and before you get upset about that, let me tell you what they did. Judaliel and her sidekick created a weapon of mind control and mass destruction for the angel versus demon war the higher ups have brewing. Not very angelic behavior if you ask me."

I was about to make some snappy wisecrack when I noticed a change come over the shepherd. He went very still, his gaze wide and his expression full of astonishment. Uh oh. Did I burst his bubble about the so-called benevolent archangels? Surely not. After all, he'd come to earth because of persecution by the higher celestials.

So what was his deal?

Before I could blink, Nisroc flew down the corridor with unearthly speed, heading straight for the cells holding Judaliel and Pinstripe.

I didn't think the celestial shepherd was powerful enough to release the prisoners, but we couldn't take any chances. Who knew what kind of havoc these two could cause if they got out and teamed up with the other archangels and their warriors. Dr. Khatri and I ran after him, dodging the floating bodies of bleating charoum that had apparently decided to follow their master at a more leisurely pace.

Just as the doc and I reached the end of the corridor, Nisroc stopped and bowed low before the prison cell. Shortly after, and much to my relief, Judaliel's wailing stopped. The formerly weeping celestial, who was wearing her humanoid glamour with tears streaming from only one pair of eyes, stared in wide wonder at the shepherd.

Pinstripe looked mildly annoyed. No idea why. The weeping and gnashing of teeth surely had been more irritating.

"My lady," said Nisroc, his voice full of reverence. "Oh, my great lady, how is it that you've come to this? Imprisoned by these wretched creatures instead of sitting in your power and glory."

Wretched creatures? Wow. So much for gratitude. I looked to the doc, but she shook her head and put a hand on my arm to hold me back. Right. We should let this play out and see if we could use it to our advantage.

"I—" Judaliel paused to clear her throat before continuing in a low, hoarse voice. "I was recruited to save our realm from the demons when the war was renewed. I designed a great weapon, one that could have ended this dreadful business once and for all, and—"

"And then she squandered it on her worthless demon of a sister."

That was the first time Pinstripe had spoken since we captured the pair. Maybe because no one could hear her over the banshee wails of her cell mate, or maybe because it was because she had a friendly audience. The charoum gathered around the cell and began bleating with what seemed to be excitement.

Or maybe they were just hungry. Hard to tell with the overgrown mops.

"I could have saved her," Judaliel said, her glamour warping to reveal flashes of eyeballs and feathers from her true from. "And I could have ended the war. But these fiends interfered!"

She pointed a feathered finger in my direction with an eyeball on the tip, spilling from the glamour of her hand. Ick. And totally unfair.

"Your sister screwed you over before I got involved," I said, shrugging. "You've got only yourself to blame for that. As far as I'm concerned, the rest was a war crime of Biblical proportions. The only fiends here are you and your secretary."

Pinstripe shook with barely suppressed fury. "I outrank her. And war crimes can only be perpetrated upon civilized beings, which you and your kind are not."

"I'm half your kind. The rest is around one-quarter human thanks to Haniel and Belial, and a quarter demon thanks to my colleagues from the other side who sacrificed parts of themselves to save me. From where I'm standing, the only uncivilized beings in this conflict are you and your band of murderous angels and the power-hungry demons you're fighting."

Nisroc stared at the cell with horror. He'd stopped bowing at some point during our verbal tennis match and picked up enough to realize that Judaliel was not, in fact, the hero he'd thought her to be. "You sided with the warmongering archangels? You know what they did to me and my flock. What they would have done had you not helped me escape."

Wait a minute...

"I thought Cassiel brought you here. Was she working with these clowns?"

The baby charoum I'd ridden back in the space between nudged me with its giant head. I gripped its silken fur as my hands balled into fists. Cassiel knew these two. And we'd let her guard them.

What had they talked about? Had they been conspiring?

But if they had been, why hadn't Cassiel busted them out and took them along on her mission to steal the Sigillum Dei?

"Cassiel is a traitor and a fool," Pinstripe said. "Instead of helping with the war effort to rid the universe of the scourge of demon kind forever, she helped traitors like you escape to earth." She pointed a finger at Nisroc and glared at him. Nisroc glared back, clearly not cowed by the angry archangel.

I took the opportunity to get Judaliel's attention while the shepherd and Pinstripe resumed bickering and trading insults. We'd learned some useful information but not the full story. Now that Judaliel was talking, I hoped to put the pieces together.

"So you aren't really a warmonger, are you? Did you want to rescue your sister and run away, or did you want to stop the war entirely?" I asked. Judaliel's glamour had settled back to her human form, but a pained expression crossed her face with the second question.

"I wanted to save Bella and I wanted to save the lesser angels like Nisroc. Cassiel helped many celestials escape to earth through the space between. She's very skilled at using the space between to travel between realms."

I'd let go of the charoum and started to pace. "So you and Cassiel know each other and have worked together. And when we sent her here to guard you and Pinstripe—"

Pinstripe dropped her glamour revealing a mass of eyeball-laden tentacles and a giant octopus-like head. Just what we needed. Her true Lovecraftian form.

"My name is Soriella, you welp of a half-breed!"

I snorted. "Soriella? Someone named an ugly giant squid with too many eyes a name fit for a princess? I may be a half-breed, but at least I'm not covered with suckers and eyeballs."

Okay, that was kind of mean. Beauty was in the eye of the beholder and all that, but as far as I could surmise, the higher the rank of the celestial—or demon—the more monstrous and inhuman the form.

Besides, she'd been insulting me since her capture and before that she'd tried to mind control me, drain me of my lifeforce, and then made a valiant effort to kill me.

"Anyway, I wasn't talking to you," I said. "I was talking to Judaliel. Unlike you, she has an opportunity to cut a deal, right her wrongs, and save some celestials in the process."

Soriella opened what passed for her mouth, but before she could speak, Judaliel assumed her celestial form and shoved a giant bundle of feathers into Soriella's maw. Nice!

Judaliel turned her attention to Nisroc. "I failed to protect you and others who fled the celestial realm. I failed to see the treachery of my sister until it was too late. I will not fail you now."

She turned her multi-eyed gaze to me and the doc and said, "I do this for my fellow celestials, not for you."

"Fine," I said. "I don't care why you do it as long as you help us stop a rogue summoner the demon invasion of earth using the space between. I also need you to track down Cassiel and the other celestial refugees so we can get them to safety. Do that, and I'll grant you sanctuary on earth—with conditions, of course. But you'll be free, and you can do some good for folks like Nisroc."

She considered while Soriella pulled wads of slimy feathers out of her mouth using her tentacles. Gross. I'd totally make the twins clean that up.

Dr. Khatri said, "It's a good deal. The celestial refugees need a powerful protector to look out for them. That's what you wanted to do for your sister. That's your purpose. It will help you heal."

I reached into my shirt and pulled out the chain that held the ring of power from my father, letting some of its magic out for the two celestials to feel. "Soriella won't protect you, and the other archangels will destroy you the first chance they get. I can protect you, and I will if you keep your end of the bargain."

I held my breath. Same deal, different celestial, but maybe this would work out better. Nisroc vouched for her. I could have him keep an eye on her while she worked to make sure she didn't double cross us.

After a long silence broken by pleading from the shepherd and the bleats and groans and what I suspected were charoum farts from the livestock, Judaliel resumed her human glamour and asked, "What are the conditions?"

CHAPTER THIRTEEN

Exhausted from negotiations with archangels, from reining in the power of my father's ring, and from herding charoum into makeshift pens on the lower levels of HQ, I headed to my room for a bit of rest. Sam would work out the details of the bargain with Nisroc's help—apparently demon bargains were similar to celestial bargains, but different enough that Nisroc could make sure to close any potential loopholes.

Plus, Judaliel trusted the shepherd.

I opened the door to my room and was greeted by a torpedo of black fur flying toward my face.

Fortunately, Sully was in her tiny cat form.

I leapt into the air and caught my demon cat in my arms. We collapsed on the floor in a tangle of limbs and wings, me giggling and Sully purring louder than a Mustang engine. She gave me a thorough sniffing as was her custom. Sometimes, I was convinced she was protecting me, looking for injuries or any signs of imminent magical danger I might have picked up while in the field. Other days, I figured she was looking for snacks she could swipe or sucker me into giving her.

Perched on my chest, she wrinkled her feline nose and opened her mouth, making one of those stinky cat faces that was actually a way to blend taste and smell into information.

Cocking her head to one side with perked ears, she said, "Animal?"

Wow, she'd made an "l" sound and pronounced the word perfectly. I didn't think her anatomy would let her do it, but I'd learned not to estimate this wonder cat of the demon realm.

"Yup," I said, scratching her between her ears and what appeared to be tiny horns sprouting in front of them. She leaned in, moving her head until I got just the right spot. "Celestial sheep. Big balls of silky fluff that unfortunately do not poop rainbows."

I'd left my shoes outside the elevators to avoid carrying charoum poop through HQ. Some things were universal, and the notion that every living thing did, in fact, poop, was one of them. Judging from the funk that permeated the air in the vicinity of the charoum, the beasts could give any demon a run for its money in the stink department.

And I'd had to clean up the bathroom after the twins destroyed it.

Sully did her best to mimic a human smile. "Stu-pid sheep."

I laughed. "Not sure about that, but I do know we need to relocate them. D was supposed to do that."

Sully went still and looked away.

I sat up, sliding her down into my lap before scooping her in my arms and moving to the bed. After some snuggle time with chin scratches and plenty of ear rubs, I said. "What's going on with D?"

Clearly my kitty, who shared a fondness for Mr. Tall, Dark, and Demon, had insider information. Either she'd been eavesdropping on Trinity—again—or D had been ranting in her vicinity. Not that I blamed him. I ranted to the cat all the time. She was a pretty good listener, and now that she could purr *and* talk back, she was a little bundle of serotonin that should come with one of those caution-habit-forming labels.

"Bad," Sully said. "Bad Trin-ity."

"Bad?" I asked. "Bad Trinity?"

Sully shook her head and jumped off my lap. Turning away from me on the bed, she hissed while raising her hackles. She wasn't threatening me, just frustrated. Either her lack of vocabulary or my lack of under-standing was pissing her off.

"Oh, okay. Not bad Trinity. Sad Trinity?"

The cat hissed again. I'd guessed wrong.

"Mad Trinity? She's still mad at D, then."

Sully shook her head and stood on her hind legs, stretching her wings and growling. "De-mor-iel and Trin-ity."

"Right," I said, encouraging my clever cat. "I think I get it now. D's mad. He's mad at Trinity. Why"

Sully sat up, her tiny face screwed up in concentration. I wish I had Cooper's skill to speak with Sully in her native language. She was doing her best, but this conversation might prove too complex and difficult with her limited human speech capabilities.

"Guessing game," I said, straightening to sit cross-legged on the bed. "He's mad because Trinity cut down his field work."

"No."

Of course not. That would have been too easy.

"He's mad because I told Trinity we wouldn't go after Pendergrass."

She considered, but then said, "No."

I remembered how D and I had fought back-to-back in the space between, me channeling more of my celestial magic and him going mega-demon, his true form or part of it emerging from his human guise. Was it a glamour? If so, he'd need a lot of power to maintain it for such long periods of time. I had my suspicions about how much power and magic he held, but I hadn't pushed him on it since our second big fight shortly after he returned to earth from the hell realm. Our relationship was progressing, but it was still such a fragile thread, a bit frayed and in danger of snapping if I said or did the wrong thing.

But if Trinity thought he was holding out on the team, she'd rip him a new one and demand that he discloses the full extent of his powers.

And maybe she'd be suspicious and less inclined to trust him.

Her paranoia was going to be the death of us all, or at least the death of my love life.

"Did Trinity bench him because she doesn't trust him?"

"Bench?"

I scooted closer and took her tiny face in my hands, staring into her eyes and willing her to understand. "Did Trinity say he couldn't work with us because she thinks he lied about his powers?"

Sully's cat pupils dilated to their full extent, and she wiggled, nodding her head up and down as best she could.

Damn it. This was bad. Not just for me, but for the team and for our chances of defeating Beelzebub and stopping Pendergrass. We couldn't afford any discord or in-fighting. I could talk to Trinity, but that might make thing worse. I had a pretty substantial conflict of interest as she would see it. I'd have to talk to D and find a way to convince him to do what he could to regain Trinity's trust—which would require swallowing his pride and proving himself.

"Why me?" I groaned, collapsing on the bed and rubbing my hands over my face. "Dr. Khatri needs to step up her sessions with Trinity. This is really a job for her. I'm no good at diplomacy."

"Ink," Sully hissed, swatting at me with her tiny paw using just enough claw to sting.

"Ow!" I yelped, keeping my hands over my eyes in case kitty mood swing decided to get really nasty. "What the hell?"

I didn't dare uncover my face until I was off the bed with some distance from me and the cat. When I dropped my hands and opened my eyes, the sight of a full-blown miniature Halloween decoration greeted me. Fur standing on end, her puffed tail swishing back and forth, black eyes wide and promising violence from needle sharp claws and wicked little fangs.

"Ink stupid. Ink dumb ass butt. Ink love De-mor-iel. Ink De-mor-iel no fight. Kick ass butt."

Wow. I would have given her a pound of jerky for completing so many sentences if she wasn't being such a little shit. But insulting me dampened my enthusiasm.

Still, she was right. I loved D. It wasn't a simple love, like the love I had for my family or my team, and it wasn't lust and yearning, though I lusted and yearned enough that I'd set a priest on fire if he heard my confession. No, this love was the kind that could make me whole or tear me asunder if I ever lost it. He was my partner, my found family, the other half of my soul.

Good grief, when had I become such a sap?

Since I met D.

"Okay, okay," I said. "Point taken. I need to find D and talk some sense into him. Or kick his ass. Maybe both."

"Both. De-mor-iel bitch boy. Kick ass butt," Sully said, dropping the fierce little kitty act and unceremoniously turning her back on me.

Dissed and dismissed.

But at least she hadn't called me a little bitch.

CHAPTER FOURTEEN

Finding D wasn't a problem. He'd shared part of his demon essence with me. I could locate all the demons from whom I'd received grafts. D's grafts had also enhanced my fighting skills and my ability to tap into my own celestial magic.

What they didn't do, unfortunately, was give me any insight into what was going on in his head.

Even without the grafts, I would have guessed where he'd be. I took the exit on autopilot and drove into a neighborhood that sat directly beside the noisy motorway. The newish concrete barrier helped, but it would never be the most desirable parcel of real estate in Nashville—nowhere near the splendor of Swan Springs.

Still, it had a warmth and realness that the upscale planned community lacked, even if it hadn't been created by a demon. The people who lived here were real, working hard to keep their slice of the American dream and fighting the wave of gentrification that had swept through the city. They had community, a rare commodity in this day and age.

It had once been my home. It was D's home, too, even if no one but me had known it when he lived there.

I pulled into the driveway of mom's house behind D's Mustang, pleased to see that the folks I'd hired to keep up with the lawn care and maintenance had been doing a stellar job. The azalea bushes that spanned the front of the house on either side of the smooth concrete front porch were neatly trimmed and glowed in the waning sunlight. They bloomed red all summer. Red was Mom's favorite color. The lawn was a brilliant green and peppered with mature trees, flower beds filled with a mixture of blooming annuals and leafy perennials. I smiled at the cardinal that was taking a dip in the weathered old bird bath.

I used to play in that water and in plastic swimming pools filled with freezing water straight out of the hose. Megan and I spent hours splashing and playing in our kiddie pool as it warmed in the summer sun. The memory warmed my heart and made it ache at the same time. It was an odd sensation.

The days of kiddie pools and carefree summer play ended the day my father left me saddled with Haniel and then bailed on our family.

I pushed that memory back into the vault where I kept my darkness, next to every memory I had of my father. Bringing that negativity with me wouldn't help me help D.

I focused on the birdfeeder again and the chickadee that had chased off the larger cardinal to claim the water for itself. Even before the house had been given a facelift, it had been a haven for birds, as well as chipmunks, squirrels, box turtles, and one stray demon boy. My old tire swing had been replaced by a more respectable wooden contraption that looked nicer but was probably less safe than the original. But the tree the swing hung from was the same. The yard and its charm were the same.

Home was the same.

Home was where you went when you were down and had no other place to go.

I got out of the car and made my way to the front door, wading through more bittersweet memories as I pulled out my key and let myself in.

The lights were all out and the house was as silent as a tomb. I had to play this just right. Did he need gentle and understanding, or did he need a wrecking ball?

Screw it. I was going full on bulldozer.

I flipped the master switch and flooded the foyer and living room with lamplight. Then I started yelling.

"D! Get your emo ass out here. I've got a bone to pick with you."

No answer. My demon was playing hard to get. Or sulking. Probably both.

I sighed and walked to the room that had once been my bedroom. After I'd started making money as a demon hunter, I'd secretly invested in my mom's personal finances and, through Megan, encouraged her to renovate. My old room had been given a facelift worthy of HGTV, complete with modern wood flooring, a fresh coat of paint, and décor that was a far cry from the second-hand furniture I'd grown up with. Yeah. We'd struggled after dad left and forgot that he had a wife and two children to support—one of whom he'd saddled with possession by an angel who thought she was a demon.

He'd pay for that. Later.

I left the lights off and walked in, planting my ass on the comfortable full-sized bed covered by a fluffy duvet and way too many pillows. The closet door was ajar, and I caught a flash of red from D's eyes. I also caught a whiff of bourbon. Sulking and drinking. Bad combination.

Been there, done that, bought the T-shirt.

After about five minutes, I said, "You going to hide in there all night? You're not a little demon anymore. There's a whole room out here, attached to a whole house, that leads to a great big old world—"

"Not in the mood." The deep growl from the closet gave me pause.

He'd never growled at me before.

It made me mad and was more than a little insulting. I regularly dealt with maaks, wraiths, master demons out for my blood and my soul, and a demon cat whose roar could wake the dead when she was in her battle cat form. He didn't seriously think he could make me go away by growling, did he?

"You're not impressing anyone," I said, trying to sound bored. "And this is childish. If I had a quarter for every time Trinity handed me my ass, I could retire. We all could. She's the boss and she's under a lot of pressure. All you have to do is go explain yourself to her and she'll see you as an even bigger asset to the team. You may even get a cookie."

It took a moment for him to answer, since he decided to take another swig from the bottle, swallowing with a large audible gulp. I got that. True, I hadn't drowned my sorrows in alcohol since I started working on my issues, but damn, everyone needed an outlet. These days I blew off steam by sparring with my teammates and with Sully. And the cat was totally therapeutic when she wasn't calling me names and swiping at me with her claws.

"You need a healthier outlet, you know."

"I could always go back to rampaging. Most of the demons in this realm aren't on par with my father's legions, but my lash would help motivate them."

He was still talking in that weird, growly voice. But at least he was talking.

I sighed. "So you're bored being the good guy? Looking to join your father in glorious battle? Not buying it. You could've double crossed us all and let his legions loose on earth any time before we closed the portals and Trinity warded the city."

"I could've. I still could."

I snorted. "You'd have to work with Pendergrass, and overcoming that pesky problem that we sent him back one way using the Sigillum Dei would be a neat trick. Or you could always torture him until he did your bidding I suppose. That one of those terrible things you did in the hell realm?"

The floor creaked as he rose. He was a big guy, but I didn't remember him being *that* big.

The thing that emerged from the closet was enormous. How he managed not to damage doors and drywall, I'd never know. Probably magic.

As he unfolded himself from the small space, he grew impossibly tall —and that was saying something. I was five foot nothing and everyone was impossibly tall to me. But in this form, D stood at least eight feet tall. Tension sizzled down my spine like I was preparing for battle. Fight or flight? I was all fight. But the rich scent he carried, like aged bourbon and sweet tobacco laced with woodsmoke transformed battle readiness to delicious tension of a different sort. I inhaled deeply, drinking in the warm spice that was familiar and new, heady and dangerous.

It called me. Something dark and hungry within me answered and I took a step forward.

His magic had done something to my bedroom space to accommodate his height and the mass of his body. There was no way he'd stand eight feet tall in my room. We didn't have fashionably high ceilings in this house, not even after renovations. Whatever he'd done made the ceiling disappear. The sky above filled with stars and faint moonlight, perfect for dark creatures and dark deeds.

I had more than a few in mind.

Great black wings unfolded, revealing a body covered with muscles that made Mr. Universe look puny. Those muscles were covered with red skin. The demon stood before me shirtless, his jeans ripped and torn by his giant thighs. Those horns I'd seen in the space between were longer.

Then there was his face. It was still D, with the same lines and symmetry. Sharp cheekbones and a strong jaw—those were familiar. And his eyes were the same dark brown, almost black, with red sparks. I'd fallen into those eyes more times that I cared to admit. True, they were hooded by more prominent brow ridges that furrowed in menace right now, but they were his eyes.

This was D in one of his many forms, maybe even his true form. It was larger and more terrifying than the form he'd used in the space between—the one that had freaked Trinity out. Big and scary didn't begin to cover it.

But fear had no place in this room or in me. Not with Demoriel.

He threw his head back, looking through whatever magic gave us X-ray vision through the ceiling, attic, and roof of our childhood home, and roared.

It was a sound that could, and no doubt had, sent scores of lesser demons, celestials, and mere mortals fleeing in abject terror. This was a demon fit to lead the legions of Belial's finest warriors as a hell realm general, with a body built for battle, a mind made for strategy and cruelty, and the cunning of an apex predator who would crush his enemies.

Hell, his roar was a weapon itself. It shot through me and tried to tell my hindbrain to run.

But I was me. I didn't run away from danger. I relished it.

And D would never, *ever* hurt me.

An image suddenly flashed through my mind, breaking my concentration, and making me want to laugh in the face of this monstrous demon. What the hell was wrong with me?

I tried to keep a straight face. I really did, but I pictured D walking into Trinity's office and plopping his giant ass into one of her chairs before kicking up his feet onto her immaculate desk. Then, he leaned back, put his hands behind his head so his biceps bulged, and the chair groaned in protest, and he grinned at Trinity, saying, "How do you like me now, boss?"

In my head, he was chewing gum. I snorted, trying not to fall over in a fit of giggles.

He leaned down and got in my face, glowering. "Are you laughing at me?"

It was too much. I collapsed on the floor and whooped, rolling around and clutching my sides. Holy guacamole, I hadn't laughed so hard in ages. My face hurt. I'd bruise a rib if I didn't stop. But I couldn't.

It was wonderful.

When I recovered enough to pay attention to my surroundings, I spotted D, or rather his backside, as he rooted around in the closet. It was a mighty fine view, but what the hell was he doing?

When he emerged, he had the bottle of booze to his lips and was soon chugging what was left. After he'd downed the alcohol, he dropped the empty bottle on the floor. Fortunately, it didn't fall on the hardwood.

Unfortunately, it spilled the last bit of amber liquid on the high-end rug I'd placed between my bed and the closet.

"Hey!" I said between bouts of coughing as my stomach settled into rhythmic jumps. Apparently, I'd laughed so hard I'd given myself a case of the hiccups, ensuring that he would not take my scolding seriously. "I don't care what kind of big feelings you're dealing with. I paid a lot for that rug. You're totally cleaning that up."

D stared at me and then bent over to pick up the bottle.

"Where are you going?" I asked as he brushed past me and out the bedroom door.

"To get some carpet cleaner. Does your mom keep it in the same place?"

Wow, I'd been half joking, but he was actually going to clean it up. The big, bad, scary demon who'd tried to terrify me—as if I hadn't seen Biblically accurate angels—was following my orders.

Okay, I could work with this.

"It's under the kitchen sink," I yelled. "While you're in there, grab me a soda. We'll talk while you scrub."

CHAPTER FIFTEEN

There was something so endearing and so sad about watching D the Mega Demon clean the rug while I lounged on my childhood bed sipping whatever fancy organic high end soda mom had stocked in the fridge. Megan got her hooked on the stuff.

I had to admit, it was tasty.

"So," I said, trying not to stare in wonder at my demon's big badass form. "What's this all about?"

Instead of answering, he scrubbed harder. Mom always kept our house immaculate. Even when we'd filled it with hand-me-down furniture and ratty old rugs, the house had been clean, and she'd turned me and Megan into her own little minions of spic-n-span. D had learned, too. He did his chores quietly in the dead of night when Mom couldn't see or hear him.

Or using some kind of magic that kept Mom asleep.

I'd taken credit when she stumbled into the kitchen each morning, exhausted from the double shifts she pulled to keep a roof over our heads and food on the table. These were one of a handful of times she smiled at me.

"Thank you," I said.

"For what?" he asked. "This?"

He rose to his full height and pointed at the spot on the rug, now only discolored by cleaning fluid. The room smelled lemony fresh, too.

"No." I put down my soda and stood to face him. At his current height, I faced his groin, which gave me all kinds of naughty ideas. He must've guessed what I was thinking since he rolled his eyes and gave an exasperated huff. "I'm thanking you for all you did when we were little. I don't think I ever thanked you for making me look good with the world-class cleaning."

He turned his gaze away. "It was the least I could do for room and board."

"But that's not why you did it."

D stooped so he could look into my eyes, searching for answers. I stood still and put my best game face on. He was talking. And if I kept him guessing and made it a game, he'd keep talking instead of shutting down or roaring or going out for a case of booze.

We stared at each other for a long moment, but he blinked first. Holy guacamole, I won. I'd never won that game before. Maybe I wasn't so terrible at diplomacy after all.

"So tell me, Jane, why did I do it?"

I snorted. "Because you're a good person. And good people do good things."

He smiled. It didn't reach his eyes. His eyes were cold and calculating, brimming with cruelty. "I'm not a person. I'm a demon. And I am not good."

Oh, for the love of lollipops, was he wallowing in self-loathing about his nature? Again? Why couldn't dudes work out their shit in therapy? I knew he'd been seeing Dr. Khatri along with the rest of the team. Clearly, he wasn't making as much progress as yours truly. I was a paragon of self-awareness and actualization.

Okay, who was I kidding, I had more issues than the longest running tabloid, and doc regularly called me her "problem patient." The twins called me a hopeless case, and my cat called me stupid. But damn it, even the most neurotic of people would recognize what was going on with D. Was he that thick?

No.

It was easier to see other peoples' issues than to see your own. He needed a cosmic kick in the ass, and I was just the gal to give it to him.

I squared my shoulders and went nose to nose with him, trying not to go cross eyed in the process. "I got two words for you, buddy. Bull and shit."

He grinned wider. Still with the cold eyes, but it was a start. "That's technically one word. And you're wrong, little girl. I found out what I was in the bowels of the hell realm. Oh, I played at being human while I was stuck in this world. And I learned to disguise and hide it. Came in handy while I worked my way up the demon hierarchy. Then again," he said, rising to his full height again so he could look down on me, the bastard, "so did this."

I assumed the "this" referred to his demon form.

I cocked my head to the side and put a finger under my chin as I looked up at him. "Hmm, is this the part where I'm supposed to scream in terror or faint? Don't get me wrong, I'm sure you were *very* impressive in the demon realm, but I've seen you in Spiderman underoos when we were kids, remember? You were watching cartoons and eating cereal with marshmallows. Sorry, dude, but that's the real you. This," I gestured to his form, "is a big fat shield you're using to hide from your issues."

He roared again.

I fought not to flinch. After he was done, I yawned. "You're boring me."

"Jane, I swear to Lucifer if you don't leave now, I'll—"

"You'll what?" I said, a deviously wicked plan forming in my mind. I backed up, grinning at him, and let my butt hit the bed. Then I climbed on it. Good thing I'd taken off my boots when I came in the house. Trying to get the docs off now would ruin the effect I was going for. Somehow, I managed to look dignified being height challenged. Sliding back, I put my head on the pillow and arranged my body to display my best features, plastering on my best come hither face that I may or may not have stolen from our resident succubus Mara, and said, "Punish me? You're such a big, bad scary demon, but talk is cheap. So is roaring. Show me who's boss."

CHAPTER SIXTEEN

He stared at me with his red, glowing eyes, mouth agape and head cocked to the side, confused. It was irritating.

"Did this whole transformation make you deaf, or did you just trade brain cells for bulk? I'll speak slowly and use small words. You, big bad demon. Me, Jane. Big bad demon make Jane shut up by fucking her brains out. It's about time."

At last, he spoke. "You can't be serious."

Oh, for the love of lemons, why was he making this so difficult? Time to bring out the big guns.

I got up from my comfortable recline, scooted ungracefully down to the end of the bed—cursing my lack of stature—stood up, marched up to the idiot, and pulled off my sweater.

"Jane, what are you doing?"

I tossed the sweater on the floor and jerked off my bra. Then I pulled down my pants and undies, making sure to ditch my socks in the process, because standing naked except for socks would be ridiculous. I was in the buff, hands on hips, waiting for D to make his move. Judging from the impressive bulge in what was left of his trousers, he was very happy to see me.

I fought not to gulp. There was big, and then there was big. I mean, there would be worse ways to die, but I'd rather not. Maybe I should see what type of oversized celestial form I could muster.

"Do you like eyeballs?"

D muttered, "Excuse me?" He wasn't paying attention. He was staring at my breasts. Good. They were one of my best features.

"Do. You. Like. Eyeballs?"

He smirked. "Is this your way of telling me to keep my eyes on yours instead of on those gorgeous breasts?"

I snorted. "Good one, but no. I was just thinking about what kind of celestial form I might assume to, ah, accommodate your...impressive demon form. And whether you'd find it attractive."

His face fell and he turned his back on me. Shit. We'd been doing so well and then I'd put my foot in it. I needed to think. But I was a little having trouble concentrating myself. Sure, he was big and no longer fit the human aesthetic, but he had a killer ass in this form. I wanted to squeeze it as I climbed up his body. I wanted to see if his skin was as smooth and salty in this form as it was in his human guise.

I wanted.

He wanted, too, but he needed to get out of his stupid head and get with the program.

I took two steps forward and pressed myself against him, reaching my arms up and around to caress his firm abs before trailing my fingers down. His skin was blazing, its heat bathing me in comfort and a growing desire that called to me, all of me—human, demon, and whatever else I truly was and would become. His muscles clenched. I teased them with my fingertips before using my nails.

"Mmm," I said, letting my fingers travel down to the waistband of his ripped jeans. He hissed when I gently stroked his length through the fabric, a thin layer between me and paradise.

"Jane," he warned. "Stop."

It took every ounce of willpower I had to move my fingers back to his abs. Ending the seduction, I embraced him, placing my cheek against the skin of his back and hugging him so close, just like I did when he would creep into my bed at night when we were young and one of us was afraid. This was right. If I had a home, this was it.

He was my home. And I was his.

I stood there, holding him until my arms ached and a chill crept over my bare skin. He must've felt my shivers since he ran his warm hands over my arms to warm them. I released him and let him turn to face me. I stood and regarded him, my body as bare as my soul.

He gently scooped me up and walked me to the bed, pulling back the covers and gently setting me down. After he tucked me in, he sighed, looking around as if at a loss. At last, he lowered himself to the ground and leaned until his head rested on the pillow next to mine.

"Sorry," he muttered.

"For what?" I reached out to stroke his hair before moving my hand up to tweak one of his massive horns. "Consent is key. I mean, if you have a headache, all you had to do was say 'not tonight, honey.'"

He gave me a lopsided grin. That was a good sign. If I could make him smile in the middle of whatever turmoil was roiling through his brain underneath that thick, stubborn skull, we would be okay.

"It's not that. I'm...not myself. Not just this," he lifted his head and gestured to his face and body. "In here."

He pointed to his head. "I haven't taken this form since I left my father's service. When I used it in the space between..."

I had a million questions, theories, light-hearted comic responses, and snark on deck, but for once I kept my big fat mouth shut. Better to let him talk when he was ready. If I pushed too hard, he might shut down.

Or shut me out.

He swallowed hard and met my gaze. "Jane, I remembered how good it felt to have power. I didn't just kill those demons to save the celestial refugees or to defend you. I did it because I *liked* it. My demon nature comes from my father and the lineage of master demon warlords before him. We revel in slaughter, feast on the fear of our enemies and victims as we tear them limb from limb. We grow stronger and become filled with insatiable battle lust with each victory. Trinity was right to send me away. I scared her. I scare myself when I'm like this."

"I get it," I said. He gave me a scowl and I thwacked him on the horn I'd stroked just moments before.

"Ow!" He moved away from me and rubbed the horn as if I'd really hurt him. Maybe I had. But that's what he got for scoffing before I shared my ugly secret.

"Listen, buster, I do get it. Remember when we took Belphegor out and I lost it?"

He nodded and shrugged. "Not the first time. You're untrained in your celestial powers and you let them loose. That was scary, but it's not the same."

I shook my head. "It wasn't celestial power. Whatever my father gave me is way stronger and more consuming than that. The power was...god-like. I wasn't just protecting our team and battling a master demon. It made me want to conquer and make all who beheld me bow down in obedience and worship, like it was my purpose and what I was owed. That was what scared me."

I ran my fingers along the chain around my neck, moving past my black mirror and over the ancient ring that served as a focus, allowing me to channel the dark power within me. I cracked the vault and let a bit of that power out. Just a sliver. Enough to show D that I under-stood the lure of that kind of power and the destruction it longed to unleash.

His gaze went wide, and he stilled. Damn it. Maybe I scared him now, too. He shook his head as if clearing it and said, "No, that's not your nature. You don't need to be feared or even liked, let alone worshipped. You protect because it's who you are. That's your nature."

With some effort, I reined my power back in, letting the strain and weight of it show on my face and body.

After I regained my composure, I raised my brows, waiting for him to put the pieces together.

"I fought it, D, and I'll keep fighting it. But I'm not going to do it alone. I can't. I need you to watch me and help me keep it in line. Just like I'll do for you. I lost you once to hell. I'll be damned if I lose you again. Your father can't have you. Your demon nature can't have you."

I sat up and took his face in my palms. I leaned in and said, "You're mine."

Then I kissed him.

CHAPTER SEVENTEEN

I meant the kiss to be an invitation, but once my lips met his and I tasted his sweet, hot mouth, I lost myself to sensation. His tongue was velvet and it danced with mine, teasing, tempting, taking my former desire to dizzying new heights as he sucked my bottom lip into his mouth and gently bit.

Then he licked my lips to soothe the sting, delighting me with an irresistible and heady mixture of pleasure and pain. I tried to pull him closer, but he was immovable as granite. He took my hands and moved them to my sides in an unspoken demand for stillness. The move let me know that he was in charge of the game, and I was to submit to him and the pleasure he promised.

I would play his game. For a while.

He teased my mouth, pulling back when I moved closer in pursuit of his tongue. Setting a maddeningly slow pace, D began to trail gentle kisses down my neck far too slow for my liking and too fast for me to catch my breath. My demon was working me into a frenzy, and we'd barely begun.

He caressed my collar bone with his tongue, and I gasped at the heat, trembling with anticipation as he dipped below to my breast. I needed his mouth on my aching nipples, but he kept teasing and taunting me with what was just out of reach, holding me in a vise grip so I had to endure the delectable torture.

He looked up, gaze meeting mine, and he flashed a wicked grin, the bastard.

"Now, D," I said, my voice breathy and gasping.

"Not yet," he said, rising back up so we were face to face. "I've waited far too long to rush this. You'll scream, beg, and curse my name before we're done, and you'll love every minute of it."

Oh, that was it. He was *so* going to pay for this.

Suddenly, he pulled me against him, keeping my arms braced at my sides while he lavished my mouth and, by luck or some bit of mercy granted from his wicked demonic soul, pulled me onto his lap so I straddled him. I ground against him, seeking friction that would grant me the release I needed. He let me do as I wished for a few moments until the hitch in my breath gave me away. I was getting too close.

He wasn't having it.

D pulled me off his lap, and I did scream in frustration. Just a little, but it must've been enough to satisfy him since he finally took my nipple into his mouth, turning my scream into a moan of satisfaction that he answered with a low rumbling chuckle of smug male satisfaction. Hot mouth, flicking tongue, pressure, then an abrupt end. He blew on my swollen, aching nipple before lavishing my other breast with the same attention.

Too soon, he released my breast and flipped me over. I balanced on trembling arms and legs as he ran his big hands over my hips and ass. "So damned beautiful," he murmured, his voice filled with reverent awe. "Better than any fantasy. I can hardly believe you're real."

"I'm real," I said. "I'm real, and I'm ready. Please, D, please, I need you inside me."

A hard smack on my ass sent a jolt of pure electricity through my body that settled in my core and left me aching, desperate. D traced the spot where he'd spanked me with the tips of those wicked demonic claws and said, "Good girl. First a delightful scream, and a bit of begging, but you can do better than that, my angel. You will do better than that."

Indignation and a dash of frustration-fueled anger heightened my arousal. "You evil bastard, I'll make you pay for this."

Damn it, I'd cursed him, just like he said I would. It wasn't fair. My brain was addled from lust and longing, and he seemed as cool as a cucumber. I looked over my shoulder and gasped at the bulge in his jeans. I grinned as heat pooled between my legs. No, I wasn't alone in my burning desire.

Quick as a snake, I put my years of training to good use. I leapt from the bed and rounded on him, tearing the remnants of jeans that barely clung to his hips to reveal his hard length.

Then I took him into my mouth.

Oh, holy wow, the soft flesh covering his hard length was even hotter than his mouth and he tasted like pure sin. I caressed him with my lips and tongue, gripping his hip with one hand and using the other to massage his shaft.

I lost my rhythm for a moment when his groans and curses made me smile. Who knew getting even could be so much fun? Teasing and tasting, licking and sucking, I brought him to the brink and released him, rising to meet his gaze and giving him my best smirk.

"You," he growled, "are going to be the death of me."

In an instant, his body morphed back to the more familiar humanoid form. D still towered over me, but at a height of over six feet instead of nearly eight. His skin had returned to a shade lighter than mine, and he'd lost the horns, heavy brows, brutish bulk, and clawed fingertips and toes.

Oh, babe, I wouldn't care if you were covered in scales and had ten arms.

I couldn't tell him that. Not yet. No, this tentative, tender moment called for something light and humorous.

"Maybe," I said, moving into his arms. "But what a way to go, eh?"

He laughed. My demon didn't laugh often. I'd have to remedy that. Later.

We kissed, allowing desire to build between us again. No more games. Just the two of us savoring a well-earned respite from all that life and the universe had thrown at us for so long. There was only me and D, our passion, our hearts, and our souls.

"You were right," D whispered as he lowered me onto the bed and covered me with his body. "I am yours."

"And I'm yours. Always have been. It's always been you."

He kissed my forehead and gently spread my legs, stroking my slick, wet heat with skilled fingers. I sighed, savoring the moment. At long last, he said, "May I?"

"Yes, please."

He entered me slowly. When I enveloped him fully, he stilled, gaze locked on mine. All that he was, the good, the bad, and the ugly, were bared to me in the glow of the red sparks that danced in the depths of his brown eyes. I knew he saw all of me, too. We were matched in so many ways, and as long as we had each other, nothing could defeat us.

I clung to that thought as we rocked against each other, meeting his thrusts and finding a rhythm that slowly, steadily built to a quiet storm that broke within me first as I cried out his name. "Don't you dare close your eyes," he said.

I didn't.

And he returned the favor as his climax swept through him. The power of it had me squeezing my thighs together until I came again while he spilled himself inside me.

Before I drifted off to sleep in his arms, he said, "Oh, Jane. You were worth the wait."

CHAPTER EIGHTEEN

I woke with sunlight streaming through the blinds hanging from my bedroom window and surrounded by the strong arms of my demon. I rolled gently so I could face him without waking him up. He looked younger in sleep, peaceful, without the weight of the hell realm on his shoulders. Good. My demon could use a bit of respite from everything he'd been through.

Plus, the war he was fighting with himself and his deep, dark demonic urges.

I'd loved D since I was five. He'd been my secret friend, best and only friend, the only creature on the planet who knew my secret and loved me anyway. Now that we'd consummated our long courtship, I realized that love was a deep, endless sea that I would happily drown in. But I didn't have to worry. D wouldn't let me, and I wouldn't let him sink to the depths of despair.

"You're well and truly mine now, mister," I said, stroking his stubbled cheek. "I'll never let you go."

The corners of his full, sensual lips crept up into a lazy smile. "Hmm, is that a threat or a promise?"

That gave me an idea. I leaned in and kissed him gently on the lips, then I ripped back the covers and climbed on top of him, pinning his arms over his head and teasing his hard length with my core. He groaned and closed his eyes, leaning back and letting me stroke us both.

"That," I said, leaning down to trail kisses along his throat, "depends on you."

He rose and captured my lips in a passionate kiss. I stopped thinking all together.

———

After a third round, we reluctantly got out of bed and showered. Thank goodness for home renovations. We'd knocked down a few walls and rearranged the space, transforming the rickety old bathroom Megan and I had shared as kids into a luxury mini spa with modern amenities that included a claw foot tub, lighted mirrors, and a huge walk-in shower tiled floor to ceiling in blue slate with grey accents. The shower floor was covered with tilework modeled after river stones. A teak bench sat beneath chrome racks that held towels, loofahs, and space for hanging bathrobes. A built-in nook on the wall beside the bench held all kinds of shampoos, conditioners, and body washes.

Mom had sprung for heated floor tiles in the bathroom, which she preferred to her own en suite bathroom.

I groaned in delight as warm water streamed from multiple jets, and melted when D massaged my scalp as he washed my hair with a fresh, minty shampoo. He rinsed and conditioned my hair after, managing to wrangle the tangles in my hair without hurting me. I returned the favor, but we silently agreed to soap up and wash ourselves by ourselves, so we'd stay clean and get out of the shower before the hot water ran out.

I made coffee while D went out to get breakfast, teleporting since I'd parked behind his Mustang.

I couldn't wipe the stupid grin from my face. Damn, I could get used to this.

Nights of passion and mornings in domestic bliss. Was this what normal people did? I'd always wanted normal.

Whatever it was, I'd enjoy it while it lasted.

D returned with chocolate croissants, a cheese and fruit platter, and breakfast sandwiches. I poured him a mug of coffee and brought him up to speed on everything from our undercover operation at Swan Springs, what we'd learned from the rallmath, and the deal I'd made with Judaliel to go after Pendergrass and his portal-in-the-making.

D stiffened and scowled when I brought up Pendergrass, the summoner who'd taken him away from earth—and me—and sent him to the cruelty of his father Belial's service. We both held a grudge against the man for that, and I hated him for whatever he'd done to damage Cooper. You didn't get as unstable as our paranoid, forest dwelling resident summoner and portal guardian without some serious trauma. And based on what little I'd found in the dossier our old boss kept on him, most of that had happened in childhood at the hands of dear old dad.

There were worse things than absentee parents.

"So, you're letting the crazy archangel go after Pendergrass with only the shepherd to supervise her?"

"Not just Judaliel and the archangel. Alexi will be trailing them, and the twins will be on deck with all their favorite weapons of mass destruction in case things go south. I can't do it for the same reason you can't—it's personal for us. We can't afford to let personal grudges interfere with the mission, no matter how justified."

"And we can't trust the word of an archangel cutting a deal to save her own skin. What's to stop her from using Pendergrass to bring legions of warrior angels to earth?"

I wanted to bang my head against the table. Ugh. We'd been doing so well. This stupid work argument was really ruining my post-orgasmic Zen.

"I trust our teammates as much as I trust you, which is completely. You should trust them, too."

He put his coffee mug down on the table with more force than necessary. He didn't yell or rage, but his tight jaw and the vein bulging at his temple showed me just how hard he was working to keep his temper in check. He stood and began pacing the kitchen floor. While we'd expanded my mom's kitchen during the renovation, there was only so much we could expand. There wasn't enough room for him to cool his jets.

"It might be easier to trust the team if they trusted me," he muttered.

"It's not the team," I said, sounding a little too whiny. "It's Trinity. And she's just got her panties in a wad because of whatever deal she cut with the demons to protect the city."

He stopped and stared at me. "You think the others don't follow her lead?"

I snorted. "The twins don't, and neither does Megan. Lacey thinks you're the best fighter on the team, Mara worships the ground you walk on for saving her from the Angel of Death, Alexi respects the hell out of you, and Sully told me that I needed to stop being a bitch and come find you last night. Unless you've done something to piss off Dr. Khatri, you're cool."

D kept scowling but plopped his fine ass back down in his seat at the kitchen table and devoured his fourth breakfast sandwich—switching forms must've burned a ton of calories—and poured himself another cup of coffee.

"She's not going to let me back in the field. And...maybe I shouldn't be."

I leaned back and mock groaned, rolling my eyes like a pissed off teenager. "That's ridiculous. By that rationale, I shouldn't be allowed in the field either. Hells bells, any of us could snap at any moment with the power we're packing. We all fight it every single day. You didn't go on a rampage of slaughter and mayhem in the space between. You *protected* the innocents and brought them to safety."

He appeared to consider what I was saying and nodded. "Okay, well, since you and Lacey are neck deep in infiltrating Beelzebub's inner sanctum, why don't I join up with Alexi and the twins to keep an eye on your double agent angel?"

I opened my mouth to protest, but he held up a hand. "I won't go after Pendergrass Senior. Capture and containment is best for the mission. Alexi and the twins can handle that. But if Judaliel goes off the deep end, I'm not so sure they could take her. It's you or me, babe, and you've got your hands full, otherwise you'd have my full support. I guess the question is, do you trust me?"

I trusted him completely, and he'd proven himself over and over, but I was biased. Trinity was, too. We didn't really have a neutral third party, but the doc was as close as we could get.

"Okay, talk to Dr. Khatri and tell her what you told me last night. If she agrees that you're fit for duty, she can override Trinity. One-time emergency case and fighting on two fronts qualifies as an emergency. I'll give Sam a call so he can be ready for any fall out."

D got up and walked to my chair, then leaned down to give me a slow, sensual kiss.

I liked it.

"So, does this mean we're officially going steady?" I asked.

He flashed me a wicked grin, one that had red demon sparks dancing in his eyes. "Oh, yes. We need to wrap up this mission ASAP. I have such plans for you."

Well, if that wasn't motivation, I didn't know what was.

CHAPTER NINETEEN

When I walked back into HQ, the team took one look at me and then money started changing hands.

"You assholes had a betting pool? About when I'd hook up with D?"

Boice took a fifty from his brother and said, "You're an endless source of entertainment, not to mention income."

Roice scowled. "Couldn't keep it in your pants until after another date, could you?"

Sam and Trinity scowled. We would have to have a little chat about that and soon. They had no idea how hard D fought his father's influence and cruel lessons. I wouldn't let them torment my demon with their fears and doubts. Those two had enough to occupy them without worrying about Demoriel.

Lacey passed Megan cash.

"*Et tu*, sis?" I asked. Damn, had I known everyone was all up in my love life, I'd have played it cooler, kept them guessing.

Nah, I would have rigged the dates in favor of anyone but the twins. And I would have taken a cut.

"Sorry not sorry, Jane. I'm just so damned happy for you." She came over and gave me a hug, but I caught the slight tremor in her embrace.

She was hurting. Of course she was hurting. I was going to find Brad, neuter him, and give her his balls in a mason jar that she could keep on her mantle.

I hugged her back. "Just please tell me mom didn't get in on the betting pool."

"Of course not. But I do plan on asking Demoriel what his long-term intentions are toward my youngest daughter."

I let go of Megan and jumped about a foot in the air at the sound of my mom's voice. Not that I wasn't grateful that she liked D and that she was happy for me, but we'd never had the whole tell-each-other-every-thing kind of relationship. I wasn't sure I wanted to start now. It was too weird.

Changing the subject, I said, "We've fooled around long enough. Lacey and I need to get ready for our meet and greet with the board at Swan Springs. Alexi, you and the twins good to go for assisting Judaliel with finding Pendergrass?"

Roice waved a dismissive hand. "I was born ready, and so was my bro. Big dog looks like he's chomping at the bit, too."

Alexi held his human shape, but the wolf showed in his eyes. It called to my inner wolf, the phantom demon creature Alexi's graft had gifted me. I promised her we'd hunt soon, and she would satisfy her appetite by battling enemy demons.

Okay, here goes nothing...

"So," I said, striving for casual. "How about we add another demon to your team to keep an eye on our little busy bee angel?"

As predicted, Trinity was less than thrilled about D going out into the field, but she surprised us all by acquiescing before D even talked to the doc. We needed all hands on deck for this mission, and our fearless leader had weighed the risks and found them to be acceptable.

After donning our glamour, Lacey and I headed to Swan Springs for our interview with the Illuminati of Snobbery to see if we qualified for the swanky planned community. Simon was set to map out the tunnels beneath the subdivision and see where they led, while we played nice with the neighbors. Sully, wearing her "stu-pid dog" rottweiler glamour and a large white collar embroidered with tiny peaches and sporting a giant bow on the side sat in the back and glared at me.

"Oh, come on. I fed you two large pepperoni pizzas and a gallon of rocky road. You need to get over your snit and get in character."

"Ink stu-pid shit-head," she yowled.

I glared at Lacey, whose snort was very much out of character while wearing her big boobed, arm candy glamour and a tight blue cocktail dress.

"Shithead? Really? What else did you teach my cat?"

Lacey looked offended. "It wasn't me. You need to stop letting her hang out with your roomies. They're teaching her how to swear in ten languages, including demon."

Great...

Lacey turned around and wagged her finger at Sully. "Don't talk to your mother that way. You think you're in this by yourself? I'm wearing enough shapewear to permanently rearrange my organs and Jinx spent about five hours learning to swagger like a dude bro while wearing a tux. It's for the mission, so get with the program."

Sully sneezed and turned around to show us her giant canine butt-hole before woofing and settling on the backseat.

"That's better," Lacey said. "Okay, so I'll charm the rich bitches while you schmooze with the guys. Remember to dazzle them with that stock tip Boice gave you."

I ran a hand over my beard, grateful that it didn't itch. My man bun sat atop my head, secured with a discreet hair tie. Mara had helped me get my hairline perfectly straight along with the lines of my beard. Surprisingly, it worked well with the tuxedo. "Yeah, yeah. We go in, we dazzle the neighbors, nail the interview, and try and get a feel for Beelzebub. Then we get the hell out after Simon and Sully do the recon thing. We've got this."

The guard at the gate adjacent to the carriage house/sales office checked our IDs, called to verify that we were, in fact, on the guest list, and gave us the once over. I thought they might search the car, but after a bit of back and forth on the walkie-talkie, they buzzed us in.

The gates opened and we drove down a long stretch of cobblestone road flanked by tall, mature magnolia trees. The trees hid most of the house as we approached, but as it came into view, Lacey and I gasped.

There were mansions. And there were *mansions*.

"Looks like we're going to the big house," I muttered, hackles rising. The chip on my shoulder from growing up poor grew three sizes as I surveyed a scaled down version of the Biltmore Estate or one of those Gilded Age mansions in Newport. It screamed elegance, New England class wrapped in Southern charm. New construction for old money. Surrounding the impressive stone and marble structure were grounds worthy of the home. No McMansions here. Acres of manicured lawn and gardens sprawled around and, in the distance, illuminated by elegant exterior lights.

No expense or detail spared on this baby. It screamed I'm-better-than-you-and-I-want-you-to-know-it. Made me wonder if the Master Demon of Envy had a hand in the design.

We drove around the circular driveway, where I tossed the valet the Mustang's keys and slipped him a wad of cash before holding the door open for Lacey. Probably shouldn't have been so gauche but fuck these rich assholes. A group of men in tuxes milled around the massive front portico, chatting, drinking, and smoking. Lacey flashed them a megawatt smile along with a generous amount of leg and thigh as she exited the vehicle. I smiled and took her hand, nodding at the men with a wicked grin that screamed, "Eat your hearts out. She's mine." We ascended the stairs where we were greeted by Lindsey, looking a little out of place in a business suit.

Lindsey must've read my thoughts on my glamoured face. "Didn't have time to change before the event," she muttered, giggling nervously as she tucked a loose lock of hair behind her ear.

"Working you that hard, sweetie?" Lacey asked with just the right amount of condescension.

Lindsey smiled brightly showing her perfectly white teeth. Was she a demon? Her mannerisms were spot on human for the most part, but that grin was just a little too feral, like she had sharp fangs underneath the veneer of demure business lady.

"Oh, I work plenty hard. And between you and me—" she leaned in to whisper conspiratorially. "My fiancé will see to it that I have the good life when we build our dream home in Phase II." Lindsey made certain that the light caught the platinum band with a giant diamond mounted in the center.

"Oh, you don't live here yet?" Lacey examined her French manicured nails and her own glamoured engagement ring, pretending to be bored.

I smirked like the smug douchebro part I was playing. Not a chore. I loved watching my partner work, especially while tormenting the enemy.

Lindsey widened her smile. "Not yet. Neither do you. Best get inside and mingle if you want the chance to call this exclusive community home. The board has exacting standards—not just money. We also go for class."

Ouch. What a snooty patootie. I hoped for her fiancé's sake that she was worth the aggravation. I wouldn't date her.

Figuring I should smooth things over, I said, "Well, I'm more than a little outclassed by both you beautiful ladies. Come on, darlin'. Let's go meet our future neighbors."

I took Lacey's arm and walked toward the door. I glanced over my shoulder, offering Lindsey a flirtatious wink. "Hope you'll be our neighbor real soon."

An honest-to-God butler opened the door for us—or was it a door-man? I had little experience with the finer things. At any rate, the man smiled, bowed, and ushered us in with a soft, "Good evening." The house, presumably belonging to Beelzebub, was as impressive inside as it was out. Marble floors, antique furniture, and classic paintings of landscapes and equestrians frolicking on horseback drew my gaze first. A fountain served as the centerpiece of the large central space. It was bronze with a column adorned with sculptured ladies in togas holding pottery from which water poured. The column supported an upper platform with a multi-faced lion's head spitting water from its gaping mouths. Lights were low enough to give the space a somewhat cozy feeling, at least as cozy as a freaking mansion could get, and provided shadowed nooks for quiet conversation. Unlike some older mansions, the interior of this house wasn't crowded with furniture and fancy knick-knacks. Not that those things weren't around, but the whole floor plan and design was open and spacious. There was room to move in this home with its high ceilings, large hallways, and extra-large windows.

The real stars, however, were the people.

Men and women—mostly older men and younger women—filled the space, decked out in perfectly tailored tuxedos and cocktail dresses. The women were dripping with jewels and sipped champagne from glasses delivered by smartly uniformed waiters and snacked on hors d'oeuvres offered by waitresses wearing uniform dresses. Most of the men held tumblers filled with amber liquid. Probably good Scotch. No beer or cocktails in sight, but I decided to go bold with my first move.

I stopped one of the waiters and asked, "I don't suppose you have any beer."

The waiter smiled. "Of course, sir. May I offer you a Scottish ale, or perhaps a Belgian lager?"

Wow. Fancy beer. Say what you want about the rich, but those mofos knew how to drink in style. "I'll take the Scottish ale, please. And my fiancé would like a martini."

He bowed and headed off to fetch our drinks. Lindsey leaned against me, playing the role of adoring arm candy with a touch of tasteful PDA. "Daring to be different?" she asked.

"Thought I'd give them something unexpected. Something that says we're confident enough to make ourselves comfortable and don't care about impressing the crowd."

She laughed. "Good one. For a minute there I thought you were trying to get me drunk so you could take advantage of moi."

"Mara would kill me, and D...well, I don't think D is all that forgiving. You're safe with me."

Lacey gave me a speculative look. "You and D on the outs again?"

"No," I said. Crap, I sounded defensive. "We're just busy. And the celestial rescue wore him out. He needs to rest before turning big bad demon again to protect our team from Judalieil if things go south."

"I'll bet." Lacey snuggled closer, offering me comfort. "That transformation was really something. He packs a lot of power."

It didn't sound like an accusation. More like an observation and opening to elaborate. I might have taken up her invitation. My partner always had my back and was a good ear to bend.

A familiar voice spoke from behind us. "Mr. Dixon and Ms. Branson. So glad you could join us."

We turned to face Mr. Rich White Privilege himself, Lawrence Duneberry. He wore a tux, of course, and held a tumbler of Scotch. His brows raised when our waiter returned to deliver my beer and Lacey's martini, but he didn't comment. A woman who didn't look that much younger than Duneberry joined our party and introduced herself as Mrs.Viola Duneberry. She wore a flattering gold cocktail dress that complimented her honey-colored highlights, making small talk before whisking Lacey away to mingle with the ladies.

Duneberry led me through a short hallway to his study, where we were greeted by men smoking cigars and drinking Scotch. No beer in sight. I raised my glass and took a long swig, earning chuckles from my companions. Who had the biggest balls in the room? I did.

The study was a masculine space in the old-fashioned sense, decorated with dark woods and well-worn chairs upholstered in forest green and probably worth more than my first apartment. Paintings that featured hunters, the fancy kind on horseback instead of the more familiar camo-clad redneck hunters I was used to, hung on the walls between the perfectly taxidermized heads of dead deer, elk, and big-horned sheep. Cigar smoke hung thick in the air along with the scents of expensive cologne and an undercurrent of sweat. Fear sweat. Beneath the veneer of civility lurked an undercurrent of doom. Humans would sense it and assume it came from the powerful men occupying the room. That was partially true.

But it was the demon menace that really set the tone. Beelzebub's essence clung to the space, as did the essences of other demon minions. Dangerous. My kind of party. Time to wheel and deal with the big boys.

We spent the next hour talking stocks, real estate, local politics, and, to my surprise, sports. Like, regular sports. I'd been afraid they would be into horse racing or sailing. Instead, we talked football—one of the resident's family owned an NFL team—and hockey. My stock tip from the twins was a hit and appeared to impress the younger men in the crowd. A few of the older men found my down-to-earth manner "refreshing." I was new money, but they assured me that, unlike Belle Meade, Swan Springs didn't care whether money was old or new.

They just cared about money.

"Well, I'm so glad to hear that, Bob," I said to the HCA executive who was also new money. "This is America. A self-made man is worth at least as much as a man with a rich daddy."

"True, but there is something to be said for family wealth."

I didn't turn around to see the man who spoke.

I didn't have to. I'd know that voice anywhere.

Having heard it for a decade, in person and in my nightmares, it was as familiar as it was unexpected.

Shit. I couldn't afford to freeze or panic and blow my cover.

I didn't know what he was playing at, but I suspected he couldn't afford to blow his own cover.

Assuming he wasn't working for the other side now.

I plastered on what I hoped was a confident smirk and turned to face my formerly AWOL boss Sameal, the Angel of Death.

CHAPTER TWENTY

Shit, shit, shit...

The bastard hadn't even bothered to change his glamour.

He looked the same as he had the last time I saw him—a devilishly handsome older man with fine features and enough gray in his salt and pepper hair to give him an aura of authority. Only this time, he wore a perfectly tailored tuxedo instead of a perfectly tailored business suit. If he wasn't hiding his glamour, he was either working with the master demons now or he was still working against them in secret.

Or he was playing both sides. That tracked. No matter what, I couldn't trust him, and I couldn't afford to have him blow my cover. I sized him up, going for cocky young buck bravado in the face of an older, more experienced man, hoping he couldn't see through my glamour.

I raised my glass to him and said, "All wealthy families got their start somewhere. I'm the start of mine."

Sameal gave a small smile and raised his glass to me. "Your reputation precedes you, Mr. Dixon."

I gave him a cool smile. "And who might you be?"

Another older gentleman laughed, clapping Sameal on the back. "No need to wheedle our new neighbor. Mr. Dixon, allow me to introduce Dr.

Neal Dormer, an esteemed member of our board and HOA. In his spare time, he guards and grows the assets of Nashville's rich and famous."

"Not just Nashville's elite, Bob," Sameal, a.k.a. Dr. Dormer, muttered. The boss, the Big Bad Boss or BBB for short, the Arbiter, Sameal the Angel of Death, and now Dormer? I needed a spreadsheet to keep up with the guy's names and titles.

He probably had more.

I'd have to settle for Jinx McGee, the one and only, Demon Hunter and, according to the stupid Grimoire back at HQ, the warrior imbued with the power of three realms destined to rise against Sameal and Haniel, who'd formerly possessed me and knew way too much about my mind, body, and soul and would use it against me in battle.

But I knew her, too. And I knew Sameal. Sort of. He took mysterious to the next level and then some.

But hey, at least I had nearly as many titles. I wasn't the same person I'd been for the decade Sameal had ruled my life and Haniel had resided in my soul. I was my own person and I'd proven myself against some pretty powerful demons and celestials.

"Of course, of course." Bob's voice brought me back to the conversation. "You're an international wolf of Wallstreet and beyond. Young Dixon here seems to know his way around the markets. Looking for a protégé?"

"Perhaps," said Sameal, offering his hand. Damn it, if we touched, there was a decent chance he'd see through my glamour.

But if I didn't shake his hand, I'd never be able to infiltrate Beelzebub's inner circle on earth.

I grasped his hand and gave it a firm shake. His gaze narrowed as he gripped my hand with more force than I'd expected. I'd been made. Fine. I raised my brows and grinned wider, letting him know that I knew who and what he was.

"Mr. Dixon," Sameal said. "Would you care to join me in our host's study? I'd love to hear everything about you and your investments. I think we can be of use to one another."

The way he said be of use made my skin crawl. Creepo. At least he hadn't blown my cover. I hoped Lacey didn't spot him. She was more intimidated by him than I'd ever been. Smart woman.

Smarter than me. If I'd maintained a healthy fear of the guy, we might not be in this mess.

"I'd be delighted," I said. "Lead the way."

We left the room full of men, cigars, and Scotch, walking in silence through the central area where the well-dressed ladies and lesser men—those not invited to schmooze with the big boys—mingled while waiters and waitresses kept the food and booze flowing. I followed Sameal down another short hallway and through the study door. The space was lit with a small lamp that bathed the room with gentle light, illuminating a fancy desk that was a little too much like my former boss's old desk and built in bookshelves along the walls, filled to capacity with books that the owner of the home had probably never read, at least not since his private school days.

Sameal rounded the desk and took a seat. Power move that said, "I'm so confident that I won't bother to stand at the ready in your presence." Dominance games sucked, but at least the glamour made me look more formidable. Mr. Dixon was fit and knew how to fight thanks to me.

"Before we begin," he said, flicking his hand and sending out a wave of powerful demon magic that coated the room, "I'll give us a bit of privacy. Don't worry. Beelzebub and his ilk won't pay attention. They'll assume you are the mortal you pretend to be and that I'm toying with you. Screams ruin a good party."

I glowered at him. "I won't be screaming. Not for you. I'm guessing you don't want your new friends to know you're talking to the enemy."

He leaned back and grinned. "Enemy? What bravado. I wasn't certain who you were under that glamour until now. Only Jane Aurelia McGee would be so foolishly smug in my presence. A nasty habit I've found I rather missed."

Taking a page from my Mega Demon fantasy play book, I plopped down in the chair across from Sameal, kicked up my feet onto the fancy desk and crossed them, leaning back and looking bored. "So, ex-boss man, where've you been?"

He smiled. "Working. Like you and your team, only without the sloppy execution."

Asshole.

"Well, our sloppy execution took out Belphegor, her archangel sister and sister's sidekick. What have you got to show for your work?"

He sighed and gave me a withering stare. "More than you'll ever know. For starters, I'm the reason you do not have to dispatch the Archangel of Temperance. She's working for our side now to sabotage the war effort. I assume you're in charge of the little ragtag band I left behind?"

If he was waiting for a thank you, he'd be waiting until hell froze over. If he'd taken out Beelzebub's counterpart, it wasn't for us. It was for his own twisted agenda.

Smiling wide and settling more comfortably in my chair, I said, "Nope. That would be Trinity. I put her in charge and she's doing a splendid job."

Aside from her deal with a powerful demon that protected the city and was giving her ulcers and raging paranoia, but he didn't need to know that.

"Excellent choice. I spent the better part of a decade preparing you and your associates for this. You've survived and prevailed, but I doubt you're ready for the next salvo."

"Is that why you came back?" I asked, tamping down on my anger. He was working hard to get my goat. I couldn't afford to let him succeed. "Sorry, you can't have your old job back, but we may hire you as an unpaid intern."

He didn't even flinch at the insult. No, the jerk-face kept right on talking. The more he talked, the more I wanted to punch his stupid face for abandoning me and my team after the trauma of our first encounter with Belial and then having the gall to reappear like it was no big deal.

I should probably listen to his rundown of infiltrating the ranks of master demons and gathering intel to feed to the celestials—at least he wasn't stupid enough to trust them—but I was spitting mad and itching for a fight.

A fight I doubted I could win.

"Blah, blah, blah," I said, rudely interrupting him. "Are you going to get to the point anytime soon? Like, while I'm young?"

That got a reaction. It was only a slight tightening of his jaw, but for the boss, that counted as a major tell. He was pissed. Good.

He stood, buttoning his jacket and wiping invisible debris off his pants. I stayed seated. I could play the dominance game, too, especially since I had a better handle on my demon powers and whatever super-charged powers I'd inherited from my father. I pulled the chain from beneath my collar that held my black mirror and the ring that allowed me to access my father's powers when I needed them. Not reliably, but they'd come to me as I fought Belphegor and while fighting demons in the space between.

It was a gamble. That power was seductive and treacherous. Flaunting it was a risky move.

But it made for an outstanding power move.

Sameal stopped in his tracks and stared at the ring. Surprise, surprise. Betcha didn't see that coming.

"You are indeed your father's daughter. He was more sledgehammer than scalpel." His voice was cold and full of disdain. "Your rashness will be your undoing. You aren't ready for this level of power."

It took a monumental act of will to remain calm. His words were a slap in the face and a dig at my deepest, darkest fear. I looked like the bastard who sired me, infected me with a crazy and powerful celestial, and then ran away like a coward.

I was made of stronger stuff.

"I am my mother's daughter," I said, matching his tone and malice. "I don't run. I'm not like him. Or you."

"I didn't run, you foolish creature. I am death. Mortals, celestials, and demons cower in the face of what I bring. You've always been too rash and stupid to fear what I am and what I can do."

Oh, had I hit a nerve? Good.

He was wrong. I'd always been terrified by him. But I wasn't that same scared, confused, directionless teenager I'd been when he'd swooped in and gave me an outlet for the power inside me—I thought it had only been Haniel's power then, but my father's curse had always been there beneath the surface.

Okay, he hadn't so much given me and the rest of the team a choice about working as demon hunters, but it had helped us. All of us. And I'd grown up since then. Enough to see that the Angel of Death who ruled by fear also feared what I was and what I could become.

"From where I'm standing, you ran. You left our team in shambles and left us to face a pack of master demons and archangels alone. And you could have killed me a decade ago. You kept me around because you knew what was in that grimoire."

I was destined to be a great warrior and force of destruction, maybe even his own.

Keep your friends close and your enemies closer.

My father's power flared in the wake of my anger. It shook the wards Sameal had set and threatened to melt my glamour. Dangerous power. The kind of power that could level mountains and scorch forest and plain. It ached to be unleashed.

I wanted to unleash it, that seductive and destructive force.

No. No, no, no, no, no.

I was not my father. I would not become my father. Oh, D. He thought he was a monster. He had nothing on me, and part of me wanted it. I could be great and terrible and revel in my darkness and savagery.

"Jane, rein it in." The boss's voice was commanding, but too calm. I was scaring him.

I was scaring me, too.

"I'm trying," I said, my own voice escaping the glamour I wore. "You started this. Always bringing out the worst in me." I gritted my teeth, tensing every muscle in my body to hold back the tsunami coursing through me.

A soft knock came at the door, and I turned to find Lacey in her buxom blonde glamour sliding through the door in a move that rivaled her succubus girlfriend. Shit. My power had totally fried Sameal's wards.

"I hate to interrupt, darlin', but we've got more mingling to do if we want—"

She spotted our former boss and froze.

"Holy shit, where the fuck have you been?"

I was about to high-five her when a wave of demon magic hit the building, leaving screams of agony in its wake.

CHAPTER TWENTY-ONE

Lacey and I were out of the study door and running down the hall when Sameal grabbed us and almost knocked us over.

"Get your fucking hands off me," Lacey hissed, kicking him in the shin. She'd been going for the knee, but the Angel of Death was too quick. "You've got a lot of nerve."

I was proud of Lacey. She'd also spent a decade under his thumb. He'd used fear and her own guilt to keep her in check and make her into his willing instrument of demon capture and containment. Like me, she'd assumed she was a bad person and that was why her little greed demon Simon latched onto her. Bad people attracted demons, right?

That wasn't always the case.

For lesser demons, it was a matter of survival. They often protected their human companions. Simon was loyal. Lacey and Simon together were a dream team. Instead of using their powers to get five-finger discounts at local malls and high-end retailers, they now used their combined powers patrolling and protecting the Nashville demon population to keep them and the unsuspecting humans in Music City safe.

Lacey and her demon had been through the meatgrinder on our last two mission and come out on the other side as sharp as tempered steel. It would take more than our former boss to cow her.

I didn't take a shot at the boss. My power was still too close to the surface. One little act of violence could still unleash it. Instead, I smirked. The screams had faded, but demon energy still hung thick in the air around us.

"Listen to me very carefully," he said. "And do exactly as I say if you want to keep your cover—and mine."

Lacey opened her mouth to protest but quickly shut it as Simon appeared, babbling frantically. Since I'd returned the essence he'd given me to save my life recently—in order to save his—I could no longer understand him. But he'd seen something that set him off.

"Sully," I said, fighting a gasp of panic.

"She's fine," Lacey said, dismissively. "She's apparently gathered all the rallmaths and herded them to safety."

"Safety from what?"

"Immaterial demons," the boss whispered with a hiss. "They used the tunnels to infiltrate our little soirée to deliver a message. Follow me and act like you're in my thrall. You're both good at looking stupid. Shouldn't be too difficult."

Rude. Lacey gave him a calculated look, but I shook my head. Sameal was an ass, but he was right. We had to play our part to get the intel we needed. Immaterial demons were bad. The kind who possessed humans were the worst.

I was pretty sure that we were dealing with the possessing kind.

Sameal jerked Lacey and I and dragged us back to the central gathering area. The crowd now consisted of humans in a stupor and humans with unnatural grins and red-eyed gazes that signified the lights were on and the demons were home.

"What is the meaning of this?" Sameal yelled, pushing us in the room and forcing us to our knees. We kept up the act, but I was going to kick his ass for this later. "We are here to woo new humans, not terrify them into divesting from the property."

The demon wearing Mr. Duneberry's skin stepped forward and said,

"Plans have changed. Someone has recruited enemy archangels to interfere with our new portal. They have the summoner. We no longer have the luxury of time."

I smiled inside. Good. Judaliel had come through. With any luck, Pendergrass was locked up at HQ and our team was interrogating him and his demon guards.

Now, if only the demon in Duneberry spilled the tea on their nefarious new plans...

"What exactly do you intend to do to correct your monumental failure?" Sameal asked, his voice low and emanating danger.

I had to hand it to the former boss man—he infused enough menace in his voice to make Duneberry's demon step back. The other demon possessed occupants of the room stood perfectly still in an unsettling and inhuman way in contrast to the unoccupied humans near them, who twitched and stumbled until their designated demon guardians secured them. I counted at least twenty possessed humans. Not good. Extracting a demon without harming the human host was no easy task.

The last time I'd done it, the poor human had ended up in the ICU.

I figured I could pull out one or two with my black mirror. I'd used it to summon Haniel when she still possessed me and kept it after her escape because it was still useful for storage and transport of bad immaterial demons. But that would leave far too many humans in the clutches of demons. Rich assholes or not, that was a fate I wouldn't wish on anyone, and I had a duty to protect the humans.

But Lacey and I couldn't fight them all.

Duneberry's demon scowled and took a step forward, squaring his shoulders and staring at Sameal. Didn't matter. He'd lost the dominance fight and face in front of his fellow demons. Everyone knew who was really in charge here.

"We proceed with infiltration. Scaled down, for now, but we have someone else who can open the portal for us."

Shit. Of course they'd have a backup. Sameal grabbed my arm and jerked me to him, reminding me to act the part of stupefied human.

"It would take a skilled summoner to accomplish the task, and humans are nearly as unreliable as you, Vor'il," Sameal said. Then he leaned over my shoulder, pressing me against his chest so he could stroke my bearded cheek. Ick. "I'd wager this cocksure idiot would be more effective."

Vor'il laughed, the other demon-possessed humans joining him in synchronized creepiness. Was Sameal bluffing? Pendergrass was the only summoner I knew with the skills and lack of morals necessary to open a portal and shepherd an invading army through the space between.

Except his son.

Cooper. Oh, man, did they have Cooper?

Sameal must've read my mind. "His son is mentally unstable. Your usual methods will damage his addled brain beyond repair. You're wasting my time and you're wasting Beelzebub's time. I'm taking over this operation effective—"

Vor'il interrupted and his words turned the blood in my veins to ice. "Belial's son has joined us at last. He shall open the portal and lead our legions to victory."

No. Impossible. He would never betray us.

D, what kind of game are you playing?

A dangerous game, a game that could cost us everything if his demon nature overtook the good man who kept it on a tight leash. I understood the struggle all too well. Even now, my father's power fought my hold, itching to get out and make the pathetic mortals and demons, lesser beings meant only to serve, bow down in awe and terror.

I pulled against Sameal's hold, sending him a wrap-it-up message as best I could. Lacey and had to get out of there and back to HQ—and then I had to find D.

Next thing I knew, a crash and familiar roar filled the space along with breaking glass and low, rumbling growls birthed from the depths of the hell realm.

We were being invaded. Again.

CHAPTER TWENTY-TWO

Sully landed in the middle of the room, crashing into the fountain in her massive, winged battle cat form. Her horns had grown three inches and the fangs filling her maw were massive. The immaterial demons unleashed wails like emergency vehicle sirens as what could only be described as an army of rallmaths burst through the marble flooring and began attacking.

Wait a minute.

The broken flooring didn't shatter like stone. It cracked and split, revealing a thick layer of foam and wood beneath the veneer of marble.

Those cheap bastards hadn't built an opulent mansion. This whole thing was a lie.

If I'd needed confirmation, it came as the "fine" furniture tossed about cracked to reveal plastic beneath. The wall art, the supposedly aged porcelain vases, and the jewels bedecking the demon-occupied women were all fakes.

If they weren't my enemies, I'd applaud the demons for duping so many humans with more money than sense.

Instead, I had the pleasure of cheering Sully on as she turned and swatted the offending fountain that had the audacity to get her butt wet, sending chrome-painted foam soaring in a shower of debris. She'd never been bothered by water before, but this water was probably contaminated with demon magic and/or whatever toxic waste lurked beneath the neighborhood. The twins had confirmed the toxicity of the samples we'd taken on our last visit. Was it part of Beelzebub's plan, or was it just a bonus?

More rallmaths emerged from the fake marble flooring, pouring out of existing holes and creating a few new ones. Sully chittered at them, sounding like a lion doing one of those housecat aak aak aak chitters they used on birds. The rallmaths stood at attention, listening to Sully, and then resumed their mission of destruction and mayhem.

My kitty had been busy.

Raus emerged from the floor, living up to his name. Gone was the oddly cute, if rather large, vole-like creature. He stood at least seven feet tall after emerging from the hole in the floor, his paws tipped with wicked talons and his yellow fangs promising pain and a slow death from a festering infection should you be unfortunate enough to get your flesh near enough for a bite.

Sameal let me go and shouted, "Motiaummerr. Evacuate, you fools!"

The humans collapsed as the immaterial demons left their bodies and disappeared into vents and out broken windows. Lacey and I dropped our glamour and ran for Sully.

"In the name of all that is holy and unholy, do not engage with the motiaummerr," Sameal yelled. "You don't know what you're dealing with."

Lacey and I shared a look of perfect understanding. Simon appeared and lifted her into the air as I leapt onto Sully's back, nailing the landing and—I hoped—giving Sameal an aneurysm. Before I could gloat, Sully spoke in a deep, rumbling feline growling voice that made the Angel of Death recoil.

"Demons, Ink. Bad demons."

"I know, baby. Bad demons. You scared them off."

"No. Bad demons down."

Her hackles rose as she looked to the holes in the floor. I looked into the hole closest to us and understood. The holes led to tunnels. That was why Beelzebub had Pendergrass bring rallmaths. They weren't just Guinea pigs to test the portal. They were brought to create tunnels beneath Swan Springs and who knew where else to support the full-scale invasion.

And bad demons were down there and getting ready to burst forth.

I turned to Sameal. "Reinforcements are on the way. I'm fighting." I conjured a celestial spear and shield.

"Me, too," said Lacey, drawing her demon steal knife.

"Me, too, too," Sully growled, showing Sameal her big, big teeth. Sameal was afraid of her, and it was activating her hunting instincts.

Scared prey. Fun to chase.

Sameal pointed at Sully, sporting the same look of horrified fascination that the twins had worn when I first brought the demon cat in her kitten form home. What was it with these demons? Sure, she was scary, but they had maaks and wraiths and master demons with legions of warriors. What made Sully so terrifying?

"You think you've tamed that beast, but sooner or later it will destroy you."

Sully hissed at Sameal. I bared my teeth and said, "I trust her more than I ever trusted *you*."

Sameal locked his gaze on mine. "She eats lesser demons, celestials, and any other magically imbued creature from the three realms now. When she's fully grown, she can consume master demons, archangels, and the world. The creature is a danger to all she encounters."

Wowzers. So that was why the immaterial demons had high-tailed it out of there. A grin split my face and my demon graft tats glowed. "Well, she likes pizza and ice cream, too. If she's hungry, we'll let her eat whatever's in that tunnel for dinner and Beelzebub's immaterial minions can be dessert. I won't blow your cover but stay out of my way if you don't want to be on the menu."

Sameal threw his hands in the air. Good grief, I'd never seen the old entity so agitated. He'd always been cool, calculating, menacing, threatening, and in control. If he hadn't left me and the rest of the team to fend for ourselves, we'd still be reliant on the Angel of Death. And we'd never have seen this side of him. Witnessing his behavior would have put me in a panic attack six months ago, before I'd learned what real danger and trauma were. Now, it made me angry and a little sad.

I'd outgrown him.

I'd seen the real monsters, and probably not the worst. If he was scared, I should probably be, too. But I just didn't have it in me. I had a mission and I had to go save D from himself if he'd really switched sides.

And I wasn't afraid of Sully. She was my ride or die.

After a long look that I couldn't read, Sameal disappeared, teleporting to parts unknown just as a pack of wraiths emerged from the tunnels and circled the space. At least until they caught sight of Sully.

Too late for them. She executed a running takeoff that had me holding on for dear life as she gave chase, chomping three wraiths in one gulp while I speared two more. Lacey wasn't slacking. She and Simon dispatched four more. The rallmaths managed to subdue several more, tossing them to my demon cat when she flew over. No need for pulling out my magic to blast them away like I had in the space between—my partner and the demon critters destroyed them with efficiency and the zeal of battle.

I'd never had so much fun fighting demons.

I'd never been much for sports. I'd grown up too poor and too possessed to play softball, tennis, basketball, or to even be picked for Red Rover. But, as it turned out, I would've made one hell of a polo player. My celestial spear slapped wraiths, their immaterial bodies growing solid at points of contact. I'd tacked more than a few to the fake marble columns so Sully could take a bite as we flew by or so Simon and Lacey could whack them like pinatas.

One managed to take a bite out of my shoulder. It hurt like a mofo and would leave a scar if we ran out of demonic medicinal supplies.

That really pissed me off.

I fashioned the end of my celestial spear into a noose and grabbed the bitey demon around what would have been its neck. It wailed with outrage as I reeled it in, and the shoulder it had bitten screamed in protest while bleeding profusely. Probably should have used my celestial weapon as a torniquet or bandage, but adrenaline made everyone stupid, including me.

Once I yelled in its face and slapped it a few times—because punching hurt too much—I used my good arm to fling it around the room and into Simon's clutches. He grabbed the wraith with his sharp talons of his giant raven form and flung it back to me, and we had a fun game of catch until my bad shoulder and blood loss ended the game.

Too bad, but by then we'd run out of loose wraiths.

While Sully did her grab and go dinner thing, I used my good arm and the last of my energy reserves to plunge my celestial spear into the tunnels, sealing them off to prevent more wraiths from escaping and to contain the toxic waste that flowed through them. It wouldn't hold forever, but hopefully long enough for us to either decontaminate or fill the tunnels to trap the waste inside.

Then, the immaterial demons working for Beelzebub returned.

Crap.

Sully started for them, but I tugged on her scruff and yelled, "Wait. I need to capture a few for questioning."

"Hungry."

"You've eaten two dozen demons. How can you still be hungry?"

She growled and bucked. Sameal was right. This damned cat was going to be the death of me.

"Pizza. All you can eat. And buckets of ice cream."

"More bad demons. Pi-zza and ice cream after."

Great googly moogly. "Fine, you can eat a few more bad demons, but not until I catch some first."

I tugged on the chain around my neck and chanted the incantation until the obsidian grew hot enough to scorch my fingertips. The first demon was easy. By the third, I was sweaty, had second degree burns on my hands, and almost fell off my battle cat.

"Jinx," Lacey said. "Enough. Let's wrap this up before the first responders arrive, and we need to get you checked out. You're bleeding all over the scene."

Lacey must've called, or maybe the neighbors who weren't at the party heard the ruckus and panicked. Smart neighbors. I hoped they all came to survey the damage and realize that the "dream" they'd invested in was in fact a nightmare of hellish proportions.

Struggling to wrap the hot potato of a demon trap in my shirt with burnt fingers and less-than-stellar motor skills while trying to hold onto a hungry demon cat giving chase proved to be too difficult. Good thing Simon had great reflexes and caught me before I fell on the fake marble floor. There was probably enough actual stone to crack my skull. Fatigue washed over me, a reminder that I'd unleashed too much of my magic, which was already running on fumes thanks to glamour, the stress of seeing my stupid ex-boss, and the, ah, depletion I'd enjoyed with D.

Blood loss probably didn't help, either.

Lacey was in my face. Oh, goody. Simon had dropped me on the floor. "Simon says he's not going to carry you, and Sully's looking a little green in the gills."

I blinked stupidly and turned my head to look at my demon cat. She was in the process of spilling her guts with the mother of all hairballs.

No, wait. Not hairballs, wraith demons. Uh, she'd overeaten. Wait, the boss said she could eat the world when she was fully grown. How much bigger was my cat going to get?

"I take," said a low, squeaky voice.

Next thing I knew, I was cradled in the arms of Raus. Aw, he was so sweet. I'd have to tell Sameal that he'd have a better life if he was nice to animals, and he'd have more allies. The other rallmaths lined up behind us. At least, I think they did. I couldn't really see past Raus's bulk.

"Where to?" I asked, fighting not to pass out.

"Cooper first," Lacey said. "No, wait, drive through first. We have a whole lot more mouths to feed. Then Cooper."

"We'll never fit them all in the Mustang," I said, my voice hoarse.

"Sure we will," Lacey said, grinning. "Your cat grows. These guys shrink."

Lacey held out a hand filled with itty bitty demon voles that she deposited in her jacket pocket. Neat trick. Too bad we couldn't do that with the celestial sheep.

At least we wouldn't have to feed them as much. And since Sully gagged up a putrid mass of sulfurous goo, she wouldn't be eating for a while either. I closed my eyes and wished that I could plug my nose.

"Rest while you can," Lacey said. "We've got to find your boyfriend and see if he's gone rogue."

I groaned. Lacey patted my shoulder. "Cheer up. You can vent your frustration on him."

I opened one eye and spotted Brad, my soon-to-be-ex-brother-in-law, hog-tied and suspended in Simon's phantom bird of prey talons.

CHAPTER TWENTY-THREE

I woke up on a bed of leaves, surrounded by the vomit-inspiring aromas of old, dried blood, forest floor detritus, and stinky cat butt.

Or was that fox musk? Ricky had curled up on my chest while a much smaller Sully rested next to my wounded shoulder. Aw, she was guarding me. I hope she felt better. I'd have to keep an eye on her next time we fought demons so she wouldn't overeat again. Those wraiths and immaterial demons couldn't be good for her.

The light hurt my eyes. Sunlight. Shit, how long had I been out? Not more than a few hours, I was guessing. We'd left Swan Springs in the wee hours of the morning. Apparently, Sully and the rallmaths had been busy while I was wheeling, dealing, and discovering the boss's undercover gig. They'd traveled to each of the fake fine homes in the gated community and trashed them.

The houses weren't a total loss, but the damage exposed them for what they were—cheap illusions.

Swan Springs's dirty little secrets revealed, most of the invading immaterial demons eaten or trapped in my black mirror, and Beelzebub's operation put out of commission. Not bad for a night's work.

"Jane McGee, are you feeling better?"

Cooper's voice was a welcome sound. I sat up slowly, my head spinning so fast I was afraid I'd take flight. Then, my gaze landed on my soon-to-be-ex brother-in-law. Hog-tied and gagged, someone had planted him face down in a bit of forest floor covered with rocks and secured by a survivalist-worthy hand-crafted wooden cage.

When he spotted me, he let out a muffled scream through his gag.

I tried to get up, but my body wasn't cooperating. "Shut up, Brad. Your ass whooping is going to have to wait until I get my bearings."

Cooper, who'd squatted next to me, handed me a cup filled with a thick, viscous liquid that smelled worse than it looked. He helped me sit up without passing out or throwing up. After I'd taken a few deep breaths, he said, "Drink that."

"No way," I said, fighting not to gag. "It smells like demon ass."

"You would know." Lacey sat against a tree opposite my moss-covered sick bed in Cooper's outdoor field hospital.

I shot her a dirty look. "You know *way* more about how demon nether regions smell than I do, since you're dating a shape-shifting succubus."

Cooper furrowed his brows in confusion. "I don't know what demon ass smells like, but this is a mixture of demon-realm herbs and brandy."

Lacey laughed. "Very cheap brandy. Be a good girl and take your meds, Jinx. It'll cure what ails you—physically. It won't cure whatever's going on in your stupid addled brain that makes you fight demons while bleeding out. And before you ask, yes, I had some too. Drink."

I opened my mouth to protest, but Sully lifted her head and gave us the stink eye for disturbing her slumber. After a long, feline stretch, she perched on my lap and got in my face, opening her little mouth to yell, "Ink stup-id dumb ass butt! Listen."

The stench of her cat breath was unholy and nearly burned off my nose hairs and eyebrows. Gross. It must've been the demons she'd eaten. The stench of sulfur, rotten meat, and cat gut digestive juices assaulted me.

I plugged my nose and downed Cooper's rancid herbal tea just to get the taste out of my mouth.

"Cooper," I said after a few coughs. "Do you happen to have a spell for demon cat oral hygiene?"

Of the two foul aromas, cat breath trumped demon medicine.

The summoner frowned. His camo painted brows furrowing as if he was seriously considering my question. He wore his normal survivalist gear of army green camo that blended in with his home in Percy Warner Park. Hiding in plain sight was one of our summoner's specialties. Good thing. The territory he guarded used to house one of Nashville's major portals leading to and from the demon realm. One of the major legal portals, that is. We'd cleaned out most of the illegal summoners when I first joined the demon hunting operation—except for Damien Pendergrass and Keith Pendergrass, Cooper's father and brother.

Keith died at the hands of Belial's henchmen who were tying up loose ends.

Cooper almost died, too.

Damien Pendergrass was next on the list.

Cooper's portal was currently closed, though he remained on guard duty in case someone tried to reactivate it.

The summoner's laughter brought me out of my trip down nightmare memory lane. "You need to feed her something sweet and minty, like ice cream."

"Ice cream?" My demon cat screeched, unleashing another puff of foul cat breath in my face.

Yuck. But that did give me a deliciously evil idea.

"Hey, Sully, how about you go ask ex-Uncle Brad? He's a little deaf from the fight, so you'll have to get right in his face and scream really loud. And you'll have to repeat yourself. Got it?"

Sully cocked her head to the side, looked at Brad, and hissed. Oh. So she knew about Brad's cheating ass, how he broke my sister's heart and left us high and dry, probably giving away our team secrets to Beelzebub and his minions.

"Even better, baby. Go hiss in his face."

My cat obliged and I enjoyed watching Brad's eyes water as my cat assaulted him with stinky breath and spittle that was probably contaminated with demon cooties. He coughed as best he could through the ball gag and snot started running from his nose. Bastard couldn't move his head. He deserved worse.

I picked up a few small rocks and started chucking them at his prone body through the wooden bars of Cooper's cage. Maybe I was evil. Pummeling Brad with rocks made me feel better.

Or it could've been the medicine. Probably both. I got to my feet and began dusting off my clothes and picking sticks and leaves out of my hair. At least my favorite pair of boots survived the fight. A little polish and shine and they'd be good as new.

"Ice cream?"

I spun around to find Raus—who'd shrunk to the less intimidating size of a small dog—eyeing me hopefully. Surrounding him was the army of tiny rallmaths who started chanting "ice cream" in an ear-splitting yet adorable chorus. It was a scene straight out of a fucked-up fairy tale. All they needed were little hats and mittens to tie the whole vibe together.

I could probably get Mom to knit some for them.

That settled it. I was going to adopt them all.

"Of course you can have ice cream. You saved me. You get ice cream," I pointed at Raus. "And you get ice cream," I said, waving my hands to encompass the herd of small demon rats surrounding Raus. "And Sully gets ice cream, Cooper gets ice cream, and Lacey gets ice cream. No ice cream for Brad, though. Ice cream is for loyal husbands and winners, not lousy cheating losers."

The critters squealed in delight and chittered. I got it. I, too, was food motivated.

Brad closed his eyes and wheezed. A big goose egg was forming on his head where one of my stones had landed. Good. I'd soften him up for the wrath of my sister. I couldn't *wait* to tell her.

Speaking of telling...

"I don't suppose anyone looped Trinity and the rest of the team in on last evening's events."

Lacey grimaced. "I called her."

"How'd she take the news that Sameal's back in town?"

"Better than I expected," Lacey said. "She's more concerned about Beelzebub's next move. We're supposed to report back ASAP and bring the immaterial demons you captured in for questioning."

She gave me a look, one that screamed why-don't-you-ask-about-what-you-really-want-to-know. My partner was big on tough love. Or maybe she was trying to spare me the pain her answer might cause.

I caved. I had to know. "What about D?"

She sighed. "You're definitely going to need ice cream, coffee, and maybe a few shots of tequila. Your boyfriend has disappeared, along with Damien Pendergrass."

CHAPTER TWENTY-FOUR

We got back to HQ around late morning. It took a while to find enough ice cream and other goodies to feed our demon realm zoo and ourselves. I indulged in ice cream and coffee as my partner suggested but skipped the alcohol. I needed to stay sharp and keep a clear head if I had any hope of finding D and Pendergrass Senior.

Cooper was kind enough to help load Brad into the trunk of D's Mustang. He offered some tips on other petty torture techniques I could use on Brad. A little off and a lot deranged was our resident summoner. But his heart was in the right place. He promised to keep an eye out for dear old dad, and his demon dog was there to guard him.

He was as safe as I could make him.

After settling the animals, locking Brad up in one of our holding cells, and handing the trapped immaterial demons over to Trinity and Sam for questioning, Lacey and I joined Boice and Roice at their tricked out digital surveillance center to review footage of my demon lover's mission gone horribly wrong.

"We'll skip all the boring stakeout stuff," Roice said as he skipped around on the vid streaming on one of his giant screens. Today's T-shirt read "I am magic. I know I am magic, and no one can stop my magical ass."

That tracked.

"Start where Judaliel and Nisroc make contact with Pendergrass," Boice said as he handed out cups of coffee, bless his demonic little heart. "We had the two angels approach Pendergrass with a proposition to smuggle them out of the city in exchange for intel on the celestial's war plans that he could sell to the demons."

"And a boat load of money via the dark web to sweeten the deal." Roice finally found what he was looking for and hit play. "Anyway, Cooper's intel and what he got from the rallmath led us to look around the border between Franklin and Nolensville. Close enough to the edge of Trinity's ward around the city with a clear path to Nashville, rural but not too far out in the boonies, and in an area with big houses surrounded by plenty of land. We found his base of operations in an older home near the Arrington Retreat neighborhood. He goes into Nolensville for food and supplies. Alexi and D trailed him to a local barbeque joint and sent the two angels in to make contact."

The video showed a parking lot next to a charming brick building with a tall ceramic pig out front, presumably the restaurant. I recognized Pendergrass from photos. Tall, middle-aged, and fit, he walked toward a truck with his lunch bag in hand. Judaliel in her human guise, wearing slacks and a casual blazar, and Nisroc dressed in jeans and a T-shirt approached. They talked, then the angels got into Pendergrass's white van.

A van with no back or side windows, like total serial killer stuff. Cooper's dad was such a cliché.

I spotted Alexi's shadow two spaces down. He'd follow on motorcycle since it was still daylight in the video. The wolf was faster, but it required the cover of darkness. A few seconds after Pendergrass pulled out of the parking lot, D walked into frame, dressed head to toe in black and wearing sunglasses that made him look like some kind of underworld spy. My demon nodded at Alexi before climbing into a silver sedan. The sedan drove off first, followed by Alexi on his bike.

"So far so good," Boice said, fiddling with the computer until a new video appeared on the screen. "This is a view from Alexi's cam." It showed D's sedan and other cars sharing the road. "And now from D's cam."

D drove a respectable distance behind the van. When Pendergrass turned onto a smaller side road, D kept driving.

"Alexi's following while D takes another route." So far it was a textbook mission. My stomach roiled with dread. Soon we'd get to the part where the mission went wrong.

"These cams are seriously good," Lacey said. "Great resolution and compensation for shaking from the motorcycle. Military tech? Is it attached to the vehicle or the team members?"

Roice grinned. "Military tech enhanced with a little something of our own. Magic and some mundane upgrades. We had them mounted at the rendezvous location and they're hidden on Alexi and D. Keep watching."

We watched as D's cam showed him exiting the car in what appeared to be a wooded area. He left the sedan and traveled on foot through thick woods without a trail and stopped just inside the tree line of a well-manicured lawn. The house it belonged to was big but not fancy like the homes in Swan Springs or the nearby subdivision, at least not from the back. More vinyl siding than brick, the windows were small and the back deck smaller. Pendergrass had a grill and a hot tub, not high end but decidedly more redneck with a fair amount of DIY on the cracked fiberglass and duct taped pump. There were a few small trees in the back yard, none tall enough or close enough to the house to allow for surveillance. This home was designed to blend in. Couldn't hide the security measures Pendergrass had installed. D's camera panned around the property to reveal five surveillance cameras, probably a mixture of standard and thermal.

And a silvery sheen undulated around the home's exterior.

"You did it," I said, unable to keep the awe out of my voice. Letting the twins know they'd impressed you was never a good idea. It went straight to their big fat heads. "You actually managed to detect a demon ward on film."

"We've been busy," they said in unison.

"Not like we just sit around on our asses since the great master demon and archangel invasion." Boice was just a tad defensive. None of us had ever accused the twins of being lazy. Snarky, perverted, occasionally smelly, but never lazy.

"We've got all kinds of field work upgrades for you battle grunts." Roice sounded like himself—superior and judgmental. Field work, he'd often said, was for newbies and those not intellectually equipped to grow wealth and engineer weapons.

Whatever. I was more familiar with his browser history than I cared to be. Smart didn't equal classy, at least not based on his porn preferences.

I could've called them out, but I knew the truth. At least one of the master demons that crossed over onto earth had ordered the hit on the twins' parents. Somehow, that demon or demons had figured out when and where the Lord of Warfare and Chief Demoness of Ingenuity were set to smuggle their young demon boys out of the hell realm and to the relative safety of earth. The demon realm ran primarily on magic, leaving its inhabitants far behind on the technology front. With the coming war, those rare demons who could work both magic and tech, blending the two into weapons and other tools of conquest, were in high demand.

The twins were already prodigies and therefore in danger of kidnapping and enslavement to any master demon who could capture and contain them. Their parents made a deal with Sameal to protect them on earth in exchange for service. It would allow the boys to hone their skills and fight to keep powerful master demons off earth and confined to their home realm, protecting the human and demon refugee populations on earth.

Boice and Roice made it through, but not before seeing their parents murdered.

They had a score to settle and had upped their game.

I leaned in close to the computer screen and whispered. "When we find Beelzebub and the rest of the masters, I promise you both will get a turn at them."

They didn't answer, but Roice patted my hand and Boice bumped my shoulder.

The video continued as D panned back and forth. They could've just skipped to the good part—or bad part, assuming D going off script was a bad thing. But I had to admit, the cameras gave us a world of information. Whatever protective ward Pendergrass had around his lair, it was complex and multilayered. Our team had rarely encountered wards outside the standard measures the boss and demons conjured to protect HQ and keep our prisoners confined. That all changed after the big baddies came to earth. I didn't have the control or skill to make one, though I'd managed to break a few, but I understood how they worked. The creator wove demon magic into a net that didn't allow anyone not keyed to the ward to pass through.

A simple net kept most earth realm inhabitants out. Tempter demons who made up most of the earth's refugee population didn't have the power to break them. For extra security against immaterial demons like Simon, the ward's creator tightened the weave of the magic and made a couple of extra layers to plug the magical holes that could allow a small demon to slip through.

Pendergrass's ward had at least seven layers, all tightly woven and based on the colors of the magic, it would keep out celestials, native earth creatures with magic like Fae and vampires, and powerful demons. It was like Fort Knox. Our prison cells below HQ only had four layers. I'd never seen anything like it, not even from Sameal. The summoner had friends in low places with a lot of magic.

That ward had to be made by a master demon.

The video shifted as D moved closer to the house. He just walked out of the tree line, strolling like he didn't have a care in the world. No running or dodging to avoid detection. My demon just waltzed right out in the open for Pendergrass or any demon guarding the place to see.

What the hell? This was so not part of the mission.

"What's he doing?" Lacey asked, sounding as shocked as I felt. "He was supposed to wait until the celestials were in the open and break through the weakest part of the open ward when Pendergrass let them out."

That had been the plan. Nothing on the video so far had shown any reason that justified deviating from that plan. I gripped the desk until my knuckles went white and my fingers stiffened.

D, what the hell are you playing at?

"Right," Boice said. "They had a panic signal set up for the angels to use, and a time limit before resorting to an attack. We figured it could take some time for Judaliel to convince Pendergrass that the deal was legit and worth his while. D was supposed to wait. If you look around 2:00 on the screen beside the Dogwood tree, you'll see Alexi peeking out."

I spotted Alexi, who'd already begun the transformation to his demon wolf form. Shit. D was blowing their cover wide open.

My inner wolf Zer growled.

"Yeah, that's probably what Alexi was thinking," Boice said. "Now, watch this."

Boice switched the video to Alexi's view. It showed D walking out onto the damned lawn like he was taking a little stroll in the park instead of blowing his fucking cover and risking the entire mission. I wanted to reach through the screen, grab him by the ear, and drag him off for an interrogation followed by a spanking.

And not the fun kind.

Then D transformed into his massive, red, winged demon form. In broad daylight. And then he walked up the steps on the back deck and to the back door, reached through the multi-layered ward like it wasn't even there, ripped the door of its hinges, and went inside.

"This is not happening, this is not happening, this totally cannot be happening," I chanted. It was better than screaming or cursing. Had D lost it and succumbed to his demonic nature? I didn't want to believe it, but why else would he break protocol and blow the mission?

I should have been there. If I'd been with him and had his back, this would never have happened.

A few seconds later, D came through the door with an unconscious

Pendergrass slung over his shoulder like a sack of potatoes, Judaliel and Nisroc hot on his heels. They followed D voluntarily by the looks of it. Not good. From where we were sitting, the evidence was damning. The simplest explanation was that D had cut a deal with the angels and gone rogue.

I didn't want to believe it. My heart warred with my rational mind, telling me that D would never, ever betray us. He would never betray *me*. My mind screamed at me to look at the video and see for myself.

The image blurred, presumably as a wolfed-out Alexi ran to intercept D and company. A series of growls and curses followed by a close up of D's face followed. His eyes were cold, devoid of anything save for darkness.

Then the screen went black.

CHAPTER TWENTY-FIVE

"Can you find Demoriel?" Trinity asked, her face carefully neutral. Sam scowled enough for both of them. After reviewing the video, we waited for Alexi to return from the field, relieved when he showed up at HQ unscathed.

Now, I sat at the conference table in Trinity's office with the rest of the team, but the question was for me.

Alexi, dirty and exhausted from trying to track D, Pendergrass, and the celestials, sat across from me next to Megan. Megan hadn't been down to see Brad yet. When I told her we'd found him, she'd gone quiet and disappeared until this meeting, when she'd shown up with red eyes and vibrating with anger. Anger was better. She'd wasted enough tears on that loser. Mara and Lacey sat beside me in solidarity. The twins sat together at the end of the table. Cooper, who had joined us, sat on the floor with Sully and Raus.

Dr. Khatri stood at the foot of the table opposite Trinity at the head.

I took a deep breath and gathered my thoughts. Then, I answered the boss lady's question. "If you asked me before I saw the video, I'd have said yes. But now? I don't know. I've been trying to open a link through the graft he gave me for the past hour with no luck."

"Is he blocking you?" Mara asked. "Can he do that?"

"Well, he can break a complex ward and teleport, so it's likely," Alexi said, rubbing his tired eyes. "I searched a ten-mile radius for a scent or magic trail where they may have materialized. If his range is beyond that, he's got as much power as a master demon."

"He's the son of a master demon and he's gone rogue. I think we have to assume he's betrayed us." Sam said what everyone was thinking.

Everyone except me.

I slammed my hands on the table. "No, we don't have to assume. When you assume, Marquess Samagina, you make an ass out of you and me."

The Marquess's eyes glowed with sparks of demonic red. "Your judgement is unclear when it comes to your demon lover. He's hidden his true nature and power from us since he arrival, which coincided with his father's spy invading earth. Perhaps he's in league with his fa—"

I slashed my hand through the air, wishing it was my knife across Sam's face. "Says the guy who was supposed to be a weak immaterial Wikipedia demon but all of a sudden appeared in his full power as the corporeal Marquess of Hell when Mephisto showed up. Maybe *you're* in league with him."

No matter what D was up to, there was no way he would ever work with or for his wicked father. Belial had ripped his son from earth and subjected him to brutal torture, training, and forced him to lead his demon army as a general. The things D had seen and done sickened him. Even if his demon nature had taken him over, he wouldn't forget or forgive his father. He was far more likely to attack the Demon Lord.

I wanted to scream in Sam's face and tell him all this, to make him understand. But it wasn't my story to tell. Besides, if the Marquess wouldn't give him the benefit of the doubt based on his track record and service, nothing I said would change his mind.

"For all we know, Sameal's the one in league with the demons," Lacey said. "Do we really know who to trust? I say the only people we can trust are in this room, and we need to start trusting each other. Let's all calm down and stop with the infighting. We need to focus on finding D, Pendergrass, and the portal."

"What about the celestials?" Mara asked.

Trinity waved a dismissive hand. "They don't matter."

"They matter," I said coldly. "If they're truly our allies, we owe them a rescue. If they double crossed us, we need to stop them from spilling our secrets to their fellow celestials."

Like the fact that we no longer had the Sigillum Dei. Our attempts to locate Cassiel and the artefact had all failed. For all we knew, she could be using it to hide in other dimensions.

The room fell silent. I was hoping Dr. Khatri would chime in and give us a pep talk or some sort of therapeutic team trust building exercise, but she looked as tired as Alexi. Figured. We were a mess and she'd been working her ass off trying to keep all of us functional, if not psychologically sound.

"You know," Boice said. "I miss the old days when our team meetings came with a taco bar and booze."

"Right?" Roice added. "This would go a lot better if you people weren't hangry." He got up. "I'm going to ask Mom for some snacks."

"Hey," I said. "Since when do you get to call her mom?"

"Since she chewed them a new one for making a mess in the kitchen. Mom made them clean it up and told them it was their chore until she said otherwise," Megan said, grinning.

"She's scary," the twins said in unison.

The anger and tension drained from the room as we all pictured the big, bad demons of technology scrubbing and cowering at the wrath of my mom. Bless them. This was just what we needed. A bit of humor to clear the air and calm tempers.

While the twins grabbed snacks, we all took a breather and the opportunity to snuggle miniature rallmaths. Sully curled up in my lap and Cooper came to sit next to me. "For what it's worth, I don't think Demoriel betrayed us. I believe he has a plan."

I sighed, hoping Cooper was right. The fact that he believed in D gave me hope and warmed my heart. "Thanks," I said. "I just wish he'd clued us in."

Cooper shrugged. "My father responds to power and dominance. If D is looking to find out what he's up to, storming in under the guise of blowing our team's cover and aborting the mission is a good strategy."

I stretched my neck and shoulders. Sully left my lap and wrapped herself around my neck, putting her purrs to good use by relaxing my tense muscles. Cooper's theory made sense. Leaving us out of the loop would give him more credibility with Pendergrass. The celestial's shock and outrage at being kidnapped and sold out to the demons would be real, as was Alexi's desperate attempt to intercept and pursue.

"Care to share with the class?" I asked. "They'll listen to you. Neutral third party and all."

"Not neutral," he said, his expression hard. Cooper's bastard of a father had been brutal with his sons. Cooper had a score to settle with him. "But, yes, I will."

Mom and the twins arrived with plates full of sweet and savory finger foods. I vetoed any alcohol, and Dr. Khatri backed me up, much to the twins' dismay. It was for the best. We were raw and not thinking clearly. As we ate, Cooper laid out his theory.

"Plausible," Trinity said. "But we can't know for sure."

Our boss lady looked bad. Dark circles under her eyes, lines of worry etched across her face, and she looked like she'd lost fifteen pounds. She wasn't herself. Picking at the food, she listened, but her mind was on something else. I looked at Sam. It was high time for some answers. I knew I wouldn't get them from Trinity, but I could make Sam talk. The Marquess was as worried about his girlfriend as I was. He mouthed "later."

I knew she carried the weight of the team and the mission on her slender shoulders. But her distress had to be about the deal she made with a demon to ward the city, trapping the remaining Master Demons and Archangels in Nashville to contain them. Keeping them confined to Nashville would make it easier to find and neutralize them as well as minimizing the damage they could unleash on earth. Tactically, the ward was necessary and a good move on our fearless leader's part.

But the thought of what she'd promised made me shudder.

I'd talk to Sam, and we would find a way to save her. But for now, we had to find D, figure out what he was doing, and put Beelzebub out of commission.

"Either way, we should work on finding him," Trinity said, rubbing her hands over her face. "If we don't and he is, in fact, working some deep undercover mission, we could blow his cover."

"Agreed," I said. "I'll get to work on that after—"

"Nope," the twins said.

"Bad idea," Lacey chimed in.

Sam said something about my clouded judgement while Dr. Khatri talked about how I was dealing with enough PTSD to risk the trauma of finding out that D had double crossed us. Megan had the good sense to keep her mouth shut, as did Mom, though she gave me a look filled with empathy. Shit. She was probably remembering how it felt when Dad went AWOL and left her alone with two kids to raise.

No. D wouldn't do that. Not voluntarily.

"You don't understand," I said. "I don't believe for a second that he's betrayed us, but he may be fighting his demon nature. I promised I'd keep him in line."

Just like he promised to do for me.

"No, you're too valuable." Trinity used her I'm-the-boss-and-this-is-final voice.

I wasn't having it.

"Says who?"

She pointed to the book in front of her. That stupid fucking grimoire and its stupid prophecy that said I had to save the world or some shit. Damn, I was sick of this. I stood up and glared at her.

"You benched me once. It was a mistake. This is another mistake. I can bring him back."

Instead of yelling at me for insubordination, Trinity nodded. Damn, worry had taken the fight out of her. Not good. "I'm sure you can. And we'll let you once we find him. And I'm not benching you. You and Lacey need to find Beelzebub and hit him before he regroups."

I wanted to be mad, to rage and scream about how wrong she was, but it was hard to argue with her when what she said made so much sense. Damn it.

"And you need to find Cassiel and get the Sigillum Dei back so we can send Beelzebub and Soriella back to the hell realm for good," Mara added. "Alexi and I will work on finding D for you. Sam will help."

Damn it, they were right. I'd almost forgotten about Pinstripe. She refused to cooperate, earning herself a one-way trip back to the celestial realm. Without the artefact, we could fight master demons and archangels for an eternity and still fail to save earth. We needed the Sigillum Dei, and we needed it now.

And I had an idea of how we might do just that.

I turned to my sister. "Hey, Megan, you up for a little trip to the space between?"

CHAPTER TWENTY-SIX

"It's creepy in here."

Megan shivered, and not from cold. We'd been slogging through the space between for hours, searching for celestial refugees on their way to rendezvous with Cassiel so she could help them escape the coming war. Unlike my last trip with D, we didn't find any livestock, shepherds, lost cherubs, or anything else.

Dark? Check. Misty? Check. Silent as the grave? Check.

Still. Could be worse. "It's creepier when maaks and wraiths are attacking."

Big sis didn't look convinced.

"Why don't you try conjuring celestial armor again? You were doing great! You just need to get the helmet and limb guards."

We'd been working on our mad celestial skills to pass the time. I could now make a sword and badass battle axe in addition to spears, and I was getting good at the armor thing. Naturally, Megan was learning faster, the showoff. Story of my life. But I was proud of her. I told her so.

She didn't look convinced. She just looked lost and...sad.

When we got back to HQ, I was so totally punching Brad in his stupid face.

"Come on, Meg. You're lightyears ahead of me in the celestial powers department. I can probably learn from you since you're, like, good at everything."

She stared at me for a full fifteen seconds—talk about creepy—then she threw her head back and started laughing. The laughter turned to cackling, which creeped me out even more. What the hell? We were half celestial or demigod or something and half human, not witches.

Unless Mom had been keeping some big McGee family secrets.

"Um, what did I miss?"

Megan managed to speak between bouts of maniacal laughter. "Oh, now that's funny. I'm good at everything. Everything. Yeah, I'm so good at everything except for my failed marriage. Oh, and fertility. Just two minor things, really."

Fertility? My big sister was infertile.

My heart sank. "Brad failed you and your marriage. Nothing to do with you. But fertility? What's going on?"

She conjured a giant, golden celestial rock and hurled it into the void. Hard. Since the void had no walls, she didn't get the satisfaction of hearing or seeing it shatter. It didn't stop her from magicking more objects and throwing them into the space between.

"You mean he didn't tell you? I'm surprised. It's the reason he left me. The real reason. Sure, he's scared shitless of what I am and what I have to do to help save the world from a celestial-demon war, but he was coping. No, he bailed as soon as we got our test results back."

Test results. They'd been trying for a baby. I had no idea. It made sense. It was a perfectly logical, normal thing for a young married couple to want. But she never told me.

Then again, until recently, I'd kept my family at a distance for their own protection—and mine. I thought they hated me because I'd been a problem kid. And it was better that way. It hurt, but at least I could keep them safe from a distance.

Who was I kidding? I should have been there for her, should have been a better sister so she'd feel like she could tell me these things. But no, I'd been so absorbed in my own problems, too busy wallowing in my own sea of guilt and self-loathing to be there for my family. Keeping them safe was a convenient excuse.

"Meg, I'm so sorry. I had no idea," I said. I left out the part about how I should have known. "But Brad married you, not your uterus. He made a promise to be there for better or worse, richer or poorer, in sickness and health—I was there. If he left you because you can't bear children, there's a special place in hell for his rotten, selfish soul."

And boy, would I be so happy to send it there.

"It's not just Brad," she said, lobbing another two celestial rocks into nothingness. "I can't have children, Jane. With or without Brad, it's not going to happen. And I should just be okay with it. After all, this isn't exactly a good time and I'm all kinds of busy with work."

She tried to laugh, but it came out as a sob. I disappeared my celestial armor and weapons and went to her, taking her in my arms and letting her cry out her pain and grief. I hadn't been there for her before, but I could be here now and offer comfort, love, and support.

"It's not fair," she sobbed. "I know, I know life isn't fair and bad things happen all the time for no reason and I should be grateful for what I do have...and..."

"It's okay," I said, rocking her. "You're allowed to feel what you feel. It's not fair. And you can be mad and sad about that, okay?"

She held onto me for a long time before letting go. Wiping her eyes, she said, "Thanks. When did you get to be so smart, huh?"

I smirked and leaned against her shoulder. "Learned it from my big sis. Oh, and therapy, but mostly from you."

She laughed. "Well, I guess if I'm the smart one, I'd better get busy finding this thieving angel who stole our artefact."

Right on cue, a shuffling noise echoed through the mist. Then a bright light appeared followed by a gaunt, haggard celestial holding an amulet.

"Looks like she found us."

"Knew you couldn't resist a good meal," I said, frowning at Cassiel. I had a hunch that if Megan and I wandered around the space between long enough, our anger, frustration, and Megan's sadness would draw the misery-sucking angel out of hiding.

Cassiel didn't respond, but she didn't deny it, either. She wore her grandmotherly form, which didn't help with the aura of utter exhaustion. Maybe it was her go-to form. When I'd first met her, she'd been wearing the same glamour, baking cookies for the grieving Mama Pendergrass after the death of her son Keith and feeding off her sorrow.

I didn't want Cassiel feeding off Megan.

Of course, given that Megan's mood had shifted from sorrow to anger, that probably wasn't an issue. She looked like she was ready to slap the angel into next Tuesday. I knew the feeling.

"So," Megan said, conjuring a sword and beautiful celestial body armor. "How about you hand the Sigillum Dei over so I don't have to cut you down where you stand?"

I'd never been prouder of my big sis.

She'd become a bona fide badass demon hunting celestial warrior, and she was itching for a fight. It would do her good to blow off some steam, and I'd be ready to back her up.

Bring it on, traitor pants.

Cassiel just looked at us. No emotion, no words—she just placed the Sigillum Dei on the ground at her feet with trembling hands.

Then she turned and started walking away.

I stood there, dumbfounded.

That was it? She'd stolen the damned thing and made us chase her all over the city and through the space-time continuum—or whatever the space between was—to get it back and instead of putting up a fight or offering some kind of explanation, she just walked away?

"What are we supposed to do now?" Megan whispered.

Like I had any clue. Cassiel had gone off script. I was so tempted to just let her go and wallow or crawl down a hole or whatever defeated celestials stuck on earth did.

But I couldn't.

Whatever was going on with the angel that made her give up the arte-fact she'd been using to rescue her fellow celestials on earth had to be bad. If it was bad for her, it was probably bad for us and for our current mission.

I had to find out what it was.

I jogged through the mist and followed the fading light before the space between swallowed it. Assuming I didn't kill her, I'd have to ask Cassie how she navigated in here. I had no idea where we'd been going or how far the void extended.

"Yo, Cassie," I yelled. "What gives?"

She kept walking.

I turned my jog into a run and caught up with her. When she didn't stop, I stood in her way and crossed my arms, wishing I had some kind of cool walking stick so I could yell, "You shall not pass!"

The asshole angel just switched directions and started walking the other way. Not cool.

"Enough," I yelled.

Megan caught up and conjured a fence around us. She pointed her sword at Cassiel. "My sister is talking to you. Answer her."

Cassiel scowled. Good. Maybe we'd get to have that much needed sparring session after all.

"I don't understand the question," Cassie said, a note of defiance in her voice.

"Don't give me that," I said. "We had several sessions on modern colloquialisms. You know what I mean."

Megan gave me a look.

"What? I know big words," I said, throwing my arms up in the air. "And I have to use them to explain things to Cassie the I'm-stuck-in-the-Victorian-era snooty angel. She has no idea how to communicate in the twenty-first century."

Cassiel sighed and sat on the ground. Ew. It was damp and squishy down there. The damp would soak through her pants and make her look like she peed on herself. No dignity at all. She was in a very bad way. Ugh, if I didn't get to the bottom of this, I'd start feeling sorry for her.

"If you must know," Cassie said, keeping her gaze on the ground, "I lost over two hundred refugees. I was leading them to the space between and we wound up back on earth and in a series of interconnected tunnels. Before I could get them back and open a portal, we were attacked by an angry hoard of immaterial demons."

Oh. Crap.

"When did this happen?" I asked, a knot of dread lodged in the pit of my stomach.

"Last night," Cassie said. "I failed them. I fervently hope you will make better use of the artefact than I have."

CHAPTER TWENTY-SEVEN

Megan's gaze went wide as she came to the same conclusion. Beelzebub's immaterial demon henchmen were the same demons who'd attacked Cassie's refugees.

That meant that those demons had access to the space between through the tunnels underneath Swan Springs.

If that was the case...

"Pendergrass's portal. It's connected to Swan Springs and the space between," Megan said, snapping her fingers.

"That's what I'm thinking," I said. "Cassie, did you actually see the immaterial demons destroy your refugees?"

Cassie stood up. If her wet ass bothered her, she didn't show it. "No, but they disappeared. I assumed the demons consumed them."

Again with assuming. I'd tell her the same thing I told my team back at HQ, but the joke would be lost on the angel. And it wasn't exactly the right time.

"What if they weren't consumed? Maybe they got caught by the portal Pendergrass is making."

"Keith Pendergrass is dead," Cassie said, her brows furrowed in confusion. "And Cooper Pendergrass would never create a portal to support a demon invasion."

"Well, Cassie, if you'd stuck with the team instead of running off with the artefact, you'd know that Damien Pendergrass, a.k.a. the father of Keith and Cooper Pendergrass, is very much alive."

I couldn't keep the bite out of my voice. Not that I was trying very hard. "Pendergrass Senior has been working on building a portal just outside the city. Looks like he's using the space between to get past the wards we have around the city."

Hope bloomed in Cassie's expression. "So we may be able to find and save the refugees?"

"There's a chance," Megan said. "We have to try."

Megan was about to take us out of the space between, but I held up a hand to stop her. I didn't trust the angel as far as I could throw her. And we had some unfinished business.

"I haven't heard an apology," I said, crossing my arms. "You don't just get to tag along with the team after the stunt you pulled without, at the very least, apologizing."

Cassie had the nerve to look surprised. Seriously. Celestials had no social skills, manners, or a conscience, apparently—at least when it came to their allies.

The angel glanced at Megan who shrugged. "You screwed up. Big time. An apology is the bare minimum you owe her and the rest of us. Besides, Jane won't budge until you say you're sorry. She can out stubborn anyone."

Cassiel bounced from foot to foot, practically vibrating with renewed energy to save the celestials she thought she'd lost. If I told her it would go much faster if she'd just apologize, would she listen, or would she keep acting like a toddler?

Good grief, she'd spent enough time on earth to understand our customs even if she truly felt no remorse.

I raised my eyebrows and gave her my best look of intimidation.

"I apologize for not coming to you sooner, but not for taking the artefact. Thousands of celestials would have perished or been enslaved if I didn't help them escape. I am not sorry that I did what was necessary to save them, but—"

"Wow, you suck at apologies." Megan glared at her.

"If you would allow me to finish."

"Fine," I said. "But you'd better make this good."

"But I am sorry that I broke your trust, that I didn't trust you to care as much for celestials as you do for demons. You made it clear how much you dislike my kind, even though part of you is celestial. But now I know you do care. You defend the innocent. It's who you are."

"Okay, I'll buy that," I said. "What changed your mind about me?"

"You saved Nisroc and his flock. You and the master demon you brought with you."

Master demon?

"Wait, D is a master demon?" Megan looked horrified. "As in the kind of demons we're fighting?"

"No," I said on reflex. "Just because he's Belial's son doesn't mean he's evil."

Megan clapped a hand over her mouth, but she couldn't take it back. I was so tired of everyone thinking the worst of my demon. He'd been through so much, and he already thought the worst of himself even though he fought every day to do the right thing, to be better than his father who tore him away from me and tortured him. Had he not been a good man who felt compassion and was protective, Belial might have molded D in his image.

But D had always been kind. From the moment I found him hiding in my closet and fed him, he'd done everything he could to help my family, to learn about earth and humans and grow to understand and value them.

"No, your master demon is not evil," Cassie said. "He protects the innocent, too. That is who he is. That is why you love him."

Megan nodded. "She's right. And having a master demon on our team is going to help us defeat Beelzebub, the rest of the master demons, and all the archangels waging war on our home turf."

Relief washed through me, and I hugged Megan. "Thanks, sis."

I let go. "Okay, let's grab the rest of the team and find our way to that portal so I can get my demon."

I pulled Sam into a private room at HQ on the way out. Talking to him confirmed my worst fears.

Trinity was running out of time.

"She will honor the bargain," Sam said, helpless anger radiating from him. "And I will join her in servitude to Marbas."

Shit. I'd read about him. Not a master demon, but he was powerful. Of course Trinity would make a deal with the wisest and most knowledgeable demon in the hell realm. I would have expected the Marquess to challenge Marbas to win Trinity's freedom, or to work with the team to break her out of his clutches, but join her in servitude? It wasn't like him to give up without a fight.

"Sam," I said, running my hands on my face. "What aren't you telling me?"

He scowled, his jaw clenched tight enough to crack his back molars. Demons and secrets. Now was so not the time.

"You need to spill the tea if we have any hope of getting Trin out of this mess. Surrender is not in your nature, and I don't see you being a loyal servant to anyone. What does Marbas have on you?"

Sam began pacing. "It's...complicated."

"When isn't it?" I muttered. "Start talking."

Sam sighed. "Trinity first encountered Marbas through an accidental summoning. It's not in her bloodline, but the book she found during one of her expeditions for rare occult texts had a bit of the previous owner's blood. It was enough for Marbas to manifest on earth for a short time."

Crap on a piece of toast.

Trinity had never shared how she became a part of our team or even a part of the world of demons in general. I assumed it had something to do with her scholarly pursuits. Before becoming a demon hunter, she'd worked as a museum curator specializing in rare old books. Then, one day, the boss found her in possession of a supposedly immaterial demon and recruited her. I'd only recently found out that Sam was, in fact, capable of manifesting as material and that he was more than just some run-of-the-mill scholar or cleric from the demon realm.

All we were told was that her demon came to her willingly.

There were more holes in that story than a block of Swiss cheese.

"Was this a part of her work, or did she dabble in demonology as a side hustle?"

"Part of her work," he said, flatly. "She was part of an organization preparing for a possible invasion by interdimensional beings. Headed by persons above the law, politics, and government, they've been working for millennia to ensure that angels and demons do not overrun earth as they did at the dawn of human civilization."

My jaw dropped. That was some grade-A illuminati shit. Then again, it made sense. Demon hunting teams existed, scattered throughout the world. Sameal never told us how old our so-called profession was.

"Is our team part of the same organization?" I asked.

Sam shrugged. "Loosely affiliated. At any rate, when she summoned Marbas and he asked her what she wanted to bargain for, she said she didn't want anything. It intrigued him. They spoke for hours. She answered his questions about earth and modern society, showed him unexpected hospitality by offering him food and drink, and treated him as an honored guest rather than an instrument of evil summoned to fulfill her dark desires. He was...impressed."

Not too surprising. Trinity was the smartest person I knew, and she could be charming when she chose to be. But knowing her, she did want something from Marbas.

Knowledge.

"That's how she got you," I said, snapping my fingers. "Not a bargain, but an exchange of information. She told him about earth, and he, what, gave her to you as a gift?"

That was a disturbing notion, if true. Such a power imbalance would make the relationship between Sam and Trinity even more disturbing. I couldn't see it.

"No, no," Sam said. "He asked if I wanted to go to the earth realm and share my knowledge of the hell realm with an...open-minded and intelligent human. I was intrigued. We demons are, in general, as ignorant of earth and the ways of humans as humans are of us. Even humans like you."

I wasn't convinced. "So you were just curious and decided to leave your legions and go on an extended Sabbatical to earth, and then you wound up helping Trinity hunt and banish demons." I looked up and stroked my chin as if pondering. "Nope. Not buying it."

Sam's eyes glowed with red demonic sparks. His power flared like it did before a fight. Oh, was someone having some big feelings? Too bad.

"There were other factors, but they are not relevant to the current situation. Suffice to say, Marbas was playing the long game. He knew Trinity would be back someday in need of something—information, a favor...a way to protect humans from marauding demons and celestials. When she did, he made her bargain."

Now that I believed. "She traded herself for the ward," I said, my heart sinking.

Sam nodded. "An eternity of service as his advisor in all things related to the earth realm, all the better to conquer what's left of humanity after the war."

She would be forced to betray her own species. Why would she make such a rotten deal? Not purely out of desperation...

"Trinity is counting on us to win, isn't she? If we banish the master demons and archangels, Marbas won't be able to conquer."

Then it hit me. "And if he can't conquer, he won't have any use for Trinity. What will he do with her?"

A look of desolation crossed Sam's face before he schooled his features to his usual calm and inscrutable mask. "That is why I must go with her. For protection. And, if necessary, I will offer myself and my legions as a sacrifice in exchange for Trinity's life and freedom."

CHAPTER TWENTY-EIGHT

We met up at Swan Springs after midnight.

At least, what was left of it.

Those immaterial demons and rallmaths had done more damage than I realized. Each and every single house was in shambles, exposing the subdivision's dirty little secret.

Roofs blown off and caving in, columns shattered to expose the wood beneath, brick veneers crumbled revealing rotting plywood beneath, and sinkholes.

So many sinkholes.

There were our tunnels.

"Raus, can you and the other rallmaths find your way back to where you were brought to earth?"

The giant rallmath crouched and went very still. Except for his eyes. They darted all around as if looking for danger. If his tail wasn't so small and stumpy, it would have been tucked between his legs.

"Bad place." Raus shivered. Poor thing. It was a big ask. I hated to do it, but we needed him to lead us and the others through the tunnels. We figured it would be easier to back track that way than wandering

aimlessly through the space between. Cassie had recruited a few celestials to monitor the space between in case Belial's demons showed up to
ambush us.

We would find the portal, D, Judaliel, and Nisroc—with any lucky,
they'd have Pendergrass hog-tied and unconscious. With Cassie's help,
we would use the Sigillum Dei to shut down the portal permanently.

I crouched down to stroke Raus's wiry fur. "I know. Bad place. But
we'll be there with you. I won't let anyone hurt you. And we can get you
and your friends back home if you want to go back."

"Pi-zza and ice cream?"

I grinned. "Sure thing. All you can eat. We'll grab some when we're
done."

"Pi-zza, ice cream, and jerk-y."

Sully wore her small cat form. I doubted she could fit her giant ass
through the tunnels if she grew to battle cat size. I'd lost track of her
during mission prep but trust the little bottomless pit to show up at the
mention of food.

"Yes, yes, Scooby snacks for everyone. Now, weapons check."

The team assembled, confident and ready to rumble. It gave me hope.
We'd been battle tested with Belphegor and two archangels. Scarred and
battered, but we'd won, and with that victory came confidence and hard-
won cohesion.

Trinity and Sam were decked out in demon realm battle gear and
carried an impressive array of physical and magical weapons. Trinity
wore her hair back in a tight fighting queue and rocked the combat boots.
She'd traded glasses for demon magic-enhanced contact lenses that
allowed her to transmit and receive visual information to the twins. They
were the twins' creation and Trinity, being the leader, got to field test the
prototype.

The Sigillum Dei sat secure in a transparent pocket of magic over her
heart.

Sam had traded his fully humanoid form for an enhanced demon
warrior version of himself. His olive skin was darker, his eyes pure red

and glowing with his magic. The long black hair remained. No need to pull it back. He fought with magic and specialized in long-range assault. Trinity had the same hand-to-hand combat training as the rest of us, but Sam had spent the past decade teaching her to fight with borrowed magic as well as using a version of demon realm martial arts favored by fighters who had little magic or preferred up close and personal fighting.

They were a lethal team. And no wonder. After what Sam told me, I understood why they clung to each other. I swore I'd find a way to save them from Marbas. I didn't have many friends. Trinity and Sam were two of a handful. Scratch that. They were my chosen family. No way would I leave them to rot in the hell realm.

For now, they stood ready to secure Beelzebub and send him back to hell as soon as we found him.

Alexi transformed into a two-legged wolf demon shape and bared his fangs, the stuff of nightmares. Six feet tall with shaggy black fur, razor sharp claws, and demon red eyes, he would be our rear guard and dispatch any demons who might follow us into the tunnels and to capture Pendergrass and/or the archangels should they try to escape. Zer, my phantom demon wolf born from demon graft Alexi used to save my life, stirred within me.

"Don't worry, girl," I whispered. "I have the feeling you'll get to come out and play."

Megan teamed up with the wolf demon, and she managed to create celestial armor outside of the space between, the show-off.

I was proud, but totally jealous.

I knew Alexi would keep her safe and she'd look out for him. They fought well together, and the Russian harbored some deep feelings for my sister. Being a gentleman, he kept things between them professional and maintained a growing friendship.

I hoped, when Megan was ready, he'd make a move.

Lacey stood decked out in form-fitting, flexible body armor, sporting her demon steel blade and a variety of small weapons that suited her grappling style of fighting. Simon floated above her, wings and wicked talons spread, and unleashed an unearthly screech. He certainly wouldn't be underutilized in the field tonight. The two of us would take up the front guard along with Sully.

"Wow. How about you scream a little louder. I don't think you woke all the humans in a twenty-mile radius." Boice's voice, and snark, came through our comms. He and Roice were waiting at the border between Nashville and Franklin. Somewhere along that border lay Pendergrass's portal. The twin tech demons would use their mad skills and equipment to track our progress through the tunnels and narrow down the likely location, meeting us on the other side to join the battle.

Or to intercept D, the celestials, and Pendergrass.

"Oh, we have that covered," Lacey said.

Mara and around twenty other demons disguised as a film crew stood at the ready. They'd cordoned off the area and posted demon security guards around the subdivision to divert any humans away from danger. The strategy was brilliant—Nashville was buzzing about the Sci-Fi action thriller being filmed in Music City. And Nashvillians left their celebrities and performers to go about their business without creating a scene. Perfect cover.

Plus, Mara and company would help monitor this side of the tunnel and space-between maze leading to the portal.

The crew of demons were busy setting up lights and cameras. Wow, talk about realism. I admired her dedication.

Wait, was it dedication or was she actually filming?

"Um, Mara, are those real cameras?"

Mara grinned. "Of course! The celestials flying downtown created a sensation, and the cover story about making a movie got me thinking, why not? The twins put me in contact with an indie studio. They're interested, especially since we can pull off fantastic special effects on a low budget. It's too perfect."

"She wrote a screenplay," Lacey said, beaming. "It's really good, Jinx. The suits sprung for some up-and-coming actors and they're filming half of the scenes in the studio backlot. Mara's taking care of the action shots. A little editing, a bit of CGI to hide our identities and presto—screen gold!"

"Don't worry," Mara said. "I'll share any royalties I earn."

"Good," said a familiar and unwelcome voice. "I've no doubt you've squandered the budget I left."

I spun around and came face to chest with the Angel of Death, with Cassiel trailing behind him.

CHAPTER TWENTY-NINE

I was going to murder Cassiel for bringing Sameal along on our mission.

My least favorite celestial wore a new glamour. Youthful, muscular, and ready for battle, it was a far cry from her grandmotherly form or the college co-ed glamour she often used.

Good. It would be easier to hit a warrior than a grandma or sorority girl.

Squaring my shoulders, I placed my hands on my hips and glared at Sameal. "Um, it's not your budget anymore. What part of you-can't-have-your-old-job-back did you not understand? We don't want you here. We don't need you here."

"Yes, we do," Trinity said.

"No!" I screamed, turning to face her. "He bailed on us. Left us to clean up the mess that Haniel and Belial created and left us to take on Belphegor on our own."

"Which we did," Megan said.

Sameal regarded my sister the way a cat feigns boredom before pouncing on a juicy little mouse. "And who might you be, little mortal?"

Alexi growled. So did I.

"She's not a little mortal," I said, fists clenched and held tight to my side. I had a powerful urge to punch our old boss's chiseled jaw. "She's a—"

"I'm her sister, you giant bully," Megan said, moving between me and Sameal. She stuck her finger in his face and yelled. At the Angel of Death. Brass. Ovaries.

I loved it.

"You took my little sister when she was only seventeen and made her work for you. Hunting *demons*. Who does that?"

Sameal's nostrils flared, and he glowered at Megan. "*You're* hunting demons. At least that's why I assume you're here. Another misfit given purpose. You should be thanking me. Had I not intervened, Haniel would have consumed Jane, or she would have escaped, ripping apart your sister's soul in the process."

Megan went nose to nose with him, the strands of blond hair that had come loose from her ponytail vibrating with her rage. "I chose this. Jane had no choice. You could have freed her from Haniel. At the very least you could have told her what she is—half celestial and full of power you made her suppress."

Before Sameal could speak, I touched my father's ring hanging from the chain around my neck, letting a small but potent dose of the power I held out to play.

"Megan, we aren't just celestials. Dear old dad rocked god-like powers a long time ago. I'm guessing Sameal knew about it and wanted to keep us weak and ignorant so he could control us."

"Hey," she said. "That's Dad's ring. He gave it to you?"

The whole team started speaking at once, yelling, asking questions, and generally spewing chaos. Megan barraged me with questions about the ring. Presumably, she could tap into the same power I'd used to defeat Belphegor.

"You saw me use it?" I yelled.

"I saw you grab something in that battle, but I didn't know it was a ring. I was kind of busy kicking demon ass."

Fair point. "We'll talk about it later. Look, I'll show you how it works, and you can take it out for a test drive. Don't use it until we do. Dad's power is...it'll try and turn you into a monster like him."

She nodded. Then, she put two fingers in her mouth and let out an ear-piercing whistle that made everyone shut up and grab their ears. While we'd been arguing with the Angel of Death, Trinity had climbed on top of a pile of rubble with Sam and stood at the ready.

"Sameal," she said. "We could use you in this fight, but it's up to the rest of the team. You kept a lot of secrets and broke trust." Trinity looked at each of us and asked, "What say you?"

"Fine, but I'm not following his orders," Lacey said.

"I'm not either," said Mara. Brave. The last time she'd faced off with our former boss, he'd threatened to send her back to the hell realm or let her starve in a human prison in solitary confinement. Our team was brimming with brass ovaries.

Alexi growled and looked at Megan. She looked at me. Great. They were leaving it up to me.

I heaved a sigh. "Okay, but if you betray us or bail again, I'm sending my demon cat after you."

Sully, who'd been flying around and surveying the action landed on my shoulder and hissed at Sameal. He flinched.

"Good girl."

"You have my word," Sameal said, then he nodded at Sam and said, "Marquess, it has been a long time."

Sam took Trinity's hand and said, "Not so long as all that. It is good to see you again. Shall we dispatch this rogue summoner for good?"

Sameal nodded. He and Cassiel ran toward one of the giant sinkholes and jumped in.

Guess they were going first.

I nodded at Lacey, and we ran after them, leaping into the sinkhole and into the unknown.

Lacey and I stuck close to Raus as his companions scuttled about. Small and nimble, they ran along the damp earthen floor, along the walls, and several clung to roots while traveling above. Versatile creatures. Their small forms made them perfect scouts and spies, and they were powerful fighters in the large size Raus wore. Our celestial light shone through the tunnel and the demon creatures cast eerie shadows.

Raus's claws dug into the earth as he loped on all fours. Sully flew ahead to keep an eye on our unlikely allies and then flew back to keep us updated on their progress.

"Angels good. No eat."

"You can always eat them after the battle," Lacey said.

"And wash them down with ice cream," I added.

We almost ran into Sameal and Cassie, who were stopped ahead where the tunnel split. A trio of rallmaths sniffed each entrance and then took off running, presumably to scout. We'd have to wait for them to come back and lead us in the right direction.

"We can hear you," Cassie grumbled. "I do not wish to be eaten by your beast."

"Then don't give us a reason to turn you into cat food." Lacey pointed her demon blade in Cassie's direction. Lacey had never liked the celestial. I should have paid more attention to my partner's intuition. We couldn't trust her any more than we could trust Sameal.

"So," I said, tossing my own demon blade back and forth between my hands. Perfectly balanced and comforting in my grip, I swung and jabbed to warm up for whatever waited for us on the other side of the maze of tunnels. "How do you two know each other?"

It might be good to know how closely they were associated.

Cassie looked at Sameal as if asking permission to answer. If she got back in my good graces, I would break the celestial of that habit. The Angel of Death didn't deserve that much deference.

We really needed to teach Cassie the fine art of snark and back-talk.

"Cassiel is one of the oldest operatives in our mission," Sameal said.

"Demon hunting?" Lacey asked.

Sameal gave her a withering look. "No, our true mission is to prevent another war. And during brief periods of peace, she's been working to keep her people safe."

I snorted. "What do you mean her people. Aren't you the Angel of Death? That makes you a celestial. You just pretended to be a demon all those years to cow us into being your minions."

Sameal's eyes glowed and he grew several feet taller—same trick as D used in my bedroom since he didn't go crashing through the tunnel's ceiling. No horns, but no more than the standard set of eyeballs, either. A small, Celtic-looking crown wrapped around his head and sat just above his massive brows. Long white hair hung in braids that reached his low back. Dude had wings. They weren't the leathery bat-like wings one expected from a demon, but the feathers were dusky instead of white. The armor covering his massive body looked like no other armor I'd ever seen.

Ancient and forged at the dawn of time. Ethereal. His skin tone didn't change, but his eyes turned silver.

Then they shifted to demon red.

"Like you," he said, voice booming. So much for stealth. "I am neither demon nor celestial. I am the harbinger of death. Death claims everyone and everything."

I glanced at Lacey. She was properly awed and probably terrified. I wasn't having it.

I leaned in and mock whispered, "Think he raided the set of *The Lord of the Rings* to get an elf crown?"

She giggled. Good. We couldn't afford to let this guy intimidate us. Never again.

Cassiel dropped her celestial sword and stood with a horrified and dumbfounded expression painted across her face. "Are they always this disrespectful?"

"You have no idea," Sameal said, shrinking back to his previous form. "Impertinent and rash, foolishly risky considering their fragile bodies and short lives. It is a uniquely human trait that I fervently hope they outgrow."

"Nah," I said. "It's one of our best qualities. Your kind never befriended a motiaummerr or rallmaths."

Right on cue, Raus's tiny companions scurried out of both tunnels and back into the chamber where we waited. They chittered, conferring with one another and with Raus. When they finished, Raus looked at me and screwed up his rodent face in helpless frustration. His limited human speech was a problem. We could work out most simple concepts with the human words he could say and charades.

We needed help.

I tapped the com device in my ear and said, "Boice, patch me through to Cooper."

"It's Roice, actually, and why do you need the summoner?"

Oh, for the love of lollipops, I did not have time for his bullshit. "Because, roomie, Raus and his buddies need to tell us which tunnel to take and why, but they can't. We need someone who can speak to demon animals."

The line went silent. "In your own time," I muttered.

After a long moment, Cooper's voice came through. "Jane. What are the rallmaths saying?"

"That's what I was hoping you could tell us," I said. I turned my attention back to Raus. "Can you repeat what you just said? Cooper can hear and he'll translate."

Raus's ears perked up and his beady eyes brightened. I listened to his squeaks and chitters, looking for any kind of pattern. We all needed to learn to speak demon realm animal languages. Cooper couldn't come with us on this mission. If his father escaped or we failed to seal the portal, it would be up to the youngest Pendergrass boy to shut it down.

Of course, the ability to speak to demon realm animals required making a deal with a powerful demon who could do it and share the magic. Cooper had probably racked up enough favors from visiting demons and refugees to trade for the ability. If I asked for it, I'd probably have to promise my first born.

Megan would never have a first born.

My heart ached for her. If I could trade something to give her the ability to have children, I would do it in a heartbeat.

Cooper spoke. "He says that the tunnel on your right leads to another chamber with multiple branching tunnels. The rallmaths know where some lead, but not others. Beelzebub's demons must have worked on them and made additions to keep the rallmaths from finding an escape route. Don't take that one. The tunnel on your left leads away from the subdivision and in the right direction for hitting the city border. That's your best bet."

"You're awesome and you're my favorite summoner," I said.

"I'm the only summoner you don't hate," he replied flatly.

"True, but that doesn't mean I don't adore you. Stay safe. We'll report back when—"

A rumbling from the tunnel behind us cut me off. Dust and debris poured from it as the ground beneath us shook.

The tunnel was collapsing.

CHAPTER THIRTY

"Run!" I yelled.

I swung around and conjured a large celestial shield to cover our escape. It held back the first wave of flying rocks and debris but didn't stop the ceiling from showering us with clumps of hard earth and rocks.

The rallmaths took off down the tunnel on the left. I shoved Lacey in their direction in a silent order to follow them. Sameal and Cassie just stood there.

"How about some help?" I said, groaning against the growing weight of detritus piling up from the tunnel's collapse.

Sameal grabbed Raus, who'd frozen in terror, and took off into the depths of the tunnel on the left. Suddenly, another celestial shield reinforced my own. I spun around and found Megan standing behind me. She was covered in dust and soil, apparently having made it through the tunnel before its collapse.

"What are you doing here?" I yelled. "You're supposed to be with Alexi."

"I ran ahead. Got this weird feeling that you were in danger, and he told me I should trust my instincts," she said, crouch walking to my right flank.

"Your instincts are going to get you killed!" I said, panic rushing through me.

My gaze darted to Cassie. The angel looked between us and the left tunnel with a strange expression on her face. Then she conjured a stronger shield.

"Go," she said. "And take the motiaummerr. I'll cover you."

Something was off. Megan sensed it, too, and Sully growled and swiped at the celestial's leg.

"What aren't you telling us?" I yelled.

"Sameal wants the summoner. He means to take him alive and use him to construct portals to pocket dimensions, prisons for the remaining master demons and archangels."

Son of a bitch. He knew D wanted to kill Damien Pendergrass and that I wanted to kill him, too. That's who he'd been after all along. He wasn't helping us. He was helping himself. All our old boss cared about was power and control. Pendergrass deserved to be punished, but Sameal would give him a get-out-of-jail-free pass to suit his agenda.

"Why are you telling us?" Megan said as I dragged her toward the left-hand tunnel.

"Because that's what allies do. Go. Save my people."

Cassiel's shield cracked. If she didn't come with us, she'd be buried alive. I had no idea if a celestial could survive that, but I didn't want to risk it. No one deserved to die like that or be trapped without the relief of death.

The shield broke. I screamed as Sully gripped my arm with her mouth and pulled me down the tunnel with Megan.

―――――

We ran for a long time as mountains of soil filled the tunnel behind us. How much was there? It wasn't natural. Someone or something was trying to kill us.

Or herding us into a trap.

We approached another fork in the tunnel system. Sameal's footprints went left. I pointed right. My sides ached, my lungs were on fire from running and from breathing particles of soil, but I kept going. I'd been trained to ignore pain and keep moving as if my life depended on it.

It often did.

But Megan hadn't been training as long. She wouldn't make it.

"Sully," I yelled, my voice hoarse and wheezy. "Help Megan."

My demon cat grew into a form larger than baby kitty but not so big as battle cat and swooped down, grabbing Megan by the celestial armor at her neck. They took off as I forced my body to its limits.

I had to keep running.

At last, the pursuing wave of dirt slowed. I caught up with Megan and Sully and tried not to collapse. At least my celestial armor held. Mixing sweat with layers of dirt and debris would be all kinds of gross.

Megan coughed and Sully appeared to be hacking up a hairball. With our luck, the soil in these tunnels was contaminated with toxic waste that was slowly killing us. Hopefully we had enough demon healing potions and elixirs stashed away at HQ. Once we coughed, spat, and caught our breath, we took stock of our surroundings.

"You okay, Jane?" Megan said.

No, I was not okay. We'd lost Cassie. She'd sacrificed herself to give us a chance to escape.

"We have to find Cassie's people, the celestials she lost in the space between," I said, my voice rough from debris and the shock of grief. "We owe her."

Megan took me into her arms as tears streamed down my face. "We will. It will be all right. We'll find them. And we'll tell them that a true angel sent us. I promise."

Sully rubbed her head and cheek against my leg in comfort. "Good angel," she said.

"She was," I whispered.

"Do you think there's any way she could've gotten out?" Megan asked.

"I hope so. It should have been Sameal. But I doubt the Angel of Death can actually die. Pity. Then again, he's afraid of my cat." I conjured celestial fabric and wet it with my canteen so I could wipe dirt and tears from my face and clean my hands. I handed the cloth to Megan so she could clean up, too. I had no idea how to use magic to create soap.

And I didn't have Cassie to teach me.

Megan pressed the comms unit in her ear. "Boice, Roice, this is Megan, do you copy?"

I tried mine, too. Nothing. We were on our own.

"We need to be careful," I said. "Whoever or whatever caused the tunnel to collapse likely wants us to go this way." I pointed in the direction we'd been running. "It's probably a trap."

"Agreed." Megan said as she conjured a celestial sword and shield.

I went with a spear and shield. So far, Sully had resisted all my attempts at covering her furry body with celestial armor. I wasn't sure if she was doing it on purpose or if she was immune to celestial magic.

When I asked her to stay behind us, she hissed then screeched, "No!"

Stubborn cat.

Sully shrank and stalked through the tunnel ahead of us. We'd killed our magic lights and followed in the dark, traveling at a snail's pace so we didn't trip on the uneven ground. The only sounds were our shallow breaths and dripping sounds that got closer the longer we walked. I had a moment of panic, imagining the tunnel flooding.

If we got out of this, I'd ask the twins to work on some kind of aquatic survival gear.

Megan's breathing came in shallow pants. Claustrophobia. We needed to get out of here soon.

I bumped her shoulder in reassurance, and we continued our agonizingly slow progress. Drops of water fell on us from time to time as we walked, and the ground became slick in places, sticky with mud in others.

Slowly, light crept through the tunnel. Wherever we were heading, it seemed we were almost there. Sully crept back to us, blocking our path. She'd seen something.

"Bad angels. De-mor-iel and angels. Bad angels, De-mor-iel, human, more angels..."

Sully screwed up her face, trying to make the words come out. Bad angels—Judaliel and Nisroc? Demoriel. The human had to be Pendergrass. More angels. More angels could mean Judaliel and Nisroc and bad angels could be other players. Were the archangels in on whatever scheme D concocted?

"Sully, are the bad angels our angels?"

Sully said, "No."

Right. We had new players in this deadly game. "Okay, are the more angels our angels?"

"No, more, more, angels." Sully shook her head in frustration, then hissed and did her best impersonation of a Halloween cat with arched back, fur standing on end, and a feline sideways defensive stance.

Damn, damn, damn, I would give my right arm to speak cat right now. More angels I got, but the rest?

Sully cocked her head at me and then crept behind a rock, tail tucked between her legs. I followed, she crouched and shivered, eyes wide and pupils dilated. She hissed and swatted, then cowered some more. Then she stood and shook her pelt and wings. "Angels."

I got it. Scared. There were a lot of celestials ahead at the end of the tunnel, and they were scared.

"Cassie's people," Megan said. "They've got Cassie's people. But why?"

I had a terrible thought that I pushed away. D would never, ever send innocents to their deaths or deliver them into the hands of enemies. But, what if, in his demonic logic, it made sense to sacrifice them for the greater good. I'd spent my whole life thinking he was like me. Mostly human with a touch of demon, but with the empathy and compassion of the humans among whom he'd lived for so long.

He was like me, damn it. And that was the problem.

It would be so easy to lose control and give in to the seductive power that flowed through me. It would be easy for him, too. He'd said as much. I had to get to him and stop this. He needed me to have his back.

But so did those celestials, and all the demons, humans, and entities caught in the middle of this looming conflict.

We had to get in there and do some recon before we planned our next move.

"Sully," I said, reaching down to stroke her soft black fur. I scratched her between her double set of ears and then on the sweet spot between her wings. "You are such a good girl. You are the best cat in three realms."

The cat preened, her ears pricked, tail up, and slow blinking.

"We need a distraction. I need to you to wear rallmath glamour."

Sully flattened her ears and growled. She hated glamour. The rottweiler was one thing, but a tiny rodent? While she'd grown fond and protective of them, rallmaths were prey. Taking on their form as a predator would be a huge step down for the cat.

"Please, baby? We have to save D and those celestials. I just need you to scamper across the floor and cause a ruckus. Then you find someplace to hide. When we give the signal, you come out in full on battle cat form. Deal?"

She considered, then rubbed her head against my hand. "Deal."

Megan and I pulled back our magic, disappearing our armor and weapons. We'd keep them close to the surface for when we mounted an attack, but we couldn't risk emitting such powerful magic signatures. I nodded at my sister. "Here goes nothing."

I tapped into the powers gifted to me by Mara's graft and covered myself and my sister with eyeballs and feathers.

Sully transformed and took off toward the end of the tunnel with us hot on her heels.

CHAPTER THIRTY-ONE

Sully was fast, bless her.

Right on cue, shouts and squeals echoed through the space as we crept along the edge of the tunnel's walls.

The tunnel ended in a large room that looked like the inside of a warehouse. What was it with demons and warehouses? They needed a new playbook, or better interior designers. D in his big, bad demon form and a man who looked like an older version of Cooper chased after Sully's tiny rallmath form as it bounced off walls and tabletops, knocking off bits of metal and bottles filled with foul-smelling liquid. One side of the room looked like an alchemist's lab, presumably Pendergrass's. On the other side, celestials cowered behind a ward. They were dirty, looked half-starved, and terrified.

Two unfamiliar celestials wearing humanoid glamour shouted at D and Pendergrass but didn't offer help. Taking advantage of the chaos, Megan and I joined the celestial prisoners. We couldn't risk breaking the ward, assuming we could manage. It would blow our cover. Instead, we stood as close as we could to the others and tried to look inconspicuous.

The desperate celestials had the good sense to keep quiet. "We'll get you out," I whispered. "But first we need to know what's going on."

"There are only two of you," one man said. He wore a filthy robe similar to the one Nisroc had on when we first met him in the space between. The celestial had the standard number of eyeballs, but tiny, iridescent scales covered his skin. "You cannot defeat the demon."

"Reinforcements are coming," Megan said.

I hoped she was right.

A tiny celestial child with classic cherubic features and wings that were probably white beneath layers of grime and dirt, smiled at Megan, her purple eyes full of hope.

"What do you know?" I asked the man, wincing as glass crashed from across the room. "What are they planning?"

"The demon found us wandering the tunnels. We lost our guide and were transported into them from the space between. He brought us here and warded us. The summoner said we would make good test subjects for his portal."

Shit.

Guess animal experimentation was over.

Pendergrass was planning to send these refugees through an untested portal that led to who knew where. They could be consumed by unstable magic, wind up back in the celestial realm to be enslaved or conscripted into the war machine, or they could go to the demon realm as prisoners.

"You told me the rallmaths would be diverted," Pendergrass senior yelled, slamming tools and instruments around wherever Sully in disguise darted. Good thing she was fast.

"They were," D said, standing back and watching Pendergrass's rant with a look of boredom. "This one must have managed to go the wrong way. Don't worry about it. They're stupid creatures. This one will scamper away and get lost in the tunnels or get eaten."

Pendergrass stopped and leveled a hard stare at Demoriel. "That's not what my son says. He talks to the animals, you know. He said demon realm animals are real smart, real sneaky, and some are deadly."

D shrugged. "I've met your son. Wouldn't rely too much on what that half-wit says. We should quit wasting time and get the portal up and running."

Pendergrass muttered, "Shows up after all the work is done. Typical demon..."

D's gaze grew cold. Demon light swirled within them as he stalked over to the summoner and loomed over him. "What was that?"

Pendergrass, who apparently had a death wish, said. "You heard me. Been working on this for years and finally have it up and running. Remember that. You don't get to take credit for my work, and I ain't sharing payment. Your kind owe me."

D grinned and grabbed the man by the collar, lifting him off his feet and bringing him close. Pendergrass put on a tough face, but his limbs twitched and sweat ran down his face and body, pooling in wet spots at his arm pits and where his shirt tucked into his pants.

I hoped he pissed himself.

"I'm not interested in money, and I don't care about credit. What I want is a way to bring my father's legions to earth. The demon hunters banished him back to hell with the Sigillum Dei. He can't come back to earth himself. Not yet. I lead in his place. And your portal won't work without my power."

He let go and Pendergrass tumbled to the floor in a pathetic heap. "Get up and ready the portal. We're sending this lot to hell as a gift to my father. Once we get word that they got through—and they'd better make it alive—I'll power it fully to bring Belial's army here to finish this war for good."

"What about Beelzebub?" Pendergrass asked, wheezing. D had held a tight grip on his neck

"Forget him. He failed along with his immaterial demon horde. You work for me now."

D had been looking in our direction, surveying the hapless celestials he planned to use to test the portal.

Did he give me a small nod, or did I imagine it?

My demon wasn't given to long speeches or explanations. Was he cluing me in to the plan so Megan and I would be ready to make a move?

Or was he truly planning to lead Belial's legions?

He'd led them before, and he admitted that assuming his demon form and powers made him crave war and carnage. I needed a more obvious sign that he was acting. So did Megan. The team was right. I was too close, too biased. I wanted to believe D was still working with us.

Pendergrass got up, dusted off his sleezy ass, and disappeared behind a cluster of metal shelves. When he returned, he pushed what looked like an enormous frame, maybe for a wall-sized painting or a mirror. It was decorated with sigils etched into the ancient metal, some worn and some new. The edges of the frame were engraved with monstrous figures of demons and celestials just in case there was any doubt about what it was.

This was the portal.

Pendergrass touched the sigils, activating the magic within them. They glowed and danced with light like the demon grafts that covered my body in swirls of moving tattoos. I felt the magic. It called to my father's power, making it stand up and take notice.

D pointed in my direction. "Send those two first, then bring them back."

Pendergrass whistled. Wraiths appeared, peeling off the room's walls like living shadows. So that's why D didn't just dispatch Pendergrass. The summoner had back up. Smart.

Two wraiths hovered over me and my sister. The ward beside us fell. Hopefully they wouldn't notice that Megan and I weren't confined by the ward. I wasn't as good at glamouring magic, but it must've worked. The wraiths icy fingers closed around our arms and dragged us to Pendergrass's portal.

D touched the portal, infusing it with his magic. A dime-sized opening formed in the frame's center and began growing as D and Pendergrass chanted. The landscape on the other side was alien and unearthly. The sky was golden, not blue. No clouds. No sounds of chirping birds and skittering wildlife. Trees of scarlet and purple sprouted out of what looked like sand and grew thicker near a distant hill. There was a structure that looked like some sort of stone castle in front of the hill, surrounded by a high gate.

Demons patrolled the walls. Their weapons glowed with magic. D meant to send us to the hell realm to face those demons. We weren't equipped. None of our training had covered the terrain, customs, or battle strategies and weapons used by powerful demons bred for war.

There were only two of us.

I risked a glance at D but could read nothing in his gaze.

We were on our own.

D slipped something in the pocket of my glamoured celestial rags

The wraiths shoved us through the portal.

CHAPTER THIRTY-TWO

I thought traveling to the space between was bad.

It was nothing compared to the portal.

Vertigo, pain like fire that began in my belly and radiated out to set all my nerve endings on fire. Screams. Some were mine. Some were Megan's. We fell and fell.

My body jerked, knocking the breath out of me as warm wind assaulted me. I fought the urge to vomit. The thick floral-scented air was strange and burned my lungs as I caught my breath.

The sensation was a welcome distraction from my aching limbs. Had we come through the portal? Vertigo still gripped me, so we hadn't crash landed. Not yet. Were we lost in the vortex forever?

No. I willed my breathing to slow and fought against the shivers running through my body. When I came to my senses, I realized we were flying. Something huge was wrapped around my waist. Huge and furry.

"Sully?" I muttered, my eyes burning as I took in my surroundings.

Couldn't be. I was dreaming or dying. The ground beneath us was indeed sandy, and we passed the strange trees, sailing through that golden, cloudless sky we'd seen through the portal. So, this was hell? I didn't smell sulfur. The air around me smelled of dessert and the perfume of unfamiliar flowers.

Hell had flowers?

My vision cleared and I saw fields of brightly colored blooms beneath us as the landscape changed from sand to rust colored soil. The flowers grew in neat rows in what had to be a plowed field, carefully designed and cultivated. I swiveled my head, looking for the castle and the demons that would no doubt tear us to shreds.

It wasn't there.

"Don't...think...we're in... Kansas...anymore."

My sister's croaking voice came from my left. She flew beside me, held by the same furry, black mass. It wasn't a paw. Apparently, we'd fallen out of the portal only to be snatched out of the air by some horrible hell realm predatory bird.

"You okay, Meg?" I asked.

"Been better. Where are we?"

"I assume we're in hell, but I have no idea what has us or where we're going."

A low, growly voice from above said, "No."

Holy guacamole, it *was* Sully!

I craned my neck to look up at my huge demon cat, but all I could see was her chin and the oversized fangs that protruded from her mouth. That was what D had slipped into my pocket.

"Good angels' home."

Good angels' home? I had no idea what she was talking about, but I trusted the fluff ball with my life.

We flew for what seemed like hours over the foreign landscape. It appeared to be a mixture of forest and farmland. Crops that looked like wheat and corn grew in fields that sat next to stone cottages. Fences partitioned what might have been pastures for livestock, though we didn't see any weird-looking sheep or cattle. The stone cottages were interspersed between the fields and pastures, all with small gardens filled with flowers. A gentle river flowed between the fields, sparkling in the golden light.

It was beautiful, but something was off.

Light. Something about the light.

I craned my neck as best I could and searched the cloudless sky. No sun. No moon. Okay, different realm, but magic aside, everything we learned in training about other known realms was that they followed the basic universal laws of physics. Light had sources.

Lights cast shadows.

There were no shadows.

Where the hell were we?

Sully banked left and we tumbled toward a tall building. She dropped us on a balcony where we were greeted by Nisroc and Judaliel. Sully shrank to her small cat form and walked toward my prone body. I was dizzy, disoriented, and confused as hell. It was all kinds of wrong that Sully the demon cat knew more than I did about this situation.

"Bad kitty," I croaked. "You are in so much trouble."

Sully purred and licked my nose.

"Welcome," Judaliel said, beaming, "to our humble abode."

Megan groaned, rubbing her head. "Where are we?"

Nisroc helped her up. Left me on the ground, of course, but for my sister? He turned on the charm. Figured.

"This is a pocket realm," Nisroc said, waving his hands around. "It is still in progress, but it is habitable and ready to receive celestials and demons fleeing the war."

Half an hour later, we were sitting on the balcony drinking some kind of floral tea and marveling at the impressive array of celestial weapons and highly trained celestial refugees ready to defend their new home.

"How did you manage all this?" Megan asked. "And in such a short amount of time."

Judaliel smiled. "Cassiel began building this place thousands of years ago. My magic simply enhanced it. The magic of its citizens will complete and sustain it. And time works differently here. Years in this realm are mere days in yours."

"Was this part of D's plan? Pretending to betray us so he could smuggle you to this pocket dimension along with the other celestial refugees?" I asked. "And if so, why didn't he tell me? Why didn't Cassie for that matter?"

"And how did you get here before us?" Megan asked. "Pendergrass's wraiths pushed us through the portal first.

Judaliel grimaced. "He wanted to tell you. So did Cassiel. But we decided it would be best to keep you and the rest of your team in the dark. It is difficult to feign outrage well enough to fool Damien Pendergrass and the demons he serves. As for getting here before you, the celestials you saw in Pendergrass's workshop were glamoured to look like us. We've been here for...a while."

"And we do not trust the Angel of Death," Nisroc added.

"That makes three of us," I said, pausing to sip my tea. "And since I don't have a poker face, it's probably good that I wasn't entirely sure about D."

Judaliel glanced at Nisroc, then at me, and looked away.

I put down my teacup and braced myself. "What?"

Nisroc cleared his throat. He and his mistress had been looking out the window periodically ever since Megan and I landed. Sully had started to pace, uncharacteristically restless. They were waiting for something or someone.

Judaliel kept her gaze averted. "Demoriel should have summoned you both back by now. He's late."

"We were meant to glamour you just before to fool the summoner into thinking you'd suffered horrific injuries at the hands of demons," Nisroc added.

Megan snapped her fingers. "That's why we saw the demon fortress through the portal. It was an illusion to make Pendergrass think we were going to hell."

We sat in silence. Megan and I joined the celestials in their vigil, scanning the horizon for a sign. I had no doubt that D could take Pendergrass in a fight if discovered, but he needed to keep the summoner in the dark about his plan in order to bring us back and send the celestial refugees to safety. Had Beelzebub discovered them?

"What if the portal fails?" I asked, dread tightening my gut.

Nisroc beamed. "Cassiel will fetch you and bring the others here. She and Demoriel are the only creatures who know how to code the portal for this hidden realm. Your fellow warrior is in possession of the Sigillum Dei. All is well."

Shit.

"All is not well," I said. "Cassie...the tunnel collapsed after we entered, and she stayed behind so Megan and I could escape. She..."

I couldn't say it. It was still too raw. The loss was fresh, and it still hadn't registered. Until now. Tears streamed down my cheeks. Megan's too. Nisroc froze. He stood and muttered apologies and something about needing air before leaving the room. The shepherd trembled as he walked as grief wrapped him like a cloak. Judaliel paled.

"What will become of the refugees?" she whispered.

Megan shook her head. "Our team will keep them safe until D can get to the Sigillum Dei. We just have to wait."

And hope.

CHAPTER THIRTY-THREE

Thirty-six hours later there were no signs of an open portal ready to beam us back home.

I tried not to stress. Back on earth, less than two hours had passed. Our hosts had been prepared for us to leave within an hour our time. It was a black hole relativity or Fae realm time bending situation that made my head spin, but being one hour late didn't merit a panic attack.

Megan and I spent our time comforting Nisroc, helping him and the other celestials tend to crops and livestock, and lending our magic to expanding the pocket realm, reinforcing their defenses, and forging celestial weapons.

It was strange being in a world without technology. Magic worked exceptionally well in the pocket realm, much as it did in the hell realm and celestial realms from what the occupants told us. There was no need for machines to plow fields, ease household chores, travel, or treat injuries.

Not that everything was driven by magic. Livestock served as muscle for plowing and transportation across the realm. They used fire for light, heat, and cooking. Light and dark cycles in the environment were driven by magic, which explained the lack of a visible sun. No clouds meant no rain, but irrigation systems and magical re-routing of rivers took care of crops.

They needed more wildlife. It was too quiet without cars, planes, and televisions. I suggested importing some birds and insects. Judaliel said it would have to wait until the demon-celestial war was stopped before it started or until after it was over. They had bees from earth for pollination and honey production.

Cooper would be fascinated by this place.

Maybe he could come visit and work out a wildlife introduction program, see which crops might be best suited for the soil, fiddle with soil chemistry and symbiosis with bacteria and fungi. That kind of nerdy analysis would be helpful.

Plus, the guy could use a vacation.

"What if we don't get to go back?" Megan asked, quietly.

"Well," I said, tossing a bucket of food scraps into a pen full of weird-looking celestial pigs. They were as big as the legendary Hogzilla and had horns. No tentacles or eyeballs, thank goodness. "That would throw a monkey wrench into the whole grimoire I've-got-to-save-the-world thing."

I expected a smile at least, maybe even a chuckle. Nothing. Clearly, I needed work on my material. Or maybe it was my delivery.

"What about Mom? What about the team and Nashville and, I don't know, the entire planet?" Megan threw her hands up in frustration. At least she'd put her slop bucket down. The pigs didn't care for the aggressive display of emotion, squealing in protest as they ambled to the other side of their pen.

I sighed. "I get it. I'm worried about them, too. And thanks to the time warp thing, we've been here stressing out a lot longer than they've been on earth fighting. Judaliel showed me a huge library that Cassie's been stocking—"

I stopped myself, swallowing hard. "That Cassie stocked for centuries, including books on all kinds of celestial, demon, and earth magic. Nisroc's going through it to see if there are any guides to portals, like how they work and how to build them."

Megan snorted, leaning over the fence to stare at our porcine friends. "I thought it took someone born with summoner magic."

I joined her, leaning over the fence and holding out my hand to a small piglet that left the rest of the pigs to come back to the piggy buffet. It put its cold, we snout against my hand and let me stroke its head. The fur was bristled and wiry, not nearly as soft as Sully's or the charoum wool. Still, petting the creature gave me some measure of comfort.

"I thought a lot of things that turned out to be untrue. When I joined the team, it was easy. We were taught that demons were material or immaterial, not both. Only tempter demons and lower power species could come to earth. That wasn't true. And I wasn't possessed by a demon, I was infected with a rogue archangel. I knew D was powerful, but I had no idea he held powers on par with his dad's. Not that I think he can control them all yet. We have that in common," I said, offering her a lopsided grin.

"Is there a point in there?" Megan asked.

"My point is, who knows what else we think we know about this world, the demons, the celestials, or even our world is true? At this point, I'm going to operate under the mantra of anything is possible."

My sister cocked her head to the side and stared at me. "Why?"

I got it. It hardly sounded like me. I was the jokester, the deflector, and generally pessimistic. But life happened along with a whole lot of unexpected. If we were going to survive any of this, we needed one thing.

I shrugged. "Hope. We have to hold onto hope. What else do we have?"

I finally got a laugh out of Megan. My jokes were duds, but something schmalzy and positive bordering on cliché from me was apparently hilarious.

"That hardly sounds like you, but I'll take it."

A strange sound echoed over the horizon. If we weren't in this unfinished pocket realm, I'd swear it was thunder. But that was impossible. No sun, no clouds, no rain.

Lights flashed across the sky.

Looked like it was finally time to go home. Either that, or we were under attack.

"That's our sign," Megan said. "Still feeling hopeful?"

"Hell yes," I said, face splitting into a huge grin as I conjured my celestial armor and weapons.

Judaliel and Nisroc rushed out of the villa followed by the celestials who'd made this place their home. There were more than I realized. Hundreds. And they were armed to the teeth and looked battle ready. No hesitation, fear tucked away deep inside, those with mouths bared their teeth in a fierce display. These troops would defend this realm and themselves with pathologic dedication.

Woe to any who chose to invade or attack.

"We must glamour you," Judaliel said, the skin of her humanoid form roiling as feathers fought to cover her body. Many eyes peered from beneath the Archangel's glamour. She was battle ready, too.

Once, she'd fought for her sister. Now, she fought for her people.

I nodded. Megan's warrior goddess form disappeared, replaced by a bloody and battered woman with ripped clothing, bruises covering every inch of her skin, the hair burned from her scalp. She was emaciated and half blind. One of her eyes was an empty, bloody socket. The thing that had been my sister gasped.

I must've looked just as bad. I knew it was an illusion, but it turned my stomach.

"Meg," I croaked. They'd glamoured my voice to sound weak and pained. Nice touch. "You okay?"

She nodded, pointing at her throat while opening and closing her mouth. Ah. They'd taken her voice. Sully transformed into a tiny kitten and climbed into my rags. The motiaummerr would shift to her warrior cat form in the blink of an eye, ready to rend and tear our enemies and devour any demon who crossed her path.

Even Demoriel.

It was the hardest decision I ever made, but I'd spoken to my cat and instructed her to consume D, my demon, my love, if he lost control and went rogue. I asked her to do the same for me if I ever succumbed to the lure of my father's terrible power. Sully balked, swatted at me, growled, roared, yelled no in her high-pitched, eerie cat voice, but I made her swear to me, sealing our pact in blood. She added another clause in her garbled human speech. With no other choice in the matter, I agreed.

"I'm counting on you," I whispered, stroking her tiny head with my finger. She gave me a love nibble and then rubbed her cheek against me. She wouldn't let me down.

A circle of light formed in a nearby field. Megan and I took off hell bent for leather, the celestials following close behind. The portal slowly opened, flanked by an array of floating sigils. It went from the size of a dinner plate to a hula-hoop, the scene on the other side fuzzy. Adrenaline coursed through my body, my father's power pushing against the boundaries I constructed to keep in leashed.

Megan glowed. Blue light like flames illuminated her from within, so much more than celestial power. Dad's power lived within my sister as well, and it was doing its best to build to a frenzy. Without the ring as a focus, Megan could keep it under control. I hoped.

The portal was large enough to drive a car through its center, the view from the other side coming into sharp focus.

Chaos. Pendergrass's laboratory in shambles. The team battling maaks, wraiths, and larger demons I'd never seen before. They looked like the unholy offspring of bats and mummies, skeletal with black, rotten flesh and no muscle covering their frames. Their arms were wings, the bones that would have been fingers or claws in another creature stretched and connected by leathery membranes.

Foul liquid dripped from their mouths, steaming as it hit the floor and burning Lacey's flesh as she grappled with one. Another splattered toxic saliva around the room without a care for who or what it hit.

One of the maaks screamed in agony, blinded after being hit in the eyes. Alexi clawed at its neck.

Trinity and Sam tag teamed a gaggle of wraiths, one shielding while the other attacked with demon steal.

They flanked D and Pendergrass. My demon held open the portal with one hand while holding Pendergrass's neck with the other. They were under attack, and he still opened the portal. D didn't leave us behind. Cassie's words came back to me.

"That's who he is."

I turned back to face the celestials. "We're going back. I swear that we will send the rest of your people here to safety if we survive."

Judaliel squared her shoulders, transformed into her feathered, eyeball laden form, and unleashed a high-pitched scream. A chorus of celestials joined her, shedding their glamours to reveal winged human-like creatures, strange beasts with the faces of two or more animals and chimeric bodies, tentacled nightmares, and everything in between. Their calls merged with the archangel's, first a cacophonous blend of painful screams and screeches that coalesced into the sound of a heavenly choir.

"Looks like they're coming with," Megan said, holding out her hand. I took it, we dropped our glamours, and together we entered the portal with an army of angels at our backs.

CHAPTER THIRTY-FOUR

Megan and I leapt through the portal. She stabbed a maak that had broken through the team's defenses and had a vise grip on D's shoulder with its sharp teeth. It let go with a howl and turned its attack to my sister. Blood loss slowed it down. Megan would deliver a death blow in short order.

I focused on D. The wound in his massive shoulder gaped and his body trembled with the strain of holding the portal and a struggling Pendergrass.

"You lied to me! Beelzebub is going to slaughter us when he gets here. Let me go!" Pendergrass kicked and writhed as he screamed. He didn't have the reach to land any blows on Demoriel's body, but holding the summoner steady enough to maintain the portal was taking its toll.

I focused my celestial power on conjuring a bandage to cover D's wound and stop the bleeding.

"Thanks," he said in a guttural, demonic voice. "I needed that. Glad you brought reinforcements."

He nodded toward Judaliel, who was busy shooting what looked like laser beams out of her eyes, knocking down bat-winged mummy demons one by one and leaving them to be hacked to pieces by the other angels. A few sustained injuries from acid spit and claws, but no casualties so far.

These demons were no match for an archangel.

Or a hungry battle cat.

Sully emerged from my pocket and grew to the size of lion on steroids. She took flight and attacked a group of maaks that had Lacey surrounded. Together, my partner and my cat disabled and dismembered a group of five.

Sully only ate three. She'd learned her lesson in our last battle and was pacing herself. Smart girl.

"Thanks for the ride back home," I replied. "You good?"

"I'll do for now. Cut down the demons and go find Beelzebub. He's got to be close. Keep him distracted while we get the refugees through the portal. We'll find you and bring the artefact to banish Beelzebub. Stay alive."

"I plan on it," I said. "You do the same."

I spoke to my inner demon wolf, inviting her out to play. Zer growled within me and burst forth in a flurry of phantom claws, fangs, and fur. We ran straight into a line of wraiths, slashing and tearing our way through their ranks. No blood. No meat. Zer wanted to sink her teeth into juicy demon meat and taste sweet, hot blood.

She had her chance when a mummy bat demon blocked our path. It hissed, unhinging its jaws and spraying foul, burning liquid on us. Pain. Heat. Zer lunged, clamping our jaws on the demon's neck and crushing its windpipe. No more pain or heat. Tasted nasty. Not good like maak. Zer wanted maak.

"Later," I said. "We have to get out of here and find Beelzebub."

Zer growled. Wanted to fight. Wanted to rend and tear and feast. Had been so long.

We looked over the battles unfolding around us. Alexi wrestled with the bat demons, his wolf tearing limbs from the beasts. There were too many of them. Seven took turns harrying the wolf, trying to bleed him out or burn him to a crisp. Lacey had her hands full with a pack of wraiths,

Trinity and Sam were fighting the last maaks standing as the dragon demons beat their great wings and attacked from all sides and from the air above.

Sully was too far away to save him.

Zer fought my hold. I was torn between the need to let her loose so she could save our comrade and the knowledge that failing to intercept Beelzebub would kill us all. Megan screamed, running toward Alexi. She didn't have the battle experience or magic to defeat this many demons.

They would overrun her and Alexi both.

"Let me go," Zer said. "I will save them. They are pack. Let me go."

Would Megan want this? What choice did I have? If she lived to hate me forever, at least she'd be alive.

I released the wolf demon Alexi had given me to save my life, missing her presence and strength as she left my body and soul. The tattoos that embodied my demon grafts glowed brightly then faded, lines disappearing just as they had when I'd given Simon his essence back. The loss sent me to my knees.

The phantom wolf hit Megan mid-swing. She dropped her celestial sword as phantom claws, fangs, and fur covered her body. Her gaze went wide with panic. Alexi howled, crushed under the weight of the bat demons who'd brought him to his knees and pummeled him.

Megan closed her eyes and a howl erupted from her throat as she accepted the wolf. Zer and my sister unleashed their fury on the demons, beheading two with claws and biting a third on the neck, breaking it. Alexi caught sight of my sister and the phantom wolf, now her wolf.

He mustered his strength and rose on his back paws, knocking the demons away from him before tearing into the nearest.

They were winning.

"Jane, go!" D yelled. He still held the portal open while terrified celestial refugees fled through it. They would be safe. Everything would be fine as long as I stopped Beelzebub. It was up to me now.

I got to my feet, shaking off the loss of my wolf. I raced toward a large set of double doors, the only exit aside from the tunnel. Beelzebub wouldn't use the tunnels. That was for minions and underlings. If he was coming, he'd come from that direction. I pushed open the door and raced down a dark and seemingly endless corridor.

Eventually, I hit a second set of double doors.

The doors flew open and instead of the Master Demon of Gluttony, I came face to face with Raus. He grinned at me, showing a mouth full of sharp teeth. "Good see you."

His small companions streamed down the corridor, heading for the battle in progress. I stood, stunned.

"How? I thought Sameal stole you from us."

"No," Raus said. "Fight demons."

"Good," I said, grabbing his furry body in a bear hug. "That's good. There are more demons to fight."

I let go and pointed down the corridor. "Go with the rest and help the team. I'm going after Beelzebub."

Raus nodded his giant rodent head and took off after the other rall-maths. I wondered what happened to Sameal, but there was no time to ask. The Angel of Death would be back, or he wouldn't. Didn't matter. Beelzebub's demons were losing, and we'd already weakened him with our previous attack. I had to get to him before he could muster more troops. I ran through the double doors and found myself in another large warehouse space.

Again, what was it with demons and warehouses?

Dim light filled the space from bare bulbs suspended from chains on the ceiling. It was eerily quiet except for heavy footfalls in the shadows opposite where I stood. I conjured a shield and stood my ground, waiting.

Then, he appeared.

Beelzebub, Master Demon of Gluttony, dirty, disheveled, red eyes glowing with rage. A shiver of fear ran down my spine. He held more power than Belphegor, and the next master demon would be stronger still. I didn't want to face him on my own. I wasn't ready. It had taken the whole team to defeat Belphegor.

Just keep him busy until reinforcements arrive...

"Nice of you to show up to the party," I said. "You're a little late. Your demons are dead. You're next if you don't surrender. We'll send you back to hell where you belong. What do you say?"

The demon laughed. Then he started to change into something far more terrifying.

CHAPTER THIRTY-FIVE

"You cost me my business, my infiltrators, and my portal, whelp. Now you'll pay that debt in blood and damnation."

Beelzebub's glamour fell, revealing the master demon in another form.

The Lord of the Flies took his moniker literally. In place of the well-dressed flashy real estate mogul stood an enormous insect that resembled a fly, but with more legs, more eyes, and a maw filled with razor sharp teeth surrounding a long proboscis the size of a spear. His wings were small, but I was certain he could fly high and fast by design or magic.

Terrifying, like something out of a B-movie only very real and very intent on ending my existence.

"How do you like me now, little warrior?"

His loud, metallic voice vibrated through my bones, a weapon in and of itself. The monstrous demon reared, slamming two of his front legs on the ground and piercing the earth with the razor-sharp spikes at the end.

Shit. I couldn't outrun him, assuming I could even break his ward, and I couldn't fight him without a lot more magic or my team or Sully.

My last resort was the ring and the power it would give me.

I wasn't ready to unleash my father's curse again. What if I couldn't control it? All that power would unleash the desire for conquest, especially after battling such a demon as this. I could feel the power clawing at my insides, demanding that I let it out to wreak havoc on the world.

But I wasn't going to just stand there and let him stab me with the pointy blades on the ends of his ugly fly legs. Ugh, what was I supposed to do? Stall for time and hope for a rescue?

Not likely. I was the warrior, and it was time I started acting like one.

Channeling my celestial powers, I conjured a glowing spear and armor. It was more difficult outside the space between, but I managed.

And then I had an idea. A terrible, amazing idea.

"What are you waiting for?" I asked, waving my hands. "I'm fresh out of gold embossed invitations. Let's do this, you worthless, overinflated sack of demon trash."

Beelzebub howled and reared, landing to carve chucks out of the concrete floor beneath us. His eyes were fixed on me with red sparks of angry light dancing in every segment. Sludge shot from his proboscis and landed on the floor, which sizzled and melted as the toxic liquid ate through it.

Acid. Flies vomited on their food and let it digest before sucking it up through that gruesome tube. The monster demon was toying with me like a cat playing with a frightened mouse. He was showing me all the ways he'd maim and torture me before turning me into a mass of goo and eating me.

His physical form would claim my body. His magic would eat my soul.

Oh, no. Not today. Not without a fight.

"Wow, am I supposed to be impressed? I can do that, too."

I spat on the ground and shot a bolt of celestial magic at it, setting the spot where it landed on fire. Then I shoved my spear into the concrete hard enough to fracture the floor into a series of ragged cracks.

The giant demon fly shook with rage and frustration.

That's right. Get good and angry and charge me you big, bad Master Demon.

He just stood there. For crying out loud, did I have to do everything?

I lobbed the spear at him. He dodged, of course, I wouldn't score a lethal hit that easily. But I grazed a couple of his insectoid legs. The demon howled in pain and hissed. Then he charged.

Three, two, one...

I tossed the celestial rope I'd conjured around his neck like a lasso and used a boost of magic to launch myself in the air. I took a swipe to the leg on my way up that burned like hell fire, but I landed on the fly's back. He bucked and kicked his many legs, but I'd settled on a spot he couldn't reach and held onto the rope for life and soul. I'd seen a few rodeos in my day, but I never thought I'd go cowgirl, let alone take a ride on an angry monster fly.

If those cowboys and girls had to work a quarter as hard to stay on their bucking broncos and bulls, they were indeed as tough as old shoe leather.

This wasn't exactly what I'd trained for, but aerial wrestling with Sully helped. I pulled the rope tight as I could, trying to choke the beast, but Beelzebub had apparently trained for this, too, since I wasn't able to leverage the rope past the thick carapace that protected his vulnerable neck.

All I could do was hold on with one hand while spearing with my other.

The leg the monster had swiped had gone from burning to cold and numb. He'd probably poisoned me, or I'd been infected with some awful hell realm bacteria that would eat me alive in short order.

If I didn't get this situation under control ASAP, I'd become a well-tenderized meal for the demon.

A stroke of luck let me spear Beelzebub through one of his muti-faceted eyes. Luckily, he bled red, and the splatter didn't burn me like the goop he shot out of his mouth parts. I reveled in his screams of pain as I pushed harder on the spear and twisted to inflict maximal agony and damage.

It was a bitch to pull my spear out, but worth it when I was able to slice off one of the demon's antennae.

Unluckily, Beelzebub remembered he had wings.

I nearly slid off the giant fly's neck when he shot up into the air. We were confined to the warehouse, but I wouldn't put it past the bastard to break through rafters and roof while breaking every bone in my body.

For now, he settled on pummeling me against every wall, column, and shelf surrounding us. It hurt. Damn, it hurt like hell, leaving me bloody and bruised as I held onto the rope for dear life. The armor protected me from broken bones, but I'd traded cushioning for flexibility and my body was paying the price.

I needed a new strategy.

It hit me then. I was such an idiot. Why hadn't I thought of it in the first place.

Focusing all my concentration and magic, I willed a web of armor to cover Beelzebub's body just as I had for D in the space between. The magic drain was massive and left me on the verge of passing out, but it worked.

Beelzebub crashed to the ground. I managed to jump off his back, avoiding the crushing weight of his body.

But I landed on my injured leg.

I collapsed on the ground in a ball of agony. There was pain, and there was *pain*. I'd never experienced such excruciating pain as this, not even when I'd nearly died. My mind threatened to shut down with my battered body.

No, don't pass out. The armor won't keep Beelzebub down for long.

Right on cue, he rose and shook off the remnants of my celestial armor. I no longer had the strength to hold it. I'd bloodied him and he'd injured himself while slamming me against all of the surfaces he could manage. The giant fly limped slowly forward as gore dripped from what was left of his eyes. It wasn't enough. He was still standing.

I no longer could.

He transformed, shedding the grotesque insectoid body for a tall, thin humanoid demon with red skin, large horns, and pair of impressive wings, his frame covered with wiry muscle. He'd healed. All that damage, all my effort to take him down had been for nothing. Two cold eyes stared at me with hatred and wry amusement.

He'd been playing with me this whole time.

"Nothing to say? Has your wit deserted you along with your strength? I expected a great warrior of myth and legend. Instead, I find a small girl with little magic and no tactical acumen."

He was right, damn him. I was small and lacked the skill and experience to battle plan against such a powerful demon.

Mostly right. I had magic. I just had to muster the courage to use it.

He grabbed the back of my neck and lifted me until we were face to face. I fought to maintain my composure against pain, terror, and a healthy dose of humiliation.

"You fight well for what you are. I'll give you that. You don't merit the death of a worthy opponent, but I find myself a little...regretful that we'll never see what you could have become. Annihilation of those cursed celestials and your race will soften the blow. Your story will be a footnote in the record of the great demon conquest."

I used the last of my strength to reach a trembling hand to my neck, slipping my father's ring on my finger. I grinned and twisted. "The only— footnote—in this...war—will...be...you."

CHAPTER THIRTY-SIX

Nothing happened at first. I almost panicked, but a vision of my hand reaching out to grab Beelzebub by the throat settled my nerves. My brain must be creating a nice little fantasy to help me cope with my impending death at the hands of the demon who'd just kicked my ass six ways to Sunday.

No, this could not be the end. I'd been possessed, abandoned, drafted by the Angel of Death to hunt down and capture rogue demons for more than ten years, nearly died after unleashing a horde of master demons and archangels now loose in Nashville and hell bent on destroying each other and taking humanity with them.

The fate of three worlds rested on my shoulders.

I was mending fences with my mom.

And I had to help my big sis destroy Brad. I'd just started making headway in therapy.

I'd fallen in love after D came back into my life.

No, I would not end like this. Not at the hand of the second lowest ranking master demon from the hell realm. I had too much to live for.

And Beelzebub had really pissed me off.

Wait, why was Beelzebub on the ground? And why was I towering above him. As a five-foot nothing gal with little man's syndrome, I'd been towered over but never towered above anyone over the age of ten. Weird.

What the hell was going on?

Wait, who was screaming? I wish they would stop. I could barely hear myself think.

Something tugged at my mind, trying to wrest control of my thoughts and my body. Oh, holy hell, it was like battling Hannah when I was younger, but worse.

The truth hit me then, and I finally panicked.

I was battling myself, the part of myself that came from my megalomaniac father. I had taken Beelzebub by the neck, and then I'd thrown him to the floor and was stomping on him with my giant, golden-booted feet.

What?

I wanted to stop, but my legs kept moving, kicking the prone and bloody demon beneath my feet as he cried out a word I'd never heard, and yet it called to something deep inside me, to the part of me that had wrested control of my broken and battered body, healed it, and was now using it to exact horrifying revenge on the Master Demon of Gluttony.

"*Shashuningin, tingir, shashuningin, tingir, shashuningin, tingir...*"

He repeated the phrase over and over again until the bloodied mass that had once been his mouth garbled the words into sobs of submission.

The worst part was how I reveled in his pain, his abject degradation and how he begged.

I didn't understand the language, but pleading for mercy needed no translation.

No, this was not me. I was a demon hunter. I had killed demons and banished demons and celestials—in defense of the innocents of all peoples of all realms.

But torture and craving worship? No.

But you did. You tortured your brother-in-law. Admit it. It felt good. It was right. He had it coming. So does this demon who would see you and all you hold dear destroyed.

I clutched my head, trying to shut out the hateful voice. The screaming stopped. In the fight for control of my mind, body, and soul, I'd stopped pummeling the bag of meat that had once been a master demon. This time, he did not shift forms. He didn't heal. He was on the brink of death. I could consume his essence and his power, take his legions, and...

No. I would not.

But think of what you could do with them. You could end this war and bring legions of demons and angels into your service. You could protect the humans who would worship you for your gifts of peace and prosperity.

I could. It would be so easy. All of it would begin here with the defeat of this Beelzebub. After, I would find and slaughter the demon who held Trinity's soul hostage. Brad would live out his days as eunuch in my court, serving me as I ruled and showered my sister and mother with unlimited food, jewels, and luxuries that would make them forget their days of poverty and want.

D would rule at my side, my consort. Not a king. I could not share such power with anyone, not even my beloved.

Wait. No. D was my equal. What the hell was I thinking?

He worships you. He'll follow you to the ends of the universe and do your bidding in gratitude for showing him such favor. All will worship you for the good you'll do. You know best.

Ending world hunger, ushering in an era of peace, making all realms a better place. I could do that. It would be easy.

Yes, but first you must consume this demon and take his power for your own. There are so many like him, even more powerful. Take the power within yourself and be the warrior you were born to be, the hero, the goddess. Take what's yours.

Take what's yours...that was what Beelzebub had promised with Swan Springs. Excess, more, more, and more, a hunger never to be satisfied no matter how much you fed it. It was a lie. Swan Springs was an illusion covering ugliness, death, and destruction.

"You're lying to me," I said to the voice in my head. "I don't want this."

It is your birthright. It is your destiny. You need this power to defeat your enemies. Why won't you embrace it? Feed it and let it fill you.

The thing that had once been Beelzebub, bloody, broken, and whimpering spoke, his voice rasping. "Please, please, have mercy. I did not know it was you. Heal me and I will serve you for all eternity. You are not like your father—you are kind and just. Please, do not leave me to suffer so."

The Master Demon of Gluttony was curled in a fetal position at my feet, a mass of pain, pathetic and begging for mercy. A wave of pity broke through the rush of power surging through me.

What had I done?

I stooped down and looked into his one good eye as tears spilled down my cheeks. "I don't know how to heal you. I don't know what I am, what my father was, or how to control all this power. All I know is that it's wrong. I'm sorry. I'm so very sorry."

"Do not...weep. I forgive you, benevolent one. Please, end my suffering, daughter of Anu."

Anu. My father's true name. I'd heard it, read about him in books about the earliest human civilizations. The Sumerians called him a god, one of three and by most accounts supreme among them.

That was my legacy.

Beelzebub didn't really believe I was benevolent or worthy of worship. My power lied to him, too. How horrible to adore the instrument of your destruction. I couldn't save him, but I would honor his request.

I pulled back the power deep within myself and assumed my true form. I came back to myself and all the injuries I sustained fighting Beelzebub. I hadn't beheld the creature I'd become when I gave into my father's magic, and I was glad of it. That wasn't me. I decided who and what I would be. Until and unless I learned to resist the urge to become the beautiful monster the power promised, I would lock it away. When it tempted me, I promised to remember this moment.

Suddenly, Beelzebub shuddered and began to transform. Grotesque black boils covered his body and roiled beneath what was left of his skin. I gagged as the smell of rotting meat spilled from the demon's body and shivered at the sudden burst of cold air coming from the demon. An unearthly sound came from what was left of his mouth, like claws on stone. The noise thundered through my skull until I thought it would split in two. So loud. I covered my ears and backed away. The clawing gradually transformed to a low, vibrating sound like the beating of thousands of wings.

Buzzing.

The body on the ground burst into a sea of flies that shot into the air and then hurtled toward me.

The bastard had been faking it! He wasn't dying. He was still trying to kill me.

I conjured celestial armor and a helmet with a face guard, the mesh too small for the insects assaulting me to penetrate. If they got through, they'd enter my nose and mouth, filling my lungs to suffocate me.

Instead, they covered my body, weighing me down as heat penetrated my armor. Sweat ran down my temples, back, and over my body as the temperature rose. If they couldn't suffocate me, the damned flies would cook me alive.

No. I would not die like this. And I would not tap into my father's power again. The Master Demon of Gluttony would not turn me into a power-hungry force of mass destruction. I wasn't like him.

I was who I chose to be.

Two could play his game. I collapsed on the ground and made my body shake. Using Mara's gift of glamour, I willed my armor to appear as melted and patchy, exposing blistered and blackened flesh. I imagined my body devoid of skin, my hair gone, scalp bloody and burning. A scent like burning bacon filled my nostrils. I screamed. Didn't have to fake that. I cried out in anger, frustration, and with all the pain I had endured since my father had infected me with Haniel, robbing me of my childhood. I unleashed grief at the loss of Cassiel, the brave celestial who sacrificed her life to save her fellow celestials.

If Beelzebub hadn't taken the celestial refugees as they fled to freedom, Cassie would be alive, free, and working to end this war in the making.

How many had Beelzebub murdered and enslaved during his eons of existence. Hundreds of thousands? Millions?

Then I cried out in true agony as the heat became almost unbearable. I held my breath, waiting and willing the demon to believe he'd killed me. If he would just let go and admire his work, maybe even gloat...

Don't pass out.

Don't pass out.

Don't pass out!

My strength was failing. The flies writhed and crawled along my body. Their tiny legs pricked at my armor, stabbing with enough force to bruise. It hurt. I hurt all over.

At last, the weight lifted from my body and blessed coolness washed over me. I looked through my glamour and saw Beelzebub assume his humanoid form. He conjured a flaming sword and prepared to swing.

Fighting through injury and agony, I leapt to my feet, letting my glamour fall.

I pulled out my demon steel knife and slid it across Beelzebub's throat.

The demon howled in surprise and agony, dropping his sword. I gripped my black mirror and chanted the incantation I had used to summon Haniel while Beelzebub clawed at his neck, infusing all my power into the summoning.

Beelzebub's body turned to wisps of black smoke, swirling dust that slammed into my black mirror with enough force to knock me flat on my back.

Pain and terror caught up with me. I curled into a ball on the hard concrete floor and cried until exhaustion pulled me under.

CHAPTER THIRTY-SEVEN

I woke up with a jolt. I expected to feel excruciating pain and cold, hard concrete. Instead, I was surrounded by soft bedding and fur. Sully was sprawled over my torso, asleep and purring up a storm.

"Hey, cat," I said, carefully lifting my arm to stroke her soft head. She opened one eye and stared at me, her gaze unfocused.

Then she opened both eyes, dug her claws into my flanks, and took off, flying out the door. I realized I was in my quarters at HQ, in my bed, and not dead or even injured, apparently. I'd survived.

And if I was here, my team had won.

Mom and Megan burst through the door and initiated a group hug that shocked me back to reality. I was alive. Somehow, we'd survived, and we'd won. Pulling back, I took Megan's hands in mine and said, "I'm so, so sorry. There was no other way to save Alexi, and Zer wanted to fight and save her packmate. I didn't have time to ask you if it was okay, I—"

Megan cut me off by pulling me tight against her chest, cradling me and rocking back and forth. Tears ran down my cheeks and my nose ran. Ugh. I was snot-crying, the ugly cry that gave you a headache and made your nose stuffy for hours.

So. Totally. Worth it.

"It's okay," Megan said. "More than okay. Zer and I are getting along great, and she's a terrific battle partner."

I pushed away from my sister and pulled my T-shirt up to wipe my eyes and nose.

"Stop that," Mom said, yanking my shirt down. She handed me several tissues, waiting patiently while I blew my nose, caught my breath, and pulled myself together.

"You're nob mad ab me?" The stuffy nose and hoarse voice sucked. I sounded as pathetic as I felt.

Megan grinned. "Of course not. I mean, you had a demon wolf and a demon cat, which was so totally not fair. Hoarding animals isn't nice, and neither is holding out on your big sister."

I laughed. She had a point.

"Before you ask," Mom said. "Everyone is fine. The team suffered some injuries, minor compared to yours." There was a note of steel in her voice. She didn't like me getting hurt. Mom understood that it was an occupational hazard, but she didn't like it.

That was okay. It was kind of nice having my mom worry over me.

"The refugees?" I asked.

"Safely in their pocket realm. They took the rallmaths with them. Raus sends his love and thanks."

I wished I had been able to say goodbye, but I understood. D couldn't hold the portal open indefinitely. Maybe I would see him again someday. If they let me visit, I'd be sure to bring him some jerky and ice cream.

A deep, dark, and very welcomed voice set my heart aflutter. "Beelzebub, his wraiths, and Soriella are back where they belong. Trinity banished them after the battle."

I jumped out of the bed, nearly knocking my mother and sister over, and flew into D's arms. I never wanted to let him go, my brave, beautiful demon. Whatever form he wore, whatever powers he wielded, it didn't matter. Sure, he was messed up and had daddy issues and a great big chip on his shoulder, but I did, too. We matched that way.

"What are you laughing about?" he asked, planting a kiss on my head.

"I was just thinking about how the crazy in me acknowledges and cherishes the crazy in you."

"We are quite a pair, aren't we? But you beat back your crazy. You didn't give in and unleash your father's power on Beelzebub. You did the right thing. It's who you are."

I'm glad he believed in me. I wasn't sure there for a minute. But it didn't matter. "You kept your inner master demon in line. Guess we're cleared for field work, then."

"Not yet."

D and I broke apart and assumed battle stances, our blades drawn. Sameal stood in the doorway, arms crossed and...smiling. The bastard never smiled. Loomed, grimaced, glared, menaced, sure, but smiled?

I didn't trust it for a second. Hell, I didn't trust *him* for a second.

I sheathed my blade, crossed my arms and glared at him. "You're not the boss of me. Trinity's in charge. And where were you when we were all fighting demons?"

Sameal cursed under his breath, lowered his head and pinched the bridge of his nose. Maybe I'd finally pushed him off the cliff of sanity and into the abyss of madness. Or irreversible exasperation. I wasn't sure what that would do to the balance of life and death. "I was fighting the demons who didn't get to your team. You would not have survived their onslaught. Neither would the rallmaths."

"He's not lying," Boice said, strolling into the room with a plate of sandwiches, Sully perched on his shoulder. "We fought with him."

Roice followed his brother, a tray full of glasses filled with what looked like lemonade. "Yeah, you all would have been in a world of hurt if we didn't stop the worst demons."

"Worse than those mummified bat things?" I asked.

Boice frog marched me back to the bed and made me sit down. Then he handed me a sandwich. Roice made me wash down the first bite with fresh squeezed lemonade. They repeated the process, refusing to answer any questions or let me talk until I'd eaten. I scarfed down three loaded club sandwiches and three glasses of lemonade. How long had I been out? I must've burned a lot of calories as I healed.

"Those were Garkanneths, and you're not far off the mark. Nasty creatures," Roice said, shuddering. "Sometimes, when strong warrior demons die, their master demon leaders preserve their bodies and turn them into what you called mummified bat things. They do plenty of damage but they're just as likely to hit the master demon's warriors or each other as the enemy."

Undead demons. Ick. What could be worse?

"Anyway," Boice said, picking up his brother's train of thought as he often did. The thing about twins and their special connection extended to the demon realm. It was like they were two halves of the same person—demon—sometimes. "We were fighting Xellmoren. Similar destructive capabilities but without the mindlessness. Going to have to add combat training for them to our exercises."

Great. Just what we needed. "Who found me? I need to know who to thank."

The team, including the rest who'd gathered inside my room, shifted nervously, and didn't look at me. Trinity and Sam were noticeably absent. What the hell?

Oh, no. No, no, no, no, no.

"It was him, wasn't it?" I said flatly, pointing at Sameal. Son of bitch. Now I owed the Angel of Death, and I had no doubt he'd take full advantage of it. Whatever. He'd done it to stop the war. It was business. Sameal had no more love for me than I had for him.

I could do this. It would suck, but I could be gracious and courteous, professional even. I swallowed the lump of sandwich lodged in my throat, nearly choking, and said, "Thank you."

Instead of gloating or demanding I grovel and bow—which is something I would have done in his position—he simply nodded. Maybe, just maybe, I could learn to work with him again. I'd never trust him or even like him, but he'd proven himself useful. So long as our agendas aligned, that was good enough for me.

But I'd never work *for* him again.

"Where's Trin?" I asked, braced for a fight about who was currently in charge of our team.

"Personal leave," Sameal said. "I believe she's visiting family and taking care of some legal paperwork." The Angel of Death waved his hand dismissively. I wasn't fooled. She was putting her affairs in order so she could pay her debt to Marbas by entering his service. The fool would sacrifice herself, and Sam, to keep the ward around Nashville intact.

I'd been doing a lot of thinking about that. I needed to do a bit of research, but I had the beginnings of a plan.

"Boice, did you get that research request I sent you?"

The tech demon looked offended. "Already done. Figured you'd be looking into Aeshma."

I smirked at him, passing my empty glass for a lemonade refill. "Already done." The Master Demon of Wrath would no doubt represent a bigger challenge than our first two demons. Unless, of course, you followed the Catholic order of the seven deadly sins. Maybe this demon would be on par with Beelzebub. If so, we had the fighting skills to take them on.

The mind games were another matter entirely. Belphegor's strategy was mind control and was the reason I still had nightmares and PTSD. Dr. Khatri should probably lead the missions so she could look out for warning signs. Infighting would be the death of us if we weren't careful, especially if Aeshma had the power to possess one or more of us.

Boice gave me a funny look before handing over a folder. I'd study it later when I had some quiet and privacy. And I needed some insider information from Sameal. It would put me deeper in his debt, but that would be a small price to pay.

"I'm a little sleepy," I said, feigning a yawn. "Think I'll get some more R and R before diving into work." I tucked the folder into a drawer beside my bed like it was no big deal. The others must've bought it since they offered hugs and good wishes before filing out of my room Sully stayed, of course.

"Hey, Sameal, you got a minute?" I asked, trying my best to sound sheepish. I hoped the rest of the team would think I was going to bite the bullet and offer a bigger apology in private. Mom smiled at me as if proud.

If she only knew.

Megan patted my head and let Zer flash in her eyes. I missed the wolf, but she'd found her home in my sister. I'd rest easier knowing Megan had another tool in her arsenal. And it would give Alexi an excuse to spend more time with her. Not that I was matchmaking or anything.

I would never dream of doing such a thing.

Before she left, I realized there were a few other things I didn't know. "Hey, what happened to Brad?"

My sister flashed an evil grin. "Brad is currently 'volunteering' in the pocket realm. We'll let him out in a day or so and send him back to his regular life. It was that or send him to the hell or celestial realm. In exchange, I'll sign divorce papers uncontested. And I get half the assets."

A few hours? Holy time warp, that would be a long, long time in the pocket realm. Lots of time for Brad to reflect on his life choices, his privilege, and time to get his hands dirty doing some manual labor.

I hoped they had him mucking out stalls for the charoum and shoveling giant barrels full of celestial pig shit.

Unlike Megan, Brad had grown up wealthy and spoiled. Blue collar and so-called menial jobs were beneath him.

A wide grin spread across my face. "Nice. A bit of karmic justice that won't cost him any time in earth terms. But how do we know he won't go find another master demon to serve?"

"He didn't mean to serve Beelzebub," Megan said. I was about to scold her for defending him, but she held up a hand. "Strictly business. His greed got the better of him. He's been terrified of demons since he learned about them. That's why the threat of a trip to the hell realm worked so well."

Ah. He understood that if he broke his word, we'd be sending him on a one-way trip using the Sigillum Dei. Yup. That was one hell of a deterrent.

Sameal had been standing just inside the door waiting patiently. Wasn't sure how long it would last, so I hugged Megan and shooed her out of the room, shutting the door behind her. I raised an eyebrow at

Sameal. He nodded and a ward crawled along the walls, floors, and ceiling of my room. I was getting better at seeing them.

It was my father's power. Now that I'd let it out to play, it had a firmer hold on me. I decided to treat it like Haniel when she possessed me. The power and I made a truce and a compromise. It would hold itself and its conquest and ruling tendencies in check.

In exchange. I would let it out to play again. Soon. Anticipation surged through me at the thought, and I wasn't sure if it was the power's lust for battle or my own.

"I know what you want," Sameal said, sitting down on my bed. I joined him. "It won't be easy."

"Nothing worth doing ever is. The biggest challenge will be opening a portal. Can't use the Sigillum Dei. Not if I want to come back, and I have to come back."

The Angel of Death gave me an odd look, as if I'd confused him. How on earth was that possible. Of course I needed a portal that I could use to travel back to earth. It wasn't like I was expected to save the world because a stupid grimoire said it was up to me or anything.

Wait a minute. Hold the phone. Of course he was confused. He knew I would come back. He knew I would survive my new secret mission just like he'd known I would survive every single mission I'd ever taken including the one that led to the great demon and celestial escape.

I was such an idiot.

"You know when I'm going to die, and it isn't going to be in the hell realm," I said, accusingly. I stood and pointed my finger at him. "You've always known. That's why you left us to go fight archangels and save rallmaths and do whatever other shit you've been doing."

Sameal leaned back on the bed, putting his hands behind his head and making himself comfy-womfy while I reeled at the implications. Sully hissed and swatted at him before flying off the bed and landing on my shoulder.

How dare he. I was in the middle of an existential crisis, and he was chillaxing like he didn't have a care in the world.

I was so tempted to let Sully eat him.

"Took you long enough to figure it out," he said. "Your mother and sister already asked me for reassurance. Not about their demises, oddly enough. No, they're worried about you."

Of course they were. My family cared about me. Not the demon hunter, not the warrior with the power of three realms, not the protector of earth, but me, Jane McGee, daughter, sister, beloved.

"Demoriel knew better than to ask, "Sameal said "I wouldn't share the day of your death with your family or with you—"

"I wouldn't ask," I said. "I don't want to know. Don't ever tell me."

He smiled. "You're smarter than you act. As far as the portal, we cannot trust Damien Pendergrass to send you where you wish to go. Left to his own devices, he would deliver you to Belial's doorstep. I assume you do not wish to involve Belial's son, your paramour?"

Who talked like that? Paramour? D was many things to me. Best friend, fighting partner, confidant, lover, companion, shelter in the storm of life, but paramour just sounded so skeevy.

That was beside the point, though.

"No, I don't want to involve D. He wouldn't let me go, or worse, he'd try to follow me. It's too risky for him. Sully's on board," I said, petting my cat. "She can guard my back and be my guide."

"What will you bargain for?" Sameal asked.

"Leave that to me. Can you get me there or not?"

Sameal nodded. "Cooper may be able to pull it off, but he'll need more magic than is currently available to him for the portal to remain open. You can't power it if you mean to go through it. We'll need someone with power to open it to get you there and for the return trip."

I wanted to ask why he couldn't do it, but he held up a hand and said, "My portals are one way and normally reserved for souls of the deceased bound for other realms. Powering the kind that you need is, as you say, out of my wheelhouse. But I know someone who might be willing to help."

"Okay," I said. "How do I find this someone?"

Sameal grinned, a dark, feral expression. "Don't worry. The someone will find you."

CHAPTER THIRTY-EIGHT

Phantom beings flew over city buildings, weaving in and out of clouds as people on the ground pointed and then began to flee in terror. Lightening flashed, revealing an enormous creature that resembled a white wingless dragon as it emerged from the clouds. The dragon unleashed an earth-shattering roar as its silky fur blew in the wind.

Fire shot from its mouth burning a straight line down Broadway as smaller versions of the dragon stampeded through the streets, trampling over pedestrians, throwing cars, scooters, and motorcycles into the air.

The vehicles fell to the ground in piles of burning metal and slammed into buildings. Bridgestone Arena collapsed as the white dragon flew over and kicked the dome with a massive hoof.

From the wreckage, a lone woman emerged, her cheek smeared with blood and soot, her red curly hair circling her head like a flaming crown. She held a sword in one hand and a battle axe in the other and her freckled face held a look that promised murder to the creatures who'd dared to invade her city.

She rose in the air without the aid of wings, driven by magic and vengeance. With a battle cry worthy of a highland warrior, she charged, clashing with the front paws of the white dragon. The dragon's swipe missed, and she flew under its body, slashing the creature's vulnerable underbelly with her blade before flying back over the dragon and decapitating it with her axe.

The dragon's body dropped from the sky as a few brave—or foolish—onlookers cheered the heroine on.

More warriors armed with spears, blades, claws, and fangs emerged, hacking the smaller dragon-like creatures to pieces as their red-haired leader shielded fleeing innocents as they took cover.

All the while, an epic soundtrack kept beat with the battle and cheers from the audience.

I grabbed another handful of popcorn and shoved them in my face.

Dissolving in a fit of belly laughs would ruin the experience for my fellow movie goers.

Boice and Roice, lacking manners and impulse control, were howling with laughter in the seats beside me. "Holy shit! Those aren't dragons, they're charoum. Downtown Nashville is under attack from killer sheep!"

Lacey, who sat behind them, leaned over and whacked the twins upside the head. Apparently, she took offense to the boys' critique of her girlfriend's film.

Mara had really outdone herself. *Red Raven and the Devils* was blockbuster, breaking box office records and shining a spotlight on Music City. Somehow, the succubus and her indie studio backer had cobbled together a superhero film that was a feast for the senses. Our team's actual battles were featured throughout the movie, and we all squealed with delight when we saw our characters on the giant Imax screen.

Lacey was the star.

The actress who played her character captured Lacey's spirit and fighting style perfectly. Mara would have accepted no less. Simon was her side kick, a phantom raven that served as her eyes and ears. Mara had been just as generous with the actors who played the rest of the team.

The actress who played yours truly was also five foot nothing and still kicked ass.

And she got to romance the tall, dark, mysterious vigilante who looked an awful lot like my own demon sweetheart.

D pushed up the armrest of his theater seat and put an arm around me. I sighed. An honest-to-goodness real date with my love, and I had my teammates and best friends in tow. Trinity and Sam critiqued the fight scenes, making notes for future training sessions.

Alexi sat next to Megan, sharing popcorn and quiet conversation.

Mara beamed, watching Lacey enjoy her work.

Cooper somehow managed to bring his cadejo under the guise of a service dog, glamour hiding his wings and otherworldly features. Archimedes looked the part, sleek and well-behaved. Cooper also smuggled Ricky the fox into the theater by hiding her under his trench coat. He slipped the demon dog and fox popcorn and bits of corndog as they peeked out between seats. The critters freaking loved earth's entertainment options and hogged the big screen television at HQ when they visited.

Sully had curled up on my lap and gone to sleep, clearly bored with the action on the screen. Or maybe it was the extra-large pizza we'd fed her before coming to the theater. Our team and several local demons and celestials took up three rows of theater seats. No one noticed my kitty.

I put my head on D's shoulder and said, "I could get used to this."

He chuckled. "Being on the silver screen?"

"No," I said, snuggling closer. "Popcorn, date nights, a few slices of peace and quiet and normal."

The scene had shifted. Red Raven was now indoors, walking down a dark corridor as ominous music played. She was alone except for the phantom raven perched on her shoulder, her footfalls the only sounds. The camera panned to a cell, plexiglass and magic the only thing separating our heroine from the terror inside. The magic of the wards glowed. Mara's CGI team had managed to get the weave of the multilayered ward just right.

The humans in the audience had no idea how right, thank goodness.

Most sat on the edges of their seats, anticipation painted on their rapt faces. Others snuggled with their dates or chattered in low whispers, critiquing the plot, special effects, and talking about how hot the redhead or giant blonde Russian were.

Some scrolled on their phones.

Others sat with smiles on their faces as they watched their kids get hooked on superhero films, where good always prevailed and kept everyone safe from unspeakable evil.

D caught me looking and smiled. "Yeah. A little peace and quiet is good for the soul."

It wasn't over. We have five more master demons on the loose and more archangels plotting against them with earth caught in the crossfire. Hell of a job. But we did it because of people like those in the theater, so they could go about their lives. Those lives weren't always peaceful. Wars still raged between humans. Daily life held its own personal hellish horrors for far too many. Disease, famine, misery—they plagued earth and always would.

But these rare moments of respite and joy were worth fighting for.

Unfortunately, this moment of respite and joy were interrupted by an unholy amount of soda hitting my bladder.

I wiggled out of D's embrace. Mara squealed. "Jinx, don't go. You're about to miss the best part!"

"Sorry, Mara. Nature calls. I'll catch it at the next showing."

We had tickets for five consecutive showings to make sure all the local supernatural residents of Nashville had the chance to see the film. I'd plan my bathroom breaks accordingly.

I rose from my seat and crept to the aisle. My height, or rather, lack thereof, meant I didn't block anyone's view. The bathroom wasn't far. I went in, did my business, and stood at the sink. It was one of those automatic numbers and I couldn't get the water to run without doing a series of bizarre hand motions that made me look like I was casting a spell. At last, I managed to get enough water flow to rinse my hands.

Opting for paper towels rather than the noisy and potentially germ-laden air dryer, I mopped up the water and checked my reflection in the mirror to see if anything was out of place. Another woman entered the bathroom, hoodie down low so I couldn't see her face. How she could see where she was going was beyond me.

Oh, wow. I was turning into one of those kids-these-days people. No. Nope. I was far too young for that. If this was the current fashion, I'd have to invest in more hoodies. Could work well for low profile or incognito missions when I didn't want to tap into my magic reserves for glamour.

Why wasn't she going into a stall?

Her hoodie was still down, so checking hair and makeup was out. She didn't strike me as the makeup type, though, with plain khakis that fit as loosely as the hoodie. The clothes swallowed her. Maybe she was an awkward teen and was waiting for me to leave.

Ugh, hopefully she wouldn't hit me with some weird-as-hell Gen Alpha skibidi toilet nonsense.

Boy did that ever make me feel old.

What if she was trans? I gathered myself to go with a plan to stand outside the bathroom until she came out in case anyone gave her trouble.

"You need to come with me."

I spun around. No phone, and no other people in the bathroom. Baggy khaki babe had to be talking to me.

"Excuse me?" I asked.

"You need to come with me if you want to go to the hell realm. Now."

Holy crap. Already? I expected it to take Sameal more time to make arrangements. I had my go-bag of supplies with me, heavily glamoured to look like a purse. I'd been carrying it since I spoke with the Angel of Death.

I wouldn't have time to explain what I was doing or where I was going.

No time to say goodbye.

D would be mad. I'd left him a long letter. I'd left letters for the rest of my teammates, my sister, and Mom, promising that I'd be back. Sameal would reassure them and make sure none of the team tried to follow me. They needed to stay put and get ready to battle Aeshma and protect earth while I was away.

And in case anyone, meaning Trinity, got the bright idea to use the Sigillum Dei to sacrifice herself, I'd taken it from the vault and entrusted it to Sameal.

I never thought I'd see the day I would entrust anything to my former boss. Strange times.

"Okay. I need my cat." Going back in the theater to get her would raise suspicions. I'd have to get her attention somehow and convince her to sneak out. Did we have time to stop by concessions for a personal pepperoni pizza?

"She's here," the woman said, pointing behind me.

"Prrrbt! Ink takes Sully home." She flew around the bathroom, purring and rolling in the air in excitement. Poor baby. Of course she missed her home. I hoped she would come back with me. From what Cooper told me, motiaummerrs stayed with their mothers for six months or so before kitty mama booted them out so she could find a new mate and have another litter. But female offspring often reunited with their mothers when they themselves were old enough to mate, living in colonies and helping one another raise the next generations.

Would Sully want to find a mate and have kittens?

Maybe. We'd cross that bridge when we came to it. In the meantime, I was glad I wasn't going it alone.

"Come with me," my mysterious companion said. A woman of few words. That was okay. I had enough on my mind without being forced to make small talk with a stranger.

"Lead the way."

My companion drove us to Percy Warner Park. Looked like we were going to fire up Cooper's portal. How we would keep Cooper out of the loop wasn't my problem. I doubted he'd try and stop me. I could explain it all to him and he'd probably pat me on the back, wish me luck, and send me off with homemade granola.

Walking to the portal site in the dark was a bitch, especially since my companion didn't bring a flashlight and wouldn't conjure any magical light source. I'd turned off my phone. No doubt D and the others were calling to find out where I was and what I was up to.

"Shit," I yelped, tripping over a root. "You know, I'd like to make it to the hell realm without a twisted ankle."

"Shh," she scolded. "We must not be seen or heard."

"Oh, are we on a clandestine mission?" I whispered. "No shit. But it won't matter if we're heard or seen if I'm out of commission."

"She said you'd be difficult," my companion muttered. "We can heal you before you go."

I still hadn't figured out what she was. Pulling out my glowing demon steel knife would "blow our cover" and we couldn't have that. For all I knew, she could be a cyclops or one of the weird Fae creatures running around Nashville after immigrating to the U.S.

"Can you carry me?" I asked, groaning. My companion was as catfooted as Sully. Maybe she had night vision. I'd had that when sharing my body with Haniel. It was one of the advantages I sorely missed.

Sully, bless her, grew large enough to grab me with her paws and lifted me off the ground just enough to avoid tripping. That's what a real ally did. And who the hell had told this chick that I was difficult? I hadn't had that many dealings with celestials. Maybe she cavorted with demons, too. Plenty of troublemakers in the Nashville demon refugee populations didn't like me.

Not my fault. They broke the rules, I hauled them in.

At last, we arrived at the clearing. My companion finally deigned to conjure some light so we could see the world's ugliest tree with twisted limbs, a decided lack of symmetry, and a lot of holes.

One of those holes was a portal.

Sameal stepped into the clearing. He must have disabled the wards designed to keep out demons. Either that, or the Angel of Death got a pass.

No, the ward had to be down. Otherwise, my demon-grafted self wouldn't be able to enter the clearing and get to the portal. One of the large holes glowed. I couldn't make out anything on the other side yet, but with more magic I'd get my first glimpse of the hell realm before plunging in.

I'd done my homework, studying maps of the known regions—known by people on earth. But the information was second hand. As far as we knew, no living human had ever traveled to the hell realm and come back to share their experiences. Most of what we knew came from accounts recorded by summoners from the demons they encountered. Cooper knew about the flora and fauna, but he wasn't a people person on the best of days.

I knew a little from things the twins and D had shared. The landscape and animals were not unlike earth, but generally bigger, weirder, and more dangerous. There was a lot of brimstone. If peaceful relations were ever established between earth and the hell realm, demons could do good business trading sulfur.

I didn't expect tall structures outside of master demons' kingdoms. The realm ran primarily on magic and horsepower. I'd have to travel on foot or on Sully. But my magic would be easier to access and use in the demon realm. The goal was to avoid being seen by demons in the remote areas through which I would be traveling so I could save my magic to bargain with Marbas.

Get in. Strike a bargain for Trinity's freedom that didn't involve withdrawing the protective ward around the city. Then get out.

Easy, right?

"Are you ready?" Sameal asked.

"As I'll ever be. Is Miss Congeniality here going to power the portal? I pointed to baggy khaki babe—her fault for not introducing herself.

"No," Sameal said, lifting his chin to someone behind me. "She is."

I turned around and nearly fell on my ass.

"I thought you were dead!" I yelled, running toward the celestial and tackling her in a bear hug. It surprised both of us. At first, I thought she would just stand there awkwardly while I squeezed her glamoured form.

Eventually, she put her arms around me, lifting me up and swinging me around like proud parent swings a child.

"I'm alive, and not much the worse for wear," she said, her aged voice matching her grandma glamour. The strength of her embrace shattered that illusion. "And you saved my people. It is a debt I can never repay, but from now until the end of your days or mine, I swear to serve you."

She released me and made a low bow. Wow. Had she really been a grandma, she would have killed her back to get lower than me. I yanked her up. "Stop that. No bowing, no swearing servitude or paying debts. I would have done it no matter what."

"I know," she said. "If not my service, I shall swear to loyalty, allyship, and above all, honesty."

I could live with that.

"So, you're going to magic the portal. Without the Sigillum Dei?"

"Yes," she said. "Surviving the ordeal in the tunnels imbued me with greater power. Enough to transport you to the hell realm. And I'll be here to see you safely home. You and your Sully. Be careful. Remember who and what you are. I wish you good fortune, Jinx McGee. With all my heart."

"I will. By the way, how did you survive the tunnel collapse?"

She smiled a small, secret smile. "That is a tale for another day."

A burst of magic shot out of Cassiel and into the portal. The portal grew, showing a forested landscape with small billows of smoke rolling in the background. Demon dwellings. Of course. No mechanical heating units. They used fire. Good thing I knew how to start one the old-fashioned way.

"The water is safe to drink," Sameal said. "Beware of berries and growing things. You should have enough food for a week. If you need more, the motiaummerr will hunt for you. Follow her lead and stay out of sight. If the wrong demon spots you, Belial will send his legions to the ends of the realm to find and capture you."

I gulped. That was the greatest risk. But saving Trinity would be worth it.

"You are a most unusual human, Jane Aurelia McGee," Sameal said. For once, it sounded like a compliment. "Safe travels. We shall meet again this side of the universe."

I nodded, unsure what to say. With a deep breath and a prayer, Sully and I stepped into the portal and into the depths of hell.

***

Thank you for reading! Did you enjoy? Please add your review because nothing helps an author more and encourages readers to take a chance on a book than a review.

Don't miss more of the Jinx McGee series coming soon, and check out the Soul Broker from D. B. Sieders with <u>WAKING THE DEAD</u>

Find all the details about D. B. Sieders including a bonus chapter from Sully's point of view at www.dbsieders.com

You can also sign up for the City Owl Press newsletter to receive notice of all book releases!

SNEAK PEEK OF WAKING THE DEAD

The sound of the crash struck her first.

Her tires screeched after she slammed on the brakes, barely missing the blue Sentra in front of her. It had one of those "Choose Life" stickers plastered on its left bumper, the smiling infant illuminated by the red of taillights.

The image still burned in her brain as she made a sharp left.

Her car fishtailed. She registered more squealing tires and the shriek of metal on metal signaling impact. Her heartbeat hammered above the clamor all around.

Breathe in, breathe out. The car stopped dead. But how?

Am I hit? Did I hit someone? Her airbag hadn't deployed, but the pain in her left shoulder let her know her seatbelt had gotten a workout. *Breathe, focus, look around!* Darkness had already swallowed much of the summer evening twilight's soft glow, but there was still enough light to make out her surroundings. *I'm off the road and half in a ditch, but I think I'm okay. I'm okay. I'm okay. God, what happened?*

There had been an impact. She'd felt it, heard it, but what had she hit? The car in front of her?

With a deep breath, she leaned forward with caution and peered into the ditch. The Sentra had landed in the narrow end of the gorge several feet away from danger. Its driver wrestled with his door, wedged against the side of the trench. When it didn't budge, he gave up, scooted over, and climbed out of the passenger door. Vivian's car teetered over a deeper part of the ditch. She couldn't see them, but knew jagged boulders lurked at the bottom below her front tires. She knew the road well.

It was close to home.

She managed to shift into park with a shaky hand, her right leg cramped from maintaining pressure on the brake. *Get up! Get out!* She turned off the ignition, wincing in pain, and shifted in her seat to remove her seatbelt. Unsure exactly how far her car lurched over the ditch's edge, she moved slow and easy, exiting the vehicle and closing the door. She clicked the automatic door locks and put her keys into her pocket out of habit. Shock and the surreal quality of the unfolding events kept her running on autopilot. The urge to move, to act, forced her to her feet. If she could breathe, she could move. If she could move, she could function. If she could function, she'd be all right.

Judging from the commotion further up the road, someone else involved in the accident was far from all right.

Her feet carried her away from her car and toward the small but growing crowd. The acrid stench of smoke, gas, and burnt rubber assaulted her. The glare of headlights hurt her eyes. She walked forward, ignoring the other spectators who ignored her in turn. Their chatter remained distant—conversations and comfort, tears and terrified mutterings, men and women speaking all around to one another.

No one spoke to Vivian. She spoke to no one.

Sirens wailed in the distance. She walked along the periphery of the crowd, grateful to go unnoticed so she could concentrate and just keep moving. A low rumble of dread gnawed at her gut, warning her to stop, but her legs refused to obey.

Time seemed disjointed, slowing, then skipping like a damaged film reel. She looked back at her car and realized she'd been inches from oblivion. *If I hadn't stopped when I did...if the guy behind me hadn't....* Any sooner, she'd have been rear-ended and launched full into the ditch. A moment later, her car would've been crumpled between the Sentra and the F-350 behind her. But she'd hit the Sentra, hadn't she?

No, no damage to the rear of the vehicle, and her front bumper remained intact, as far as she could tell from the distance. How had she stopped? Shifting her gaze to the F-350, Vivian saw it from the side now, the black truck adorned with a custom flame job painted across the doors and bed. The brawny owner inspected the body for damage. Flecks of dried mud and grime rose from the undercarriage and dulled the flares above. The vehicle's powerful bulk was adapted to rough terrain, like its owner. She and her sleek sedan were not. They'd all been going at least 35, maybe 40 miles an hour. She had to look away. Disaster had come so close.

I should've been knocked into that ditch. How did I miss it?

Shivering, she caught a flash of white in the periphery, but when she turned, it was gone, departing along with the warm breeze that swept in out of nowhere and chased the odd chill that surrounded her away. Infused with energy and a strange sense of urgency, she shook off the remnants of unease and continued.

She had to keep moving.

Another man lumbered across the street toward the crowd. He moved in the long shadows cast by the setting sun, looking from side to side and peering over his shoulder. He seemed as intent on his journey as Vivian was on hers, but unlike the other onlookers, he at least spared her a nod before moving along. Well, she thought he had. The dark green ball cap he wore shielded his eyes, and thus his intent, but he kept walking in the same direction. No one else paid him any mind.

When she turned back to face her destination, she saw what remained at ground zero of the evening's terror. The poor soul in that twisted and crumpled wreckage before her hadn't been so lucky. No one could walk away from this crash.

She took two steps closer. Smoke rose from the damaged engine, along with the occasional spark. Everyone around her stayed back. A man's hand emerged from the driver's side window, along with a soft groan. Another step closer and she heard his ragged breathing.

Vivian took one more step, close enough for her arm to brush the car's cooling frame. She met his stare through the window.

Oh dear God, no.

Her gaze burned a path from his face down to his torso, and then she had to look away from what remained of his body below the waist. The mangled steering column and dashboard covered much of the damage, but not quite enough. *He'll never walk again. He'll be paralyzed. If he took a blow to the head, he'll be a vegetable.*

Vivian's pulse raced. Her hands and fingers went numb.

He'd be better off dead.

Fighting the wave of revulsion, she took one more step toward the car. Every nerve in her body screamed for her to run away, to leave this *thing* that used to be a man and never look back. This was his nightmare, not hers.

She had already lived one of her own.

With palpable effort, Vivian reached for him with one trembling arm and took his hand in hers, gasping when she felt his skin.

Jesus, he's so cold!

The man's grip was iron and it caught her off guard. She hadn't anticipated the strength of it or the effect it would have on her. The bone-deep chill started where their hands joined and spread through her body. She flinched and tried to pull away.

The man squeezed her hand even tighter and tugged, pulling her closer. His brilliant green-eyed gaze was filled with fear, pain, and something she couldn't quite define. Was it anger? He closed his eyes after a moment and a shocking burst of heat traveled through her from their joined hands. His touch chased away the chill, soothing her from ragged fingertips to her battered palm.

When he opened his eyes again, the man's expression mirrored the sudden and inexplicable relief surging within her. No fear, no pain. These weren't her emotions. *They must be his.* But how was she able to experience them as if they were her own? Then a singular emotion reflected in his gaze suddenly pierced her with vivid clarity.

Regret.

Vivian swore she could *see* the gray light of this man's regret emanating from his very pores as it coursed through her.

His expression pleaded, and he spoke to her in a harsh rasp. "I'm...sorry."

"It's going to be okay," she whispered, even though it wasn't.

His chest heaved and his eyes dulled, rolling back as he gasped for air. Two more shallow breaths later, he stilled completely.

"No, please. You have to stay with me. Please, stay with me," she pleaded, shaking his shoulder with one trembling hand even as she felt his grip slipping from her other.

"Oh no, oh dear God, someone help him!"

"Ma'am, I need you to step away from the vehicle," a muffled male voice said from behind her.

"Where the hell did she come from?" asked another man.

"Easy, bro, she must've just wandered in before we put up the barricades."

"No, she didn't. She just popped up out of nowhere!"

Hands gripped her shoulders and tried to pull her away, but she struggled free, refusing to let go of the man in the car. He wasn't blinking. He wasn't moving. His pallor faded to ash even as she begged him to come back.

"Please, ma'am, let us help him."

She yelped when a second set of hands grabbed her around the waist and lifted her off the ground. She wailed in rage and agony when she lost contact with the man's hand. She kicked and clawed at her captor until he dropped her, then she spun around and lifted her hands, ready to fight.

"Jesus, lady, calm down. We're paramedics," one of the uniformed men said. "We're here to help. I'm Ed, and this is Abner." He gestured to taller man beside him. They stood between her and the wreckage. Both began moving forward with outstretched hands as she backed away.

"Why don't you come with us so we can check you for injuries?" Ed spoke in a soft voice, taking slow, measured steps toward her and holding out his hand.

"I'm not injured. I...I can't leave him."

"Were you in the car with him, ma'am?" Abner asked. His sharp tone carried a note of accusation, or perhaps suspicion.

No, not that. He was afraid of her.

"No," she muttered, confused. She shook it off, focusing instead on the overwhelming urge to return to the man in the car.

"What's your name, ma'am?"

"Vivian."

"And his?"

"I have no idea. I don't know him, I just—I saw the crash and I came over. And I need to get back to him. I—I need to help him. Let me go back to him."

"Shh, it's okay. Come on with us now."

Ed lurched forward and grabbed her wrist. She tried to pull away but his scream caught her off guard. He dropped her arm and stumbled back, clutching his hand against his chest and groaning as if in terrible pain. Looking down, she swore she saw a red spark flash out of her fingertips, but by the time she blinked, it was gone.

"Ed? You okay?" Abner stepped away from Vivian and turned his attention to his colleague.

"Jesus Christ, my hand is on *fire*. What the hell did you do to me, lady?" Ed groaned, arm still clutched to his chest and eyes wide with shock and fear.

"Let me have a look." Abner tugged on his buddy's arm. After a quick exam he said, "I don't see anything. Must've been static electricity or something."

"Static electricity, my ass," Ed muttered, wringing his hand and staring at Vivian like she'd sprouted a second head. He and Abner exchanged a few more hushed words before he turned his attention back to the mangled car and the man inside.

Abner spoke louder then, snapping Vivian back to attention. "As for you, you really should go over to the ambulance and let our team have a look at you. The police will want your statement too."

He didn't make any further attempt to touch her. Instead, he pointed to the ambulance parked behind the growing crowd of onlookers while inspecting her with a wary expression. What the hell just happened? Numb with shock and an inexplicable sense of loss, she willed her feet to carry her over to the ambulance, leaving the stranger to his fate.

She paused, glancing back over her shoulder. "Will he be okay?"

"We'll do all we can, ma'am. You just go on now and take care of you."

She made it home two hours later.

Vivian sat on the deck and looked out as far as moonlight allowed. The scent of early summer clover hung heavy in the air and almost masked the fading honeysuckle of spring. Lightning bugs twinkled in the dark while the heat of the day flowed off the land. It wasn't a boon year for cicadas, better known as jar flies in this neck of the woods, but they still sang loud enough to match the volume of the crickets. A few mourning doves cooed in their haunting altos, joined by mockingbirds from time to time.

Her cherished backyard paradise offered little respite from the evening's trauma, or the smaller terrors this night would no doubt offer.

She sighed and drew another long swallow from her glass of wine. Her late arrival back home earned her an earful from the home health-care aide and a fifty-dollar penalty. At least she'd managed to get her car out of the ditch with the help of burly Mr. F-350 and one of the patrolmen on the scene. She could still drive her sedan, but the alignment was out of whack. She'd have to take it in for service tomorrow. What if she had to replace all four tires? Could've been worse. God only knew how she'd managed not to damage her last remnant of the good life. The way things were going, this car would have to last her well beyond its shelf life as a status symbol.

Not that she had any status left, or much of a life.

While still shaken, she wouldn't risk a stronger drink. She had to function. Her sister Mae was likely to have another bad night in spite of the new medications, so neither of them would be getting much sleep. Waiting was the worst. She could only afford about six more weeks off work, maybe eight if she pinched a few more pennies. Having burned through her vacation days and time allotted for family and medical leave, she still couldn't bring herself to return to work.

The irony wasn't lost on her. In the course of her work as a loan officer, she advised countless clients on the merits of financial planning, adequate insurance, and savings. So much for practicing what she preached. But Mae's condition was deteriorating fast according to the doctors, and Vivian couldn't bear to leave her. Besides, insurance only covered twenty hours of home health care per week, hardly conducive to a full-time work schedule.

But more time out of work would be time without pay, forcing her to use more of her scarce savings and dip into her retirement fund. Mae might live even longer. No one would have thought such a wreck of a body could make it thirty-two years.

Her passing would be a mercy for both of them, though the fact didn't offer any comfort, nor did the possibility that Mae might pull through. Guilt enveloped Vivian, wrapping around her like an old worn-out sweater stretched too far. She couldn't throw it out, and she wore it often these days.

Pushing those thoughts aside, she focused on the sights and sounds of her small patch of nature. A light breeze rustled through her favorite maple as its leaves showed their white underbellies. Rain's calling card, as if the heavy slate clouds and palpable humidity weren't announcement enough. A movement in the treeline caught her eye. A deer was always a treat. There weren't many left since the developers got busy in her little corner of the county. As it moved closer, she realized it was something bigger than a deer. No, not *something*, *someone* bigger. She stood and took a step closer to the door.

A man pushed out of the trees and onto the lawn. In the half-light, she saw his hat and heard his footfalls on the soft grass. He paused at the bottom of the stairs, looked up at her, then tipped his hat and raised a hand to wave.

"Evening, ma'am," came his low, gravelly voice. "Didn't mean to startle you." He stopped, perhaps waiting for her response.

"Good evening," she replied, clutching the cell phone in her pocket. "What can I do for you?"

"I just stopped by to see if you was all right after that big ruckus tonight."

She risked a step forward then leaned over the rail to get a better look at him. Yes, she remembered him now. Her visitor was the man who'd given her the nod at the crash site. The outdoor security light let her see him a little better now. He was definitely a local. Clad in well-worn overalls, a weathered John Deere cap, and dusty old boots, the clothes and their owner had more than a few miles on them.

"I'm fine," she said. "You did startle me when you came out of the trees. I didn't recognize you at first."

"You saw me," he said, almost to himself. He seemed to be chewing on some thought or another before he continued. "Oh yes, ma'am, I saw it. Shame too. That boy didn't make it."

"No, he didn't," she said, lowering her eyes. The images were still fresh and buzzed around in her aching head like a nest of angry hornets. Flashes of twisted metal and blood, but not a lot on his face. She'd done all she could for him, holding his hand and whispering words of reassurance. He looked to be about her age, a healthy man with years of life ahead of him.

Until capricious fate cut his life with sudden brutality.

Giving what comfort she could, she'd watched the life drain out of him. The medics had tried to console her that all was not lost. She knew the truth. He was gone. She winced at the thought, closing her eyes at the unexpected pang. Maybe it was just weariness with her own troubles. Death was an old if not welcome acquaintance. Should she try to find out more about him and talk to his family? What would she say? Of course, the police or paramedics would inform them, but the moment she'd shared with the man had been so personal, made her somehow...responsible for him. The voice of her visitor brought her back.

"Hey, now, you all right? I thought you might be pretty shaken up, watching that boy die." When she offered no objection, he took slow, steady steps up the stairs. Something about her visitor dampened the fear running beneath the surface of her civility. Any other night, she'd have run straight inside. It was as if his presence enveloped her in a cocoon of calm and safety.

Maybe she was just lonely.

Once he stood on the deck in front of her, he asked, "Is there someone I can give a holler for you?"

"No, I'll be okay, but it was nice of you to stop by. How'd you know where I live? Are you from the neighborhood?" He didn't look familiar. She'd lived here long enough to know most everyone. The realization should have set off alarm bells, but the warmth in his gaze and down home manner kept her at ease.

"Oh, I'm around here a bit." He smiled. "But I don't like the idea of leaving you all alone after what you been through."

"My sister's in the house, so I'll be fine. She's...she's not feeling well. I really should check on her." Retreating, she asked, "Did you know the man in the accident?"

"Not exactly, but I think we might have something in common," he said with a knowing smile.

His statement and smile poked a big hole in the cocoon of calm, giving Vivian a case of the creeps. Good down-home charm aside, she should never have let him get this close or stay this long. This wasn't like her, especially in light of the evening's stress. Time to end the conversation before the guy went all Jack the Ripper on her.

"Thank you for stopping by. I need to get back inside now. Rain's coming. You should get home before it starts. Good night, Mister...."

"Oh, you can just call me Ezra. It surely was a pleasure to meet you, Miss Vivian," he said, extending his hand.

She hesitated for a moment, but then accepted, tilting her hand slightly to hide the unsightly nails, chewed to the quick. His roughened skin and gnarled knuckles chafed her skin before the warmth of his grasp overwhelmed her.

The shock of it froze her in place, even as warmth suffused her fingertips and beyond—the same heat she'd felt with the wounded man in the car, only more intense and powerful.

When she didn't release his hand, Ezra pulled away gently. He tipped his hat and began his slow descent down the stairs as she stood dazed, still swathed in the pleasant warmth of his presence. Halfway down, he glanced over his shoulder and said, "I'll be seeing you soon. Get on in the house and rest easy now."

"Good night," she said politely, then nipped inside and bolted the door behind her with a sigh of relief and irrational regret.

She tiptoed down the dark hall to check on the shell that held her sister. Entering Mae's room with practiced quiet, Vivian listened. Her sister's breaths were shallow and still plagued by rasps and wheezes. Vivian stood over the narrow bed, regarding her sister with a mixture of love, pity, and resentment.

All of that time they'd borrowed and bought for her, and for what?

God, she was *loathsome* to think such things. What decent person questioned the value of life, especially the life of a loved one? Hell, Mae was the only family she had left since their parents were gone. Good people didn't think of their flesh and blood as burdens, especially someone like Mae. She hadn't asked to be born with her condition, and Vivian had long ago promised to assume responsibility for her should the time ever come.

Still, standing there in the dark, Vivian recalled the horror with which she first contemplated her sister's level of awareness. When she'd prayed as a child, Vivian had hoped God's mercy had spared Mae awareness. She didn't want to think of an intact mind trapped in such a body.

Without thinking, she stroked her sister's cheek and ran her hand over Mae's soft hair. Mae shifted and inhaled deeply. Vivian stiffened, bracing herself for a coughing fit or worse, Mae choking. Instead, Mae's breathing evened out and she drifted further into a peaceful rest. Stranger still, the air around them seemed warmer.

Perplexed, though relieved, Vivian left her sister and forced her own weary legs in the direction of her bathroom. Halfway there, realization dawned. She hadn't actually told Ezra her name.

Had she?

Then again, she'd given her contact information and statement to a half a dozen cops, medics, and even one firefighter at the scene. He'd probably just overheard it. A good chunk of southeast Nashville probably knew how to find her by now.

Still, she could have kicked herself for letting a stranger know she was more or less alone in the house, and for letting him get so close to her. The news and all of those crime dramas on TV tended to blur the line between healthy caution and paranoia. The events of the past few hours weren't helping either.

She didn't notice anything unusual with her hands while completing her nightly routine, other than the slight tremor running through them as she washed her face and brushed her teeth. And the raw skin and mangled nails, of course. Maybe she'd just zapped the paramedic and Ezra with a little static discharge, like the other paramedic had said. But she hadn't been wearing a sweater and it was such a humid night.

Oh God, she'd just touched Mae with that hand. What had she been thinking?

But she'd touched Ezra with it too, and his hot touch almost burned *her*. What the hell? Static electricity didn't travel back and forth like a normal current. Since when had she turned into a battery?

She touched one tentative fingertip to the metal faucet fixture, bracing for a jolt.

Nothing.

Feeling foolish, she touched the brass-plated hoop that held her hand towel, her metal tweezers, and her scissors. Wet or dry, she felt nothing other than cold metal, which should have been a better conductor than flesh.

Vivian shook her head. Maybe things would look a little clearer in the morning.

"Go figure," she muttered, looking at her bottle of sleeping pills. She hadn't even realized she'd pulled them out of the cabinet, though it came as no surprise. Seemed her earlier brush with death had killed the mood.

She put them back with a little hesitation.

After all, they'd still be there tomorrow.

———————

Don't stop now. Keep reading with your copy of <u>WAKING THE DEAD</u>

And visit www.dbsieders.com to keep up with the latest news where you can subscribe to the newsletter for contests, giveaways, new releases, and more.

Don't miss more of the Jinx McGee series coming soon, and check out the Soul Broker from D. B. Sieders with WAKING THE DEAD

The road to hell begins when the reaper darkens her door.

A chance encounter with a dying stranger opens an empathic connection between down-on-her-luck caregiver Vivian Bedford and the world of spirits. Lazarus Darkmore, a grim reaper in a charming and seductive package, seeks to recruit her as a soul broker. Guardian spirit Ezra and his new apprentice Zeke offer protection from the reaper—so long as she works on their side of afterlife management. But these guardians are no angels, and their methods leave Vivian fearing the price of their protection.

Her ability to channel conscious energy from the living, something no guardian or reaper can do, could be a game changer. If she can control it, she can use this power as leverage. And she needs a bargaining chip, especially when she discovers that incapacitated living mortals can supply energy for the spirit realm, making her disabled sister Mae a prime target for guardian and reaper alike.

Can she move from pawn to major player in order to save Mae, and herself, from a horrific fate beyond the simple and fleeting terrors of death?

All reviews are **welcome** and **appreciated**. Please consider leaving one on your favorite social media and book buying sites.

Escape Your World. Get Lost in Ours! City Owl Press at www.cityowlpress.com.

ACKNOWLEDGMENTS

I am super grateful to the team at City Owl Press for supporting me as an author. My amazing editor Tee Tate always brings out the best in me and in my stories. She ROCKS! Huge thanks to SiederTree Studios (a.k.a. my insanely talented daughter) for creating the graphic for chapter headings. And, of course, thanks to all my readers. You're the reason I keep writing, and every review inspires me to create bigger and better stories. Finally, I'd like to thank my family for their love and support and my three cats for purrs, cuddles, and daily entertainment.

ABOUT THE AUTHOR

Award-winning author D.B. Sieders was born and raised in East Tennessee and spent her childhood hiking in the Great Smoky Mountains and chasing salamanders, fish, and frogs. She loved to tell stories while sitting around the campfire.

She is a working scientist by day, but never lost her love of telling stories. Now, she's a purveyor of unconventional fantasy romance featuring strong heroines and the heroes who strive to match them. Her heroes and heroines face a healthy dose of angst as they strive for redemption and a happily ever after, which everyone deserves.

www.dbsieders.com

f facebook.com/DBSieders

X x.com/DBSieders

g goodreads.com/dbsieders

a amazon.com/D.B.-Sieders/B00D18ZPOY

ABOUT THE PUBLISHER

City Owl Press is a cutting edge indie publishing company, bringing the world of romance and speculative fiction to discerning readers.

Escape Your World. Get Lost in Ours!

www.cityowlpress.com

 facebook.com/CityOwlPress
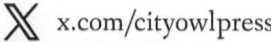 x.com/cityowlpress
instagram.com/cityowlbooks
pinterest.com/cityowlpress
 tiktok.com/@cityowlpress